Nebula Award Stories 3

D1798365

9780586034132

edited by
Roger Zelazny

Panther Science Fiction

A Panther Book

First published in Great Britain by Victor Gollancz Limited
1968.   Panther edition published 1970.   Copyright © Science
Fiction Writers of America 1968.

This book is published at a net price and is supplied subject
to the Publishers Association Standard Conditions of Sale
registered under the Restrictive Trade Practices Act, 1956.
*Printed in Great Britain by Richard Clay (The Chaucer Press),
Ltd., Bungay, Suffolk, and published by Panther Books, 3 Upper
James Street, London, W.1*

Seven SF stories—and something special about each of them
(otherwise they wouldn't be here).

They were all of them nominated for the 1967 Nebula Awards
of the Science Fiction Writers of America—*the* SF accolade.
Moorcock's 'Behold the Man' took the novella award, Leiber's
'Gonna Roll the Bones' the novelette award, and Delaney's
'Aye, and Gomorrah' the short story award. The remaining four
were runners up. The annual Nebula Awards reach over the
whole field of imaginative literature, always seeking new SF experiences and because of this no two of the anthologies are
alike—but each anthology is always the cream of the year's SF
cream: pace-making, mind-stretching, and first-class as enter-
tainment.

Reviewing *Nebula Award Stories 2*, the *Tribune's* critic wrote,
'The mouth waters for number three.'

Here it is—in all its wayout brilliance.

Also in this series in Panther Books

Nebula Award Stories 2

Contents

This book is dedicated to
Robert Silverberg.

Thanks for the love, sweat
and miserable hours, Bob.
We'll remember you for each.

INTRODUCTION

Here are seven stories. There is something special about each of them, or they wouldn't be here.

They were all of them nominated for the Nebula Award, a thing presented at the annual Science Fiction Writers of America awards banquet, a thing which represents our collective opinion as to what is the very best work our area of literature produced in the year in question.

Three of these stories won that award. Some of the others came close.

What is a Nebula?

Physically, it is a 9 in. $\times$ 4$\frac{1}{4}$ in. $\times$ 4$\frac{1}{4}$ in. piece of lucite with a black base, containing a chunk of quartz and a stylized representation of the spiral nebula. It is an expensive, and as such things occasionally are, a lovely thing to behold. It is our Academy Award/Emmy/Edgar/What Have You. It is the thing we give to the people we respect, for what they have written. A full list of winners, for this and previous years, occurs at the end of this book.

Now, let the Nebula, with its arms reaching out, turning, represent the human imagination, seeking new things. Okay. Because of this, no two of our anthologies (or stories) will ever be alike. Know this, because you need to know it before you start reading these or any other works of science fiction. The imagination is a funny thing. By nature, it reaches out; and this nature is a pleasure–pain thing. As Robert Conquest has said, nobody reads science fiction out of a sense of duty. Since it has not yet been academicized, you read it, if you read it at all, for pleasure, impure and unsimple.

And that is what this award represents; recognition of the highest fruits of the imagination, impure and unsimple.

An individual story of this sort may hold the fascination of a spider or a butterfly. When I say that they give pleasure, I do not mean that you are holding a collection of fairy tales with happy endings. I mean only that these are stories people will read because they want to, not because they have to, I mean that they are alive, with heatbeats, metabolisms, EEG readings.

I mean that they can be sad, happy or neither of these. The pleasure I mentioned comes from contemplating the many aspects of the human condition in whatever variant environments it may be cast, the same as in any other form of literature.

Two things please bear in mind: like opera, nobody kicks because people sing instead of talking, or if *medias res* means Medieval Germany or Italy; likewise, we live now in an age when the really big philosophical ideas are born of Science (cap 'S', yes), rather than debate over the horse's teeth.

So . . .

This is, as a mass-media magazine once observed, and correctly, the folk-literature of the machine age. Without the industrial revolution, the folk-literature, you might be reading re-writes of the *Faerie Queene*. But this is not the case. No. Those antipodal themes, Pygmalion and Frankenstein, are with us still. Our creations may kill or love. In this sense, the archetypes are still valid, and probably always will be. Otherwise, though, these writers were doing electric things long before Marshall M came along. They project, expand, guess upon and just plain fool around with themes as current as the headlines and as timeless as Auden's four terms of nonbeing: Darkness, Silence, Nothing, Death.

In short, they're all of them good, hard-working stories, calculated to play the Life–Death–Love–Hate game the same as any others, but on their own terms; the expansions of science and human awareness.

If you depart them at this point, you will be none the richer. Embrace them, and a world or three may be opened before you.

Roger Zelazny

Ever play Max Ernst games by staring up at that tent of blue we prisoners call the sky? If so, I think you will appreciate this story. If not, you can always do it over again yourself by regarding Up. It takes a true architect of the nervous system and the environment, however, to not only play this game, but to play it well. J. G. Ballard, I submit, is one of the greatest cloud-sculptors I have ever witnessed in action.

So put on the appropriate piece by Debussy, and bear in mind that despite Cervantes, last year's clouds are not so useless as they may seem. No.

I chose to open the volume with this story, to set the Magritte-mood of reality twice removed and, perhaps because of this, twice as real. I'll double-cross you later on, I promise, but for an opener, let's start with a piece that only Mister Ballard could have written.

THE CLOUD-SCULPTORS OF CORAL D

J. G. Ballard

All summer the cloud-sculptors would come from Vermilion Sands and sail their painted gliders above the coral towers that rose like white pagodas beside the highway to Lagoon West. The tallest of the towers was Coral D, and here the rising air above the sandreefs was topped by swan-like clumps of fair-weather cumulus. Lifted on the shoulders of the air above the crown of Coral D, we would carve sea-horses and unicorns, the portraits of presidents and film-stars, lizards and exotic birds. As the crowd watched from their cars, a cool rain would fall on to the dusty roofs, weeping from the sculptured clouds as they sailed across the desert floor towards the sun.

Of all the cloud-sculptures we were to carve, the strangest were the portraits of Leonora Chanel. As I look back to that afternoon last summer when she first came in her white limousine to watch the cloud-sculptors of Coral D, I know we barely realized how seriously this beautiful but insane woman regarded

the sculptures floating above her in that calm sky. Later her
portraits, carved in the whirlwind, were to weep their storm-rain
upon the corpses of their sculptors.

I had arrived in Vermilion Sands three months earlier. A
retired pilot, I was painfully coming to terms with a broken leg
and the prospect of never flying again. Driving into the desert
one day, I stopped near the coral towers on the highway to
Lagoon West. As I gazed at these immense pagodas stranded
on the floor of this fossil sea, I heard music coming from a sand-
reef two hundred yards away. Swinging on my crutches across
the sliding sand, I found a shallow basin among the dunes where
sonic statues had run to seed beside a ruined studio. The owner
had gone, abandoning the hangar-like building to the sandrays
and the desert, and on some half-formed impulse I began to drive
out each afternoon. From the lathes and joists left behind I built
my first giant kites and, later, gliders with cockpits. Tethered by
their cables, they would hang above me in the afternoon air like
amiable ciphers.

One evening, as I wound the gliders down on to the winch, a
sudden gale rose over the crest of Coral D. While I grappled
with the whirling handle, trying to anchor my crutches in the
sand, two figures approached across the desert floor. One was
a small hunchback with a child's overlit eyes and a deformed
jaw twisted like an anchor barb to one side. He scuttled over to
the winch and wound the tattered gliders towards the ground,
his powerful shoulders pushing me aside. He helped me on to
my crutches and peered into the hangar. Here my most ambitious glider to date, no longer a kite but a sail-plane with eleva-
tors and control lines, was taking shape on the bench.

He spread a large hand over his chest. 'Petit Manuel—acrobat
and weight-lifter. Nolan!' he bellowed. 'Look at this!' His
companion was squatting by the sonic statues, twisting their
helixes so that their voices became more resonant. 'Nolan's an
artist,' the hunchback confided to me. 'He'll build you gliders
like condors.'

The tall man was wandering among the gliders, touching
their wings with a sculptor's hand. His morose eyes were set in
a face like a bored Gauguin's. He glanced at the plaster on my
leg and my faded flying jacket, and gestured at the gliders.

'You've given cockpit to them, major.' The remark contained a complete understanding of my motives. He pointed to the coral towers rising above us into the evening sky. 'With silver iodide we could carve the clouds.'

The hunchback nodded encouragingly to me, his eyes lit by an astronomy of dreams.

So were formed the cloud-sculptors of Coral D. Although I considered myself one of them, I never flew the gliders, but I taught Nolan and little Manuel to fly, and later, when he joined us, Charles Van Eyck. Nolan had found this blond-haired pirate of the café terraces in Vermilion Sands, a laconic teuton with droll eyes and a weak mouth, and brought him out to Coral D when the season ended and the well-to-do tourists and their nubile daughters returned to Red Beach. 'Major Parker—Charles Van Eyck. He's a head-hunter,' Nolan commented with cold humour, '—maidenheads.' Despite their uneasy rivalry I realized that Van Eyck would give our group a useful dimension of glamour.

From the first I suspected that the studio in the desert was Nolan's, and that we were all serving some private whim of this dark-haired solitary. At the time, however, I was more concerned with teaching them to fly—first on cable, mastering the updraughts that swept the stunted turret of Coral A, smallest of the towers, then the steeper slopes of B and C, and finally the powerful currents of Coral D. Late one afternoon, when I began to wind them in, Nolan cut away his line. The glider plummetted on to its back, diving down to impale itself on the rock spires. I flung myself to the ground as the cable whipped across my car, shattering the windshield. When I looked up, Nolan was soaring high in the tinted air above Coral D. The wind, guardian of the coral towers, carried him through the islands of cumulus that veiled the evening light.

As I ran to the winch, the second cable went, and little Manuel swerved away to join Nolan. Ugly crab on the ground, in the air the hunchback became a bird with immense wings, outflying both Nolan and Van Eyck. I watched them as they circled the coral towers, and then swept down together over the desert floor, stirring the sandrays into soot-like clouds. Petit Manuel was jubilant. He strutted around me like a pocket

Napoleon, contemptuous of my broken leg, scooping up handfuls of broken glass and tossing them over his head like bouquets to the air.

Two months later, as we drove out to Coral D on the day we were to meet Leonora Chanel, something of this first feeling of exhilaration had faded. Now that the season had ended few tourists travelled to Lagoon West, and often we would perform our cloud-sculptures to the empty highway. Sometimes Nolan would remain behind in his hotel, drinking by himself on the bed, or Van Eyck would disappear for several days with some widow or divorcee, and Petit Manuel and I would go out alone.

None the less, as the four of us drove out in my car that afternoon and saw the clouds waiting for us above the spire of Coral D, all my depression and fatigue vanished. Ten minutes later the three cloud-gliders rose into the air and the first cars began to stop on the highway. Nolan was in the lead in his black-winged glider, climbing straight to the crown of Coral D two hundred feet above, while Van Eyck soared to and fro below, showing his blond mane to a middle-aged woman in a topaz convertible. Behind them came little Manuel, his candy-striped wings slipping and churning in the disturbed air. Shouting happy obscenities, he flew with his twisted knees, huge arms gesticulating out of the cockpit.

The three gliders, brilliant painted toys, revolved like lazing birds above Coral D, waiting for the first clouds to pass over-head. Van Eyck moved away to take a cloud. He sailed around its white pillow, spraying the sides with iodide crystals and cutting away the flock-like tissue. The steaming shards fell towards us like crumbling ice-drifts. As the drops of condensing spray fell on my face, I could see Van Eyck shaping an immense horse's head. He sailed up and down the long forehead and chiselled out the eyes and ears.

As always, the people watching from their cars seemed to enjoy this piece of aerial marzipan. It sailed overhead, carried away on the wind from Coral D. Van Eyck followed it down, wings lazing around the equine head. Meanwhile Petit Manuel worked away at the next cloud. As he sprayed its sides, a familiar human head appeared through the tumbling mist. Manuel caricatured the high wavy mane, strong jaw but slipped mouth from the cloud with a series of deft passes, wing-tips almost touching each other as he dived in and out of the portrait.

The glossy white head, an unmistakable parody of Van Eyck in his own worst style, crossed the highway towards Vermilion Sands. Manuel slid out of the air, stalling his glider to a landing beside my car as Van Eyck stepped from his cockpit with a forced smile.

We waited for the third display. A cloud formed over Coral D, within a few minutes had blossomed into a pristine fair-weather cumulus. As it hung there Nolan's black-winged glider plunged out of the sun. He soared around the cloud, cutting away its tissues. The soft fleece fell towards us in a cool rain.

There was a shout from one of the cars. Nolan turned from the cloud, his wings slipping as if unveiling his handiwork. Illuminated by the afternoon sun was the serene face of a three-year-old child. Its wide cheeks framed a placid mouth and plump chin. As one or two people clapped, Nolan sailed over the cloud and rippled the roof into ribbons and curls.

However, I knew that the real climax was yet to come. Cursed by some malignant virus, Nolan seemed unable to accept his own handiwork, always destroying it with the same cold humour. Petit Manuel had thrown away his cigarette, and even Van Eyck had turned his attention from the women in the cars.

Nolan soared above the child's face, following like a matador waiting for the moment of the kill. There was silence for a minute as he worked away at the cloud, and then someone slammed a car door in disgust.

Hanging above us was the white image of a skull.

The child's face, converted by a few strokes, had vanished, but in the notched teeth and gaping orbits, large enough to hold a car, we could still see an echo of its infant features. The spectre moved past us, the spectators frowning at this weeping skull whose rain fell upon their faces.

Half-heartedly I picked my old flying helmet off the back seat and began to carry it around the cars. Two of the spectators drove off before I could reach them. As I hovered about uncertainly, wondering why on earth a retired and well-to-do Air Force officer should be trying to collect these few dollar bills, Van Eyck stepped behind me and took the helmet from my hand.

'Not now, major. Look at what arrives—my apocalypse . . .'

A white Rolls-Royce, driven by a chauffeur in braided cream livery, had turned off the highway. Through the tinted communication window a young woman in a secretary's day suit spoke to the chauffeur. Beside her, a gloved hand still holding the window strap, a white-haired woman with jewelled eyes gazed up at the circling wings of the cloud-glider. Her strong and elegant face seemed sealed within the dark glass of the limousine like the enigmatic madonna of some marine grotto.

Van Eyck's glider rose into the air, soaring upwards to the cloud that hung above Coral D. I walked back to my car, searching the sky for Nolan. Above, Van Eyck was producing a patische Mona Lisa, a picture postcard gioconda as authentic as a plaster virgin. Its glossy finish shone as if enamelled together out of some cosmetic foam.

Then Nolan dived from the sun behind Van Eyck. Rolling his black-winged glider past Van Eyck's, he drove through the neck of the gioconda, and with the flick of a wing toppled the broad-cheeked head. It fell towards the cars below. The features disintegrated into a flaccid mess, sections of the nose and jaw tumbling through the steam. Then wings brushed. Van Eyck fired his spray gun Nolan, and there was a flurry of torn fabric. Van Eyck fell from the air, steering his glider down to a broken landing.

I ran over to him. 'Charles, do you have to play Von Richthofen? For God's sake, leave each other alone!'

Van Eyck waved me away. 'Talk to Nolan, major. I'm not responsible for his air piracy.' He stood in the cockpit, gazing over the cars as the shreds of fabric fell around him.

I walked back to my car, deciding that the time had come to disband the cloud-sculptors of Coral D. Fifty yards away the young secretary in the Rolls-Royce had stepped from the car and beckoned to me. Through the open door her mistress watched me with her jewelled eyes. Her white hair lay in a coil over one shoulder like a nacreous serpent.

I carried my flying helmet down to the young woman. Above a high forehead her auburn hair was swept back in a defensive bun, as if she were deliberately concealing part of herself. She stared with puzzled eyes at the helmet held out in front of her.

'I don't want to fly—what is it?'

'A grace,' I explained. 'For the repose of Michelangelo, Ed Keinholz and the cloud-sculptors of Coral D.'

'Oh, my God. I think the chauffeur's the only one with any *money*. Look, do you perform anywhere else?'

'Perform?' I glanced from this pretty and agreeable young woman to the pale chimera with jewelled eyes in the dim compartment of the Rolls. She was watching the headless figure of the Mona Lisa as it moved across the desert floor towards Vermilion Sands. 'We're not a professional troupe, as you've probably guessed. And obviously we'd need some fair-weather cloud. Where, exactly?'

'At Lagoon West.' She took a snake-skinned diary from her handbag. 'Miss Chanel is holding a series of garden parties. She wondered if you'd care to perform. Of course there would be a large fee.'

'Chanel . . . Leonora Chanel, the . . .?'

The young woman's face again took on its defensive posture, dissociating her from whatever might follow. 'Miss Chanel is at Lagoon West for the summer. By the way, there's one condition I must point out—Miss Chanel will provide the sole subject matter. You do understand?'

Fifty yards away Van Eyck was dragging his damaged glider towards my car. Nolan had landed, a caricature of Cyrano abandoned in mid-air. Petit Manuel limped to and fro, gathering together the equipment. In the fading afternoon light they resembled a threadbare circus troupe.

'All right,' I agreed. 'I take your point. But what about the clouds, Miss——?'

'Lafferty. Beatrice Lafferty. Miss Chanel will provide the clouds.'

I walked around the cars with the helmet, then divided the money between Nolan, Van Eyck and Manuel. They stood in the gathering dusk, the few bills in their hands, watching the highway below.

Leonora Chanel stepped from the limousine and strolled into the desert. Her white-haired figure in its cobra-skinned coat wandered among the dunes. Sand-rays lifted around her, disturbed by the random movements of this sauntering phantasm of the burnt afternoon. Ignoring their open stings around her legs, she was gazing up at the aerial bestiary dissolving in the sky, and at the white skull a mile away over Lagoon West that had smeared itself across the sky.

At the time I first saw her, watching the cloud-sculptors of Coral D, I had only a half-formed impression of Leonora Chanel. The daughter of one of the world's leading financiers, she was an heiress both in her own right and on the death of her husband, a shy Monacan aristocrat, Comte Louis Chanel. The mysterious circumstances of his death at Cap Ferrat on the Riviera, officially described as suicide, had placed Leonora in a spotlight of publicity and gossip. She had escaped by wandering endlessly across the globe, from her walled villa in Tangier to an Alpine mansion in the snows above Pontresina, and from there to Palm Springs, Seville and Mykonos.

During these years of exile something of her character emerged from the magazine and newspaper photographs: moodily visiting a Spanish charity with the Duchess of Alba, or seated with Saroya and other members of café society on the terrace of Dali's villa at Port Lligat, her self-regarding face gazing out with its jewelled eyes at the diamond sea of the Costa Brava.

Inevitably her Garbo-like role seemed over-calculated, for ever undermined by the suspicions of her own hand in her husband's death. The Count had been an introspective playboy who piloted his own aircraft to archaeological sites in the Peloponnese and whose mistress, a beautiful young Lebanese, was one of the world's pre-eminent keyboard interpreters of Bach. Why this reserved and pleasant man should have committed suicide was never made plain. What promised to be a significant exhibit at the coroner's inquest, a mutilated easel portrait of Leonora on which he was working, was accidentally destroyed before the hearing. Perhaps the painting revealed more of Leonora's character than she chose to see.

A week later, as I drove out to Lagoon West on the morning of the first garden party, I could well understand why Leonora Chanel had come to Vermilion Sands, to this bizarre, sand-bound resort with its lethargy, beach fatigue and shifting perspectives. Sonic statues grew wild along the beach, their voices keening as I swept past along the shore road. The fused silica on the surface of the lake formed an immense rainbow mirror that reflected the deranged colours of the sand-reefs, more vivid even than the cinnabar and cyclamen wing-panels of the cloud-gliders overhead. They soared in the sky above the lake like fitful dragonflies as Nolan, Van Eyck and Petit Manuel flew them from Coral D.

We had entered an inflamed landscape. Half a mile away the angular cornices of the summer house jutted into the vivid air as if distorted by some faulty junction of time and space. Behind it, like an exhausted volcano, a broad-topped mesa rose into the glazed air, its shoulders lifting the thermal currents high off the heated lake.

Envying Nolan and little Manuel these tremendous up-draughts, more powerful than any we had known at Coral D, I drove towards the villa. Then the haze cleared along the beach and I saw the clouds.

A hundred feet above the roof of the mesa, they hung like the twisted pillows of a sleepless giant. Columns of turbulent air moved within the clouds, boiling upwards to the anvil heads like liquid in a cauldron. These were not the placid, fair-weather cumulus of Coral D, but storm-nimbus, unstable masses of overheated air that could catch an aircraft and lift it a thousand feet in a few seconds. Here and there the clouds were rimmed with dark bands, their towers crossed by valleys and ravines. They moved across the villa, concealed from the lakeside heat by the haze overhead, then dissolved in a series of violent shifts in the disordered air.

As I entered the drive behind a truck filled with *son et lumière* equipment, a dozen members of the staff were straightening lines of gilt chairs on the terrace and unrolling panels of a marquee.

Beatrice Lafferty stepped across the cables. 'Major Parker—there are the clouds we promised you.'

I looked up again at the dark billows hanging like shrouds above the white villa. 'Clouds, Beatrice? Those are tigers, tigers with wings. We're manicurists of the air, not dragon-tamers.'

'Don't worry, a manicure is exactly what you're expected to carry out.' With an arch glance, she added: 'Your men do understand that there's to be only one subject?'

'Miss Chanel herself? Of course.' I took her arm as we walked towards the balcony overlooking the lake. 'You know, I think you enjoy these snide asides. Let the rich choose their materials —marble, bronze, plasma or cloud. Why not? Portraiture has always been a neglected art.'

'My God, not here.' She waited until a steward passed with a tray of table-cloths. 'Carving one's portrait in the sky out of the sun and air—some people might say that smacked of vanity, or even worse sins.'

'You're very mysterious. Such as?'

She played games with her eyes. 'I'll tell you in a month's time when my contract expires. Now, when are your men coming?'

'They're here.' I pointed to the sky over the lake. The three gliders hung in the overheated air, clumps of cloud-cotton drifting past them to dissolve in the haze. They were following a sand-yacht that approached the quay, its tyres throwing up the cerise dust. Behind the helmsman sat Leonora Chanel in a trouser suit of yellow alligator skin, her white hair hidden inside a black raffia toque.

As the helmsman moored the craft, Van Eyck and Petit Manuel put on an impromptu performance, shaping the fragments of cloud-cotton a hundred feet above the lake. First Van Eyck carved an orchid, then a heart and a pair of lips, while Manuel fashioned the head of a parakeet, two identical mice and the letters 'L.C.' As they dived and plunged around her, their wings sometimes touching the lake, Leonora stood on the quay, politely waving at each of these brief confections.

When they landed beside the quay, Leonora waited for Nolan to take one of the clouds, but he was sailing up and down the lake in front of her like a weary bird. Watching this strange chatelaine of Lagoon West, I noticed that she had slipped off into some private reverie, her gaze fixed on Nolan and oblivious of the people around her. Memories, caravels without sails, crossed the shadowy deserts of her burnt-out eyes.

Later that evening Beatrice Lafferty led me into the villa through the library window. There, as Leonora greeted her guests on the terrace, wearing a topless dress of sapphires and organdy, her breasts covered only by their contour jewellery, I saw the portraits that filled the villa. I counted more than twenty, from the formal society portraits in the drawing rooms, one by the President of the Royal Academy, another by Annigoni, to the bizarre psychological studies in the bar and dining room by Dali and Francis Bacon. Everywhere we moved, in the alcoves between the marble semi-columns, in gilt miniatures on the mantel shelves, even in the ascending mural that followed the staircase, we saw the same beautiful, self-regarding face. This colossal narcissism seemed to have become her last refuge, the only retreat for her fugitive self in its flight from the world.

Then, in the studio on the roof, we came across a large easel portrait that had just been varnished. The artist had produced a deliberate travesty of the sentimental and powder-blue tints of a fashionable society painter, but beneath this gloss he had visualized Leonora as a dead Medea. The stretched skin below her right cheek, the sharp forehead and slipped mouth gave her the numbed and luminous appearance of a corpse.

My eyes moved to the signature. 'Nolan! My God, were you here when he painted this?'

'It was finished before I came—two months ago. She refused to have it framed.'

'No wonder.' I went over to the window and looked down at the bedrooms hidden behind their awnings. 'Nolan was *here*. The old studio near Coral D was his.'

'But why should Leonora ask him back? They must have——'

'To paint her portrait again. I know Leonora Chanel better than you do, Beatrice. This time, though, the size of the sky.'

We left the library and walked past the cocktails and canapes to where Leonora was welcoming her guests. Nolan stood beside her, wearing a suit of white suede. Now and then he looked down at her as if playing with the possibility this self-obsessed woman gave to his macabre humour. Leonora clutched at his elbow. With the diamonds fixed around her eyes she reminded me of some archaic priestess. Beneath the contour jewellery her breasts lay like eager snakes.

Van Eyck introduced himself with an exaggerated bow. Behind him came Petit Manuel, his twisted head ducking nervously among the tuxedos.

Leonora's mouth shut in a rictus of distaste. She glanced at the white plaster on my foot. 'Nolan, you fill your world with cripples. Your little dwarf—will he fly too?'

Petit Manuel looked at her with eyes like crushed flowers.

The performance began an hour later. The dark-rimmed clouds were lit by the sun setting behind the mesa, the air crossed by wraiths of cirrus like the gilded frames of the immense paintings to come. Van Eyck's glider rose in a spiral towards the face of the first cloud, stalling and climbing again as the turbulent updraughts threw him across the air.

As the cheekbones began to appear, as smooth and lifeless as carved foam, applause rang out from the guests seated on the terrace. Five minutes later, when Van Eyck's glider swooped down on to the lake, I could see that he had excelled himself. Lit by the searchlights, and with the overture to Tristan sounding from the loudspeaker on the slopes of the mesa, as if inflating this huge bauble, the portrait of Leonora moved overhead, a faint rain falling from it. By luck the cloud remained stable until it passed the shoreline, and then broke up in the evening air as if ripped from the sky by an irritated hand.

Petit Manuel began his ascent, sailing in on a dark-edged cloud like an urchin accosting a bad-tempered matron. He soared to and fro, as if unsure how to shape this unpredictable column of vapour, then began to carve it into the approximate contours of a woman's head. He seemed more nervous than I had ever seen him. As he finished a second round of applause broke out, soon followed by laughter and ironic cheers.

The cloud, sculptured into a flattering likeness of Leonora, had begun to tilt, rotating in the disturbed air. The jaw lengthened, the glazed smile became that of an idiot's. Within a minute the gigantic head of Leonora Chanel hung upside down above us.

Discreetly I ordered the searchlights switched off, and the audience's attention turned to Nolan's black-winged glider as it climbed towards the next cloud. Shards of dissolving tissue fell from the darkening air, the spray concealing whatever ambiguous creation Nolan was carving. To my surprise, the portrait that emerged was wholly lifelike. There was a burst of applause, a few bars of Tannhauser, and the searchlights lit up the elegant head. Standing among her guests, Leonora raised her glass to Nolan's glider.

Puzzled by Nolan's generosity, I looked more closely at the gleaming face, and then realized what he had done. The portrait, with cruel irony, was all too lifelife. The downward turn of Leonora's mouth, the chin held up to smooth her neck, the fall of flesh below her right cheek—all of these were carried on the face of the cloud as they had been in his painting in the studio.

Around Leonora the guests were congratulating her on the performance. She was looking up at her portrait as it began to break up over the lake seeing it for the first time. The veins held the blood in her face.

Then a fireworks display on the beach blotted out these ambiguities in its pink and blue explosions.

Shortly before dawn Beatrice Lafferty and I walked along the beach among the shells of burnt-out rockets and catherine wheels. On the deserted terrace a few lights shone through the darkness on to the scattered chairs. As we reached the steps, a woman's voice cried out somewhere above us. There was the sound of smashed glass. A french window was kicked back, and a dark-haired man in a white suit ran between the tables.

As Nolan disappeared along the drive, Leonora Chanel walked out into the centre of the terrace. She looked at the dark clouds surging over the mesa, and with one hand tore the jewels from her eyes. They lay winking on the tiles at her feet. Then the hunched figure of Petit Manuel leapt from his hiding place in the bandstand. He scuttled past, racing on his bent legs.

An engine started by the gates. Leonora began to walk back to the villa, staring at her broken reflections in the glass below the window. She stopped as a tall, blond-haired man with cold and eager eyes stepped from the sonic statues outside the library. Disturbed by the noise, the statues had begun to whine. As Van Eyck moved towards Leonora they took up the slow beat of his steps.

The next day's performance was the last by the cloud-sculptors of Coral D. All afternoon, before the guests arrived, a dim light lay over the lake. Immense tiers of storm-nimbus were massing behind the mesa, and any performance at all seemed unlikely.

Van Eyck was with Leonora. As I arrived, Beatrice Lafferty was watching their sand-yacht carry them unevenly across the lake, its sails shipped by the squalls.

'There's no sign of Nolan or little Manuel,' she told me. 'The party starts in three hours.'

I took her arm. 'The party's already over. When you're finished here, Bea, come and live with me at Coral D. I'll teach you to sculpt the clouds.'

Van Eyck and Leonora came ashore half an hour later. Van Eyck stared through my face as he brushed past. Leonora clung to his arm, the day-jewels around her eyes scattering their hard light across the terrace.

By eight, when the first guests began to appear, Nolan and Petit Manuel had still not arrived. On the terrace the evening was warm and lamplit, but overhead the storm-clouds sidled past each other like uneasy giants. I walked up the slope to where the gliders were tethered. Their wings shivered in the updraughts.

Barely half a minute after he rose into the darkening air, dwarfed by an immense tower of storm-nimbus, Charles Van Eyck was spinning towards the ground, his glider toppled by the crazed air. He recovered fifty feet from the villa and climbed on the updraughts from the lake, well away from the spreading chest of the cloud. He soared in again. As Leonora and her guests watched from their seats, the glider was hurled back over their heads in an explosion of vapour, then fell towards the lake with a broken wing.

I walked towards Leonora. Standing by the balcony were Nolan and Petit Manuel, watching Van Eyck climb from the cockpit of his glider three hundred yards away.

To Nolan I said: 'Why bother to come? Don't tell me you're going to fly?'

Nolan leaned against the rail, hands in the pockets of his suit. 'I'm not—that's why I'm here.'

Leonora was wearing an evening dress of peacock feathers that lay around her legs in an immense train. The hundreds of eyes gleamed in the electric air before the storm, sheathing her body in their blue flames.

'Miss Chanel, the clouds are like madmen,' I apologized.

'There's a storm on its way.'

She looked up at me with unsettled eyes. 'Don't you people expect to take risks?' She gestured at the storm-nimbus that swirled over our heads. 'For clouds like these I need a Michelangelo of the sky . . . What about Nolan? Is he too frightened as well?'

As she shouted his name, Nolan stared at her, then turned his back to us. The light over Lagoon West had changed. Half the lake was covered by a dim pall.

There was a tug on my sleeve. Petit Manuel looked up at me with his crafty child's eyes. 'Raymond, I can go. Let me take the glider.'

'Manuel, for God's sake. You'll kill——'

He darted between the gilt chairs. Leonora frowned as he plucked her wrist.

'Miss Chanel . . .' His loose mouth formed an encouraging smile. 'I'll sculpt for you. Right now, a big storm-cloud, eh?'

She stared down at him, half-repelled by this eager hunchback ogling her beside the hundred eyes of her peacock train. Van Eyck was limping back to the beach from his wrecked glider. I guessed that in some strange way Manuel was pitting himself against Van Eyck.

Leonora grimaced, as if swallowing some poisonous phlegm. 'Major Parker, tell him to——' She glanced at the dark cloud boiling over the mesa like the effluvium of some black-hearted volcano. 'Wait! Let's see what the little cripple can do!' She turned on Manuel with an over-bright smile. 'Go on then. Let's see you sculpt a whirlwind!'

In her face the diagram of bones formed a geometry of murder.

Nolan ran past across the terrace, his feet crushing the peacock feathers as Leonora laughed. We tried to stop Manuel, but he raced up the slope. Stung by Leonora's taunt, he skipped among the rocks, disappearing from sight in the darkening air. On the terrace a small crowd gathered to watch.

The yellow and tangerine glider rose into the sky and climbed across the face of the storm-cloud. Fifty yards from the dark billows it was buffeted by the shifting air, but Manuel soared in and began to cut away at the dark face. Drops of black rain fell across the terrace at our feet.

The first outline of a woman's head appeared, satanic eyes lit by the open vents in the cloud, a sliding mouth like a dark smear as the huge billows boiled forwards. Nolan shouted in warning from the lake as he climbed into his glider. A moment later little Manuel's craft was lifted by a powerful updraught and tossed over the roof of the cloud. Fighting the insane air, Manuel plunged the glider downwards and drove into the cloud again. Then its immense face opened and in a sudden spasm the cloud surged forward and swallowed the glider.

There was silence on the terrace as the crushed body of the craft revolved in the centre of the cloud. It moved over our heads, dismembered pieces of the wings and fuselage churned about in the dissolving face. As it reached the lake, the cloud began its violent end. Pieces of the face slewed sideways, the mouth was torn off, an eye exploded. It vanished in a last brief squall.

The pieces of Petit Manuel's glider fell from the bright air.

Beatrice Lafferty and I drove across the lake to collect Manuel's body. After the spectacle of this death within the exploding replica of their hostess's face, the guests began to leave. Within minutes the drive was full of cars. Leonora watched them go, standing with Van Eyck among the deserted tables.

Beatrice said nothing as we drove out. The pieces of the shattered glider lay over the fused sand, tags of canvas and broken struts, control lines tied into knots. Then yards from the cockpit I found Petit Manuel's body, lying in a wet ball like a drowned monkey.

I carried him back to the sand-yacht.

'Raymond!' Beatrice pointed to the shore. Storm-clouds were massed along the entire length of the lake, and the first flashes of lightning were striking in the hills behind the mesa. In the electric air the villa had lost its glitter. Half a mile away a tornado was moving along the valley floor, its trunk swaying towards the lake.

The first gusts of air struck the yacht. Beatrice shouted again: 'Raymond! Nolan's there—he's flying inside it!'

Then I saw the black-winged glider circling under the

umbrella of the tornado, Nolan himself riding in the whirl-wind. His wings held steady in the revolving air around the funnel. Like a pilot fish he soared in, as if steering the tornado towards Leonora's villa.

Twenty seconds later, when it struck the house, I lost sight of him. An explosion of dark air overwhelmed the villa, a churning centrifuge of shattered chairs and tiles that burst over the roof. Beatrice and I ran from the yacht, and lay together in a fault in the glass surface. As the tornado moved away, fading into the storm-filled sky, a dark squall hung over the wrecked villa, now and then flicking the debris into the air. Shreds of canvas and peacock feathers fell around us.

We waited half an hour before approaching the house. Hundreds of smashed glasses and broken chairs littered the terrace. At first I could see no signs of Leonora, although her face was everywhere, the portraits with their slashed profiles strewn on the damp tiles. An eddying smile floated towards me from the disturbed air, and wrapped itself around my leg.

Leonora's body lay among the broken tables near the band-stand, half-wrapped in a bleeding canvas. Her face was as bruised now as the storm-cloud Manuel had tried to carve.

We found Van Eyck in the wreck of the marquee. He was suspended by the neck from a tangle of electric wiring, his pale face wreathed in a noose of light bulbs. The current intermittently through the wiring, lighting up his strangled eyes.

I leaned against the overturned Rolls, holding Beatrice's shoulders. 'There's no sign of Nolan—no pieces of his glider.'

'Poor man. Raymond, he was driving that whirlwind here. Somehow he was controlling it.'

I walked across the damp terrace to where Leonora lay. I began silently to cover her with the shreds of canvas, the torn faces of herself.

I took Beatrice Lafferty to live with me in Nolan's studio in the desert near Coral D. We heard no more of Nolan, and never flew the gliders again. The clouds carry too many memories. Three months ago a man who saw the derelict gliders outside the studio stopped near Coral D and walked across to us. He told us he had seen a man flying a glider in the sky high above

Red Beach, carving the strato-cirrus into images of jewels and children's faces. Once there was a dwarf's head.

On reflection, that sounds rather like Nolan, so perhaps he managed to get away from the tornado. In the evenings Beatrice and I sit among the sonic statues, listening to their voices as the fair-weather clouds rise above Coral D, waiting for a man in a dark-winged glider, perhaps painted like candy now, who will come in on the wind and carve for us images of sea-horses and unicorns, dwarfs and jewels and children's faces.

Comes now the double-cross. If you're reading these consecutively, Ellison follows Ballard like a double-shot of Jack Daniels after a whisky sour. He is about to punch you in the belly. His prose is as stark as a skull of Georgie O'Keefe and as steady as a jack-hammer. His themes are always different and always interesting. He never wastes a word, though he's got a lot of them in him. Also, though it's not why he's here, nor intended to be intrusive, he's one of the few people in the world I consider a friend. So I'll tell you a thing about him: unlike Norman Mailer, he need not refer to anything specifically as an advertisement for himself. Everything he writes fills this bill. He writes the most beautiful introductions I have ever read—for his own stories. Consider the fact that everything a man writes is really only a part of one big story, to be ended by the end of his writing life. Consider that, as so many have said, everything a man writes is, basically, autobiographical. Pick up any book by this man, and you will be entranced by learning precisely what went into the creative process. He tells you beforehand, then follows with the story. This one began in Las Vegas and ended with sickness and beauty. I tell you these things because every writer who has ever lived is unique. Harlan, though, is so damned unique that most editors don't know what to make of him. If you ever meet him, you'll know what I mean. There is no separation whatsoever between the subject and the object, the man and his work. When he writes, that's what he is. I'd also say intense, *but that's trite—and if you know him, redundant, too.*

PRETTY MAGGIE MONEYEYES

Harlan Ellison

With an eight hole-card and a queen showing, with the dealer showing a four up, Kostner decided to let the house do the work. So he stood, and the dealer turned up. Six.

The dealer looked like something out of a 1935 George Raft film: Arctic diamond-chip eyes, manicured fingers long as a brain surgeon's, straight black hair slicked flat away from the pale forehead. He did not look up as he peeled them off. A three. Another three. Bam. A five. Bam. Twenty-one, and Kostner saw his last thirty dollars—six five-dollar chips—scraped on the edge of the cards, into the dealer's chip racks. Busted. Flat. Down and out in Las Vegas, Nevada. Playground of the Western World.

He slid off the comfortable stool-chair and turned his back on the blackjack table. The action was already starting again, like waves closing over a drowned man. He had been there, was gone, and no one had noticed. No one had seen a man blow the last tie with salvation. Kostner now had his choice: he could bum his way into Los Angeles and try to find something that resembled a new life . . . or he could go blow his brains out through the back of his head.

Neither choice showed much light or sense.

He thrust his hands deep into the pockets of his worn and dirty chinos, and started away down the line of slot machines clanging and rattling on the other side of the aisle between blackjack tables.

He stopped. He felt something in his pocket. Beside him, but all-engrossed, a fiftyish matron in electric lavender capris, high heels and Ship n' Shore blouse was working two slots, loading and pulling one while waiting for the other to clock down. She was dumping quarters in a seemingly inexhaustible supply from a Dixie cup held in her left hand. There was a surrealistic presence to the woman. She was almost automated, not a flicker of expression on her face, the eyes fixed and unwavering. Only when the gong rang, someone down the line had pulled a jackpot, did she look up. And at that moment Kostner knew what was wrong and immoral and deadly about Vegas, about legalized gambling, about setting the traps all baited and open in front of the average human. The woman's face was grey with hatred, envy, lust and dedication to the game—in that timeless instant when she heard another drugged soul down the line winning a minuscule jackpot. A jackpot that would only lull the player with words like *luck* and *ahead of the game*. The jackpot lure; the sparkling, bobbling many-coloured wiggler in a sea of poor fish.

The thing in Kostner's pocket was a silver dollar.

He brought it out and looked at it.

The eagle was hysterical.

But Kostner pulled to an abrupt halt, only one half-footstep from the sign indicating the limits of Tap City. He was still with it. What the high-rollers called the edge, the *vigerish*, the fine hole-card. One buck. One cartwheel. Pulled out of the pocket not half as deep as the pit into which Kostner had just been about to plunge.

What the hell, he thought, and turned to the row of slot machines.

He had thought they'd all been pulled out of service, the silver dollar slots. A shortage of coinage said the United States Mint. But right there, side by side with the nickel and quarter bandits, was one cartwheel machine. Two thousand dollars jackpot. Kostner grinned foolishly. If you're gonna go out, go out like a champ.

He thumbed the silver dollar into the coin slot and grabbed the heavy, oiled handle. Shining cast aluminium and pressed steel. Big black plastic ball, angled for arm-ease, pull it all day and you won't get weary.

Without a prayer in the universe, Kostner pulled the handle.

She had been born in Tucson, mother full-blooded Cherokee, father a bindlestiff on his way through. Mother had been working a truckers' stop, father had popped for spencer steak and sides. Mother had just got over a bad scene, indeterminate origins, unsatisfactory culminations. Mother had popped for bed. And sides. Margaret Annie Jessie had come nine months later; black of hair, fair of face, and born into a life of poverty. Twenty-three years later, a determined product of Miss Clairol and Berlitz, a dream-image formed by Vogue *and intimate association with the rat race, Margaret Annie Jessie had become a contraction.*

Maggie.

Long legs, trim and coltish; hips a trifle large, the kind that promote that specific thought in men, about getting their hands around it; belly flat, isometrics; waist cut to the bone, a waist that works in any style from dirndl to disco-slacks; no breasts—all nipple, but no breast, like an expensive whore (the way O'Hara pinned it)—and no padding . . . forget the cans, baby, there's other, more important action; smooth, Michelangelo-sculpted neck, a pillar, proud; and all that face.

Out-thrust chin, perhaps a tot too much belligerence, but if you'd walloped as many gropers, you too, sweetheart; narrow mouth, petulant lower lip, nice to chew on, a lower lip as though filled with honey, bursting, ready for things to happen; a nose that threw the right sort of shadow, flaring nostrils, the acceptable words—aquiline, patrician, classic, allathat; cheekbones as stark and promontory as a spit of land after ten years of open ocean; cheekbones holding darkness like narrow shadows, sooty beneath the taut-fleshed bone-structure; amazing cheekbones, the whole face, really; simple uptilted eyes, the touch of the Cherokee, eyes that looked out at you, as you looked in at them, like someone peering out of the keyhole as you peered in; actually, dirty eyes, they said you can get it.

Blonde hair, a great deal of it, wound and rolled and smoothed and flowing, in the old style, the pageboy thing men always admire; no tight little cap of slicked plastic; no ratted and teased Anapurna of bizarre coiffure; no ironed-flat discothèque hair like number 3 flat noodles. Hair the way a man wants it, so he can dig his hands in at the base of the neck and pull all that face very close.

An operable woman, a working mechanism, a rigged and sudden machinery of softness and motivation.

Twenty-three, and determined as hell never to abide in that vale of poverty her mother had called purgatory for her entire life; snuffed out in a grease fire in the last trailer, somewhere in Arizona, thank God no more pleas for a little money from babygirl Maggie hustling drinks in a Los Angeles topless joint. (There ought to be some remorse in there somewhere, for a Mommy gone where all the good grease-fire victims go. Look around, you'll find it.)

Maggie.

Genetic freak. Mommy's Cherokee uptilted eye-shape, and Polack quickscrewing Daddy WithoutaName's blue as innocence colour.

Blue-eyed Maggie, dyed blonde, alla that face, all that leg, fifty bucks a night can get it and it sounds like it's having a climax.

Irish-innocent blue-eyed innocent French-legged innocent Maggie. Polack. Cherokee. Irish. All-woman and going on the market for this month's rent on the stucco pad, eighty bucks' worth of groceries, a couple of months' worth for a Mustang, three appointments with the specialist in Beverly Hills about that shortness of breath after a night on the Bugalu.

Maggie, Maggie, Maggie, pretty Maggie Moneyeyes, who came from Tucson and trailers and rheumatic fever and a surge to live that was all kaleidoscopic frenzy of clawing scrabbling no-nonsense. If it took laying on one's back and making sounds like a panther in the desert, then one did it, because nothing, *but* nothing *was as bad as being dirt-poor, itchy-skinned, soiled-underwear, scuff-toed, hairy and ashamed lousy with the no-gots. Nothing!*

Maggie. Hooker. Hustler. Grabber. Swinger. If there's a buck in it, there's rhythm and the onomatopoeia is Maggie Maggie Maggie.

She who puts out. For a price, whatever that might be.

Maggie was dating Nuncio. He was Sicilian. He had dark eyes and an alligator-grain wallet with slip-in pockets for credit cards. He was a spender, a sport, a high-roller. They went to Vegas.

Maggie and the Sicilian. Her blue eyes and his slip-in pockets. But mostly her blue eyes.

The spinning reels behind the three long glass windows blurred, and Kostner knew there wasn't a chance. Two thousand dollar jackpot. Round and round, whirring. Three bells or two bells and a jackpot bar, get 18; three plums or two plums and a jackpot bar, get 14; three oranges or two oranges and a jac——

Ten, five, two bucks for a single cherry cluster in first position. Something . . . I'm drowning . . . something . . .

The whirring . . .

Round and round . . .

As something happened that was not considered in the pit-boss manual.

The reels whipped and snapped to a stop, clank clank clank, tight in place.

Three bars looked up at Kostner. But they did not say JACKPOT. They were three bars on which stared three blue eyes. Very blue, very immediate, very JACKPOT! !

Twenty silver dollars clattered into the pay-off trough at the bottom of the machine. An orange light flickered on in the Casino Cashier's cage, bright orange on the jackpot board. And the gong began clanging overhead.

The Slot Machine Floor Manager nodded once to the Pit Boss, who pursed his lips and started towards the seedy-looking man still standing with his hand on the slot's handle.

The token payment—twenty silver-dollars—lay untouched in the pay-off trough. The balance of the jackpot—one thousand nine hundred and eighty dollars—would be paid manually by the Casino Cashier. And Kostner stood, dumbly, as the three blue eyes stared up at him.

There was a moment of idiotic disorientation, as Kostner stared back at the three blue eyes; a moment in which the slot machine's mechanisms registered to themselves; and the gong was clanging furiously.

All through the hotel's Casino people turned from their games to stare. At the roulette tables the white-on-white players from Detroit and Cleveland pulled their watery eyes away from the clattering ball and stared down the line for a second, at the ratty-looking guy in front of the slot machine. From where they sat, they could not tell it was a two grand pot, and their rheumy eyes went back into billows of cigar smoke, and that little ball.

The blackjack hustlers turned momentarily, screwing around in their seats, and smiled. They were closer to the slot-players in temperament, but they knew the slots were a dodge to keep the old ladies busy, while the players worked towards their endless twenty-ones.

And the old dealer, who could no longer cut it at the fast-action boards, who had been put out to pasture by a grateful management, standing at the Wheel of Fortune near the entrance to the Casino, even he paused in his zombie-murmuring ('Annnnother winner onna Wheel of Forchun!') to no one at all, and looked towards Kostner and that incredible gong-clanging. Then, in a moment, still with no players, he called *another* non-existent winner.

Kostner heard the gong from far away. It had to mean he had won two thousand dollars, but that was impossible. He checked the pay-off chart on the face of the machine. Three bars labelled JACKPOT meant JACKPOT. Two thousand dollars.

But these three bars did not say JACKPOT. They were three grey bars, rectangular in shape, with three blue eyes directly in the centre of each bar.

Blue eyes?

Somewhere, a connection was made, and electricity, a billion volts of electricity, were shot through Kostner. His hair stood on

*end, his fingertips bled raw, his eyes turned to jelly, and every fibre
in his musculature became radio-active. Somewhere, out there, in a
place that was not this place, Kostner had been inextricably bound
to—to someone.* Blue eyes?

The gong had faded out of his head, the constant noise level
of the Casino, chips chittering, people mumbling, dealers calling
plays, it had all gone, and he was embedded in silence.

Tied to that someone else, out there somewhere, through
those three blue eyes.

Then in an instant, it had passed, and he was alone again, as
though released by a giant hand, the breath crushed out of him.
He staggered up against the slot machine.

'You all right, fellah?'

A hand gripped him by the arm, steadied him. The gong was
still clanging overhead somewhere, and he was breathless from
a journey he had just taken. His eyes focused and he found
himself looking at the stocky Pit Boss who had been on duty
while he had been playing blackjack.

'Yeah . . . I'm okay, just a little dizzy is all.'

'Sounds like you got yourself a big jackpot, fellah,' the Pit
Boss grinned. It was a leathery grin; something composed of
stretched muscles and conditioned reflexes, totally mirthless.

'Yeah . . . great . . .' Kostner tried to grin back. But he was
still shaking from that electrical absorption that had kidnapped
him.

'Let me check it out,' the Pit Boss was saying, edging around
Kostner, and staring at the face of the slot machine. 'Yeah, three
jackpot bars, all right. You're a winner.'

Then it dawned on Kostner! Two thousand dollars! He
looked down at the slot machine and saw——

Three bars with the word JACKPOT on them. No blue eyes,
just words that meant money. Kostner looked around frantically, was he losing his mind? *From somewhere, not in the Casino
room, he heard a tingle of rhodium-plated laughter.*

He scooped up the twenty silver dollars, and the Pit Boss
dropped another cartwheel into the Chief, and pulled the jackpot
off. Then the Pit Boss walked him to the rear of the Casino,
talking to him in a muted, extremely polite tone of voice. At the
Cashier's window, the Pit Boss nodded to a weary-looking man
at a huge Rolodex card-file, checking credit ratings.

'Barney jackpot on the cartwheel Chief; slot five-oh-oh-one-five.' He grinned at Kostner, who tried to smile back. It was difficult. He felt stunned.

The Cashier checked a pay-off book for the correct amount to be drawn and leaned over the counter towards Kostner. 'Cheque or cash, sir?'

Kostner felt buoyancy coming back to him. 'Is the Casino's cheque good?' They all three laughed at that. 'A cheque's fine,' Kostner said. The cheque was drawn, and the Cheque-Riter punched out the little bumps that said two thousand. 'The twenty cartwheels are a gift,' the Cashier said, sliding the cheque through to Kostner.

He held it, looked at it, and still found it difficult to believe. Two grand, back on the golden road.

As he walked back through the Casino with the Pit Boss, the stocky man asked pleasantly, 'Well, what are you going to do with it?' Kostner had to think a moment. He didn't really have any plans. But then the sudden realization came to him: 'I'm going to play that slot machine again.' The Pit Boss smiled: a congenital sucker. He would put all twenty of those silver dollars back into the Chief, and then turn to the other games. Blackjack, roulette, faro, baccarat . . . in a few hours he would have redeposited the two grand with the hotel Casino. It always happened.

He walked Kostner back to the slot machine, and patted him on the shoulder. 'Lotsa luck, fellah.'

As he turned away, Kostner slipped a silver dollar into the machine, and pulled the handle.

The Pit Boss had only taken five steps when he heard the incredible sound of the reels clicking to a stop, the clash of twenty token silver dollars hitting the pay-off trough, and that goddamned gong went out of its mind again.

She had known that sonofabitch Nuncio was a perverted swine. A walking filth. A dungheap between his ears. Some kind of monster in nylon undershorts. There weren't many kinds of games Maggie hadn't played, but what that Sicilian De Sade wanted to do was outright vomity!

She nearly fainted when he suggested it. Her heart—which the Beverly Hills specialist had said she should not tax—began whumping frantically. 'You pig!' she screamed. 'You filthy, dirty, ugly pig you, Nuncio you pig!' She had bounded out of the bed and started to throw on clothes. She didn't even bother with a brassiere, pulling the poor-boy sweater on over her thin breasts, still crimson with the touches and love-bites Nuncio had showered on them.

He sat up in the bed, a pathetic-looking little man, grey hair at the temples and no hair at all on top, and his eyes were moist. He was porcine, was indeed the swine she called him, but he was helpless before her. He was in love with his hooker, with the tart whom he was supporting. It had been the first time for the swine Nuncio, and he was helpless. Back in Detroit, had it been a floozy, a chippy broad, he would have got out of the double bed and rapped her around pretty good. But this Maggie, she tied him in knots. He had suggested . . . that, what they should do together . . . because he was so consumed with her. But she was furious with him. It wasn't that bizarre an idea!

'Gimme a chanct'a talk t'ya, honey . . . Maggie . . .'

'You filthy pig, Nuncio! Give me some money, I'm going down to the Casino, and I don't want to see your filthy pig face for the rest of the day, remember that!'

And she had gone in his wallet and pants, and taken eight hundred and sixteen dollars, while he watched. He was helpless before her. She was something stolen from a world he knew only as 'class' and she could do what she wanted with him.

Genetic freak Maggie, blue-eyed posing mannequin Maggie, pretty Maggie Moneyeyes, who was one-half Cherokee and one-half a buncha other things, had absorbed her lessons well. She was the very model of a 'class broad'.

'Not for the rest of the day, do you understand?' she snapped at him, and went downstairs, furious, to fret and gamble and wonder about nothing but years of herself.

Men stared after her as she walked. She carried herself like a challenge, the way a squire carried a pennant, the way a prize bitch carried herself in the judge's ring. Born to the blue. The wonders of mimicry and desire.

Maggie had no desire for gambling, none whatever. She merely wanted to taste the fury of her relationship with the swine Sicilian, her need for solidarity in a life built on the edge of the slide area, the senselessness of being here in Las Vegas when she could be back in Beverly Hills. She grew angrier and more ill at the thought of

Nuncio upstairs in the room, taking another shower. She bathed three times a day. But it was different with him. He knew she resented his smell; he had the soft odour of wet fur sometimes, and she had told him about it. Now he bathed constantly, and hated it. He was a foreigner to the bath. His life had been marked by various kinds of filths, and baths for him now were more of an obscenity than dirt could ever have been. For her, bathing was different. It was a necessity. She had to keep the patina of the world off her, had to remain clean and smooth and white. A presentation, not an object of flesh and hair. A chromium instrument, something never pitted by rust and corrosion.

When she was touched by them, by any one of them, by the men, by all the Nuncios, they left little pit holes of bloody rust on her white, permanent flesh; cobwebs, sooty stains. She had to bathe. Often.

She strolled down between the tables and the slots, carrying eight hundred and sixteen dollars. Eight one hundred dollar bills and sixteen dollars in ones.

At the change booth she got cartwheels for the sixteen ones. The Chief waited. It was her baby. She played it to infuriate the Sicilian. He had told her to play the nickel slots, the quarter or dime slots, but she always infuriated him by blowing fifty or a hundred dollars in ten minutes, one coin after another, in the big Chief.

She faced the machine squarely, and put in the first silver dollar. She pulled the handle that swine Nuncio. Another dollar, pulled the handle how long does this go on? The reels—cycled and spun and whirled and whipped in a blurringspinning and metalhumming overandoverandover as Maggie blue-eyed Maggie hated and hated and thought of hate and all the days and nights of swine behind her and ahead of her if only she had all the money in this room in this Casino in this hotel in this town right now this very instant just an instant this instant it would be enough to whirring and humming and spinning and overandoverandoverandover and she would be free free free and all the world would never touch her body again the swine would never touch her white flesh again and then suddenly as dollarafterdollarafterdollar went aroundaroundaround hummmmmming in reels of cherries and bells and bars and plums and oranges there was suddenly painpainpain a SHARP pain!pain!pain! in her chest, her heart, her centre, a needle, a lancet, a burning, a pillar of flame that was purest pure purer PAIN!

Maggie, pretty Maggie Moneyeyes, who wanted all that money in that cartwheel Chief slot machine, Maggie who had come from filth and rheumatic fever, who had come all the way to three baths a day and a specialist in Very Expensive Beverly Hills, that Maggie suddenly had a seizure, a flutter, a slam of a coronary thrombosis and fell instantly dead on the floor of the Casino. Dead.

One instant she had been holding the handle of the slot machine, willing her entire being, all that hatred for all the swine she had ever rolled with, willing every fibre of every cell of every chromosome into that machine, wanting to suck out every silver vapour within its belly, and the next instant—so close they might have been the same—her heart exploded and killed her and she slipped to the floor . . . still touching the Chief.

On the floor.

Dead.

Struck dead.

Liar. All the lies that were her life.

Dead on a floor.

[A moment out of time ■ lights whirling and spinning in a cotton candy universe ■ down a bottomless funnel roundly sectioned like a goat's horn ■ a cornucopia that rose up cuculiform smooth and slick as a worm belly ■ endless nights that pealed ebony funeral bells ■ out of fog ■ out of weightlessness ■ suddenly total cellular knowledge ■ memory running backwards ■ gibbering spastic blindness ■ a soundless owl of frenzy trapped in a cave of prisms ■ sand endlessly draining down ■ billows of for ever ■ edges of the world as they splintered ■ foam rising drowning from inside ■ the smell of rust ■ rough green corners that burn ■ memory the gibbering spastic blind memory ■ seven rushing vacuums of nothing ■ yellow ■ pinpoints cast in amber straining and elongating running like live wax ■ chill fevers ■ overhead the odour of stop ■ this is the stop-over before hell or heaven ■ this is limbo ■ trapped and doomed alone in a mist-eaten nowhere ■ a soundless screaming a soundless whirring a soundless spinning spinning spinning ■ spinning spinning ■ spinning ■ spinning spinning ■ spinninggggggggg]

Maggie had wanted all the silver in the machine. She had

died, willing herself into the machine. Now, looking out from within, from inside the limbo that had become her own purgatory, Maggie was trapped, the soul of Maggie was trapped, in the oiled and anodized interior of the silver dollar slot machine. The prison of her final desires, where she had wanted to be, completely trapped in that last instant of life between life/death. Maggie, all soul now, trapped for all eternity in the soul of the machine. Trapped.

'I hope you don't mind if I call over one of the slot men,' the Slot Machine Floor Manager was saying, from a far distance. He was in his late fifties, a velvet-voiced man whose eyes held nothing of light and certainly nothing of kindness. He had stopped the Pit Boss as the stocky man had turned in mid-step to return to Kostner and the jackpotted machine; he had taken the walk himself. 'We have to make sure, you know how it is, somebody didn't fool with the slot, you know, maybe it's outta whack or something, you know.'

He lifted his left hand and there was a clicker in it, the kind children use at Hallowe'en. He clicked half a dozen times, like a rabid cricket, and there was a scurrying in the pit between the tables.

Kostner was only faintly aware of what was happening. Instead of being totally awake, feeling the surge of adrenaline through his veins, the feeling any gambler gets when he is ahead of the game, a kind of desperate urgency when he has hit it for a boodle, he was numb, partaking of the action around him only as much as a drinking glass involves itself in the alcoholic's drunken binge.

All colour and sound had been leached out of him.

A tired-looking, resigned-weary man wearing a grey porter's jacket, as grey as his hair, as grey as his indoor skin, came to them, carrying a leather wrap-up of tools. The slot repairman studied the machine, turning the pressed steel body around on its stand, studying the back. He used a key on the back door and for an instant Kostner had a view of gears, springs, armatures and the clock that ran the slot mechanism. The repairman nodded silently over it, closed and relocked it, turned it around again and studied the face of the machine.

'Nobody's been spooning it,' he said, and went away.

Kostner stared at the Floor Manager.

'Gaffing. That's what he meant. Spooning's another word for it. Some guys use a little piece of plastic, or a wire, shove it down through the escalator, it kicks the machine. Nobody thought that's what happened here, but you know, we have to make sure, two grand is a big pay-off, and twice . . . well, you know, I'm sure you'll understand. If a guy was doing it with a boomerang——'

Kostner raised an eyebrow.

—'uh, yeah, a boomerang, it's another way to spoon the machine. But we just wanted to make a little check, and now everybody's satisfied, so if you'll just come back to the Casino Cashier with me——'

And they paid him off again.

So he went back to the slot machine, and stood before it for a long time, staring at it. The change girls and the dealers going off duty, the little old ladies with their canvas work gloves worn to avoid callouses when pulling the slot handles, the men's room attendant on his way up front to get more matchbooks, the floral tourists, the idle observers, the hard drinkers, the sweepers, the busboys, the gamblers with poached-egg eyes who had been up all night, the showgirls with massive breasts and diminutive sugar daddies, all of them conjectured mentally about the beat-up walker who was staring at the silver dollar Chief. He did not move, merely stared at the machine . . . and they wondered.

The machine was staring back at Kostner.

Three blue eyes.

The electric current had sparked through him again, as the machine had clocked down and the eyes turned up a second time, as he had *won* a second time. But this time he knew there was something more than luck involved, for no one else had seen those three blue eyes.

So now he stood before the machine, waiting. It spoke to him. Inside his skull, where no one had ever lived but himself, now someone else moved and spoke to him. A girl. A beautiful girl. Her name was Maggie, and she spoke to him:

I've been waiting for you. A long time, I've been waiting for you, Kostner. Why do you think you hit the jackpot? Because I've been waiting for you, and I want you. You'll win all the jackpots. Because I want you, I need you. Love me, I'm Maggie, I'm so alone, love me.

Kostner had been staring at the slot machine for a very long time, and his weary brown eyes had seemed to be locked to the blue eyes on the jackpot bars. But he knew no one else could see the blue eyes, and no one else could hear the voice, and no one else knew about Maggie.

He was the universe to her. Everything to her.

He thumbed in another silver dollar, and the Pit Boss watched, the slot machine repairman watched, the Slot Machine Floor Manager watched, three change girls watched, and a pack of unidentified players watched, some from their seats.

The reels whirled, the handle snapped back, and in a second they flipped down to a halt, twenty silver dollars tokened themselves into the pay-off trough and a woman at one of the crap tables belched a fragment of hysterical laughter.

And the gong went insane again.

The Floor Manager came over and said, very softly, 'Mr. Kostner, it'll take us about fifteen minutes to pull this machine and check it out. I'm sure you understand.' As two slot repairmen came out of the back, hauled the Chief off its stand, and took it into the repair room at the rear of the Casino.

While they waited, the Floor Manager regaled Kostner with stories of spooners who had used intricate magnets inside their clothes, of boomerang men who had attached their plastic implements under their sleeves so they could be extended on spring-loaded clips, of cheaters who had come equipped with tiny electric drills in their hands and wires that slipped into the tiny drilled holes. And he kept saying he knew Kostner would understand.

But Kostner knew the Floor Manager would not understand.

When they brought the Chief back, the repairmen nodded assuredly. 'Nothing wrong with it. Works perfectly, Nobody's been boomin' it.'

But the blue eyes were gone on the jackpot bars.

Kostner knew they would return.

They paid him off again.

He returned and played again. And again. And again. They put a 'spotter' on him. He won again. And again. And again. The crowd had grown to massive proportions. Word had spread like the silent communications of the telegraph vine, up and down the Strip, all the way to downtown Vegas and the sidewalk casinos where they played night and day every day of the year, and the crowd moved towards the hotel, and the Casino, and the seedy-looking walker with his weary brown eyes. The crowd moved to him inexorably, drawn like lemmings by the odour of the luck that rose from him like musky electrical cracklings. And he won. Again and again. Thirty-eight thousand dollars. And the three blue eyes continued to stare up at him. Her lover was winning. Maggie and her Moneyeyes.

Finally, the Casino decided to speak to Kostner. They pulled the Chief for fifteen minutes, for a supplemental check by experts from the slot machine company in downtown Vegas, and while they were checking it, they asked Kostner to come to the main office of the hotel.

The owner was there. His face seemed faintly familiar to Kostner. Had he seen it on television? The newspapers?

'Mr. Kostner, my name is Jules Hartshorn.'

'I'm pleased to meet you.'

'Quite a string of luck you're having out there.'

'It's been a long time coming.'

'You realize, this sort of luck is impossible.'

'I'm compelled to believe it, Mr. Hartshorn.'

'Um. As am I. It's happening to my Casino. But we're thoroughly convinced of one of two possibilities, Mr. Kostner: one, either the machine is inoperable in a way we can't detect, or two, you are the most clever spooner we've ever had in here.'

'I'm not cheating.'

'As you can see, Mr. Kostner, I'm smiling. The reason I'm smiling is at your naïveté in believing I would take your word for it. I'm perfectly happy to nod politely and say of course you aren't cheating. But no one can win thirty-eight thousand dollars on nineteen straight jackpots off one slot machine; it doesn't even have mathematical odds against its happening, Mr. Kostner. It's on a cosmic scale of improbability with three dark planets crashing into our sun within the next twenty minutes. It's on a par with the Pentagon, Peking and the Kremlin all three pushing the red button at the same microsecond. It's an impossibility, Mr. Kostner. An impossibility that's happening to me.'

'I'm sorry.'

'Not really.'

'No, not really. I can use the money.'

'For what, exactly, Mr. Kostner?'

'I hadn't thought about it, really.'

'I see. Well, Mr. Kostner, let's look at it this way. I can't stop you from playing, and if you continue to win, I'll be required to pay off. And no stubble-chinned thugs will be waiting in an alley to jackroll you and take the money. The cheques will all be honoured. The best I can hope for, Mr. Kostner, is the attendant publicity. Right now, every player in Vegas is in that Casino, waiting for you to drop cartwheels into that machine. It won't make up for what I'm losing, if you continue the way you've been, but it will help. Every high-roller in town likes to rub up next to luck. All I ask is that you co-operate a little.'

'The least I can do, considering your generosity.'

'An attempt at humour.'

'I'm sorry. What is it you'd like me to do?'

'Get about ten hours' sleep.'

'While you pull the slot and have it worked over thoroughly?'

'Yes.'

'If I wanted to keep winning, that might be a pretty stupid move on my part. You might change that hickamajig inside so I couldn't win if I put back every dollar of that thirty-eight grand.'

'We're licensed by the state of Nevada, Mr. Kostner.'

'I come from a good family, too, and take a look at me. I'm a bum with thirty-eight thousand dollars in my pocket.'

'Nothing will be done to that slot machine, Kostner.'

'Then why pull it for ten hours?'

'To work it over thoroughly in the shop. If something as undetectable as metal fatigue or a worn escalator tooth or—we want to make sure this doesn't happen with other machines. And the extra time will get the word around town; we can use the crowd. Some of those tourists will stick to our fingers, and it'll help defray the expense of having you break the bank at this Casino—on a slot machine.'

'I have to take your word.'

'This hotel will be in business long after you're gone, Kostner.'

'Not if I keep winning.'

Hartshorn's smile was a stricture. 'A good point.'

'So it isn't much of an argument.'

'It's the only one I have. If you want to get back out on that floor, I can't stop you.'

'No Mafia hoods ventilate me later?'

'I beg your pardon?'

'I said: no Maf——'

'You have a picturesque manner of speaking. In point of fact, I haven't the faintest idea what you're talking about.'

'I'm sure you haven't.'

'You've got to stop reading *The National Enquirer*. This is a legally run business. I'm merely asking a favour.'

'Okay, Mr. Hartshorn, I've been three days without any sleep. Ten hours will do me a world of good.'

'I'll have the desk clerk find you a quiet room on the top floor. And thank you, Mr. Kostner.'

'Think nothing of it.'

'I'm afraid that will be impossible.'

'A lot of impossible things are happening lately.'

He turned to go, as Hartshorn lit a cigarette.

'Oh, by the way, Mr. Kostner?'

Kostner stopped and half-turned. 'Yes?'

His eyes were getting difficult to focus. There was a ringing in his ears. Hartshorn seemed to waver at the edge of his vision like heat lightning across a prairie. Like memories of things Kostner had come across the country to forget. Like the whimpering and pleading that kept tugging at the cells of his brain. The voice of Maggie. Still back in there, saying . . . things . . .

They'll try to keep you from me.

All he could think about was the ten hours of sleep he had been promised. Suddenly it was more important than the money, than forgetting, than anything. Hartshorn was talking, was saying things, but Kostner could not hear him. It was as if he had turned off the sound and saw only the silent rubbery movement of Hartshorn's lips. He shook his head trying to clear it.

There were half a dozen Hartshorns all melting into and out of one another. And the voice of Maggie.

I'm warm here, and alone. I could be good to you, if you can come to me. Please come, please hurry.

'Mr. Kostner?'

Hartshorn's voice came draining down through silt as thick as velvet flocking. Kostner tried to focus again. His extremely weary brown eyes began to track.

'Did you know about that slot machine?' Hartshorn was saying. 'A peculiar thing happened with it about six weeks ago.'

'What was that?'

'A girl died playing it. She had a heart attack, a seizure while she was pulling the handle, and died right out there on the floor.'

Kostner was silent for a moment. He wanted desperately to ask Hartshorn what colour the dead girl's eyes had been, but he was afraid the owner would say blue.

He paused with his hand on the office door. 'Seems as though you've had nothing but a streak of bad luck on that machine.'

Hartshorn smiled an enigmatic smile. 'It might not change for a while, either.'

Kostner felt his jaw muscles tighten. 'Meaning I might die, too, and wouldn't *that* be bad luck.'

Hartshorn's smile became hieroglyphic, permanent, stamped on him for ever. 'Sleep tight, Mr. Kostner.'

In a dream, she came to him. Long, smooth thighs and soft golden down on her arms; blue eyes deep as the past, misted with a fine scintillance like lavender spiderwebs; taut body that was the only body Woman had ever had, from the very first. Maggie came to him.

Hello. I've been travelling a long time.

'*Who are you?*' *Kostner asked, wonderingly. He was standing on a chilly plain, or was it a plateau? The wind curled around them both, or was it only around him? She was exquisite, and he saw her clearly, or was it through a mist? Her voice was deep and resonant, or was it light and warm as night-blooming jasmine?*

I'm Maggie. I love you. I've waited for you.

'*You have blue eyes.*'

Yes. *With love.*

'*You're very beautiful.*'

Thank you. *With female amusement.*

'*But why me? Why let it happen to me? Are you the girl who— are you the one that was sick—the one who——?*'

I'm Maggie. And you, I picked you, because you need me.

You've needed someone for a long, long time.

Then it unrolled for Kostner. The past unrolled and he saw who he was. He saw himself alone. Always alone. As a child, born to kind and warm parents who hadn't the vaguest notion of who he was, what he wanted to be, where his talents lay. So he had run off, when he was in his teens, and alone always alone on the road. For years and months and days and hours, with no one. Casual friendships, based on food, or sex, or artificial similarities. But no one to whom he could cleave, and cling, and belong. It was that way till Susie, and with her he had found light. He had discovered the scents and aromas of a spring that was eternally one day away. He had laughed, really laughed, and known with her it would at last be all right. So he had poured all of himself into her, giving her everything; all his hopes, his secret thoughts, his tender dreams; and she had taken them, taken him, all of him, and he had known for the first time what it was to have a place to live, to have a home in someone's heart. It was all the silly and gentle things he laughed at in other people, but for him it was breathing deeply of wonder.

He had stayed with her for a long time, and had supported her, supported her son from the first marriage; the marriage Susie never talked about. And then one day, he had come back, as Susie had always known he would. He was a dark creature of ruthless habits and vicious nature, but she had been his woman, all along, and Kostner realized he had been used as a stop-gap, as a bill-payer till her wandering terror came home to nest. Then she had asked him to leave. Broke, and tapped out in all the silent inner ways a man can be drained, he had left, without even a fight, for all the fight had been leached out of him. He had left, and wandered West, and finally come to Las Vegas, where he had hit bottom. And found Maggie. In a dream, with blue eyes, he had found Maggie.

I want you to belong to me. I love you. *Her truth was vibrant in Kostner's mind. She was his, at last someone who was special, was his.*

'Can I trust you? I've never been able to trust anyone before. Women, never. But I need someone. I really need someone.'

It's me, always. For ever. You can trust me.

And she came to him, fully. Her body was a declaration of truth and trust such as no other Kostner had ever known before. She met him on a windswept plain of thought, and he made love to her more completely than he had known any passion before. She joined

*with him, entered him, mingled with his blood and his thought and
his frustration, and he came away clean, filled with glory.*

'*Yes, I can trust you, I want you, I'm yours,*' he whispered to
her, when they lay side by side in a dream nowhere of mist and
soundlessness. '*I'm yours.*'

*She smiled, a woman's smile of belief in her man; a smile of
trust and deliverance. And Kostner woke up.*

The Chief was back on its stand, and the crowd had been
penned back by velvet ropes. Several people had played the
machine, but there had been no jackpots.

Now Kostner came into the Casino, and the 'spotters' got
themselves ready. While Kostner had slept, they had gone
through his clothes, searching for wires, for gaffs, for spoons or
boomerangs. Nothing.

Now he walked straight to the Chief, and stared at it.

Hartshorn was there. 'You look tired,' he said gently to
Kostner, studying the man's weary brown eyes.

'I am, a little,' Kostner tried a smile, which didn't work. 'I
had a funny dream.'

'Oh?'

'Yeah . . . about a girl . . .' he let it die off.

Hartshorn's smile was understanding. Pitying, emphatic, and
understanding. 'There are lots of girls in this town. You
shouldn't have any trouble finding one with your winnings.'

Kostner nodded, and slipped his first silver dollar into the
slot. He pulled the handle. The reels spun with a ferocity
Kostner had not heard before and suddenly everything went
whipping slantwise as he felt a wrenching of pure flame in his
stomach, as his head was snapped on its spindly neck, as the
lining behind his eyes was burned out. There was a terrible
shriek, of tortured metal, of an express train ripping the air
with its passage, of a hundred small animals being gutted and
torn to shreds, of incredible pain, of night winds that tore the
tops off mountains of lava. And a keening whine of a voice that
wailed and wailed and wailed as it went away from there in
blinding light——

Free! Free! Heaven or Hell it doesn't matter! Free!

The sound of a soul released from an eternal prison, a genie
freed from a dark bottle. And in that instant of damp soundless

nothingness, Kostner saw the reels snap and clock down for the final time:

One, two, three. Blue eyes.

But he would never cash his cheques.

The crowd screamed through one voice as he fell sidewise and lay on his face. The final loneliness . . .

The Chief was pulled. Bad luck. Too many gamblers resented its very presence in the Casino. So it was pulled. And returned to the company, with explicit instructions it was to be melted down to slag. And not till it was in the hands of the ladle foreman, who was ready to dump it into the slag furnace, did anyone remark on the final tally the Chief had clocked.

'Look at that, ain't that weird,' said the ladle foreman to his bucket man. He pointed to the three glass windows.

'Never saw jackpot bars like that before,' the bucket man agreed. 'Three eyes. Must be an old machine.'

'Yeah, some of these old games go way back,' the foreman said, hoisting the slot machine on to the conveyor track leading to the slag furnace.

'Three eyes, huh. How about that. Three brown eyes.' And he threw the knife-switch that sent the Chief down the track, to puddle, in the roaring inferno of the furnace.

Three brown eyes.

Three brown eyes that looked very, very weary. That looked very, very trapped. That looked very, very betrayed. Some of these old games go way back.

—Las Vegas and Hollywood, 1965

I had only read two stories by Gary Wright prior to this one, and each of them has spoken to me in the words of Antoine de Saint-Exupéry, when he was on the Toulouse–Dakar line:

'Old bureaucrat, my comrade, it is not you who are to blame. No one ever helped you to escape. You, like a termite, built your peace by blocking up with cement every chink and cranny through which the light might pierce. You rolled yourself up into a ball in your genteel security, in routine, in the stifling conventions of provincial life, raising a modest rampart against the winds and the tides and, the stars. You have chosen not to be perturbed by great problems, having trouble enough to forget your own fate as man. You are not the dweller upon an errant planet and do not ask yourself questions to which there are no answers. You are a petty bourgeois of Toulouse. Nobody grasped you by the shoulder while there was still time. Now the clay of which you were shaped has dried and hardened, and naught in you will ever awaken the sleeping musician, the poet, the astronomer that possibly inhabited you in the beginning.'*

Here is a story of freedom, violence, Angst. I will not insult the author by comparing him to someone else—like, say, Hemingway. No. He is himself. And he has written a man against the elements story, which I feel belongs right here. After Ballard's magical shadow-play in the sky and Harlan's jazz-discord finale, here is something as cold and clean as a bottle of akavit frozen into a block of ice, or the winds that lash the highest mountains.

* 'Wind, Sand and Stars', *Airman's Odyssey*, Heinemann (London, 1939).

MIRROR OF ICE

Gary Wright

They called it The Stuka. It was a tortuous, twenty-kilometre path of bright ice, and in that distance—12·42 miles—it dropped 7,366 feet, carving a course down the alpine mountainside like the track of a great snake. It was thirty feet wide on the straights with corners curling as high as forty feet. It was made for sleds. . . .

He waited in the narrow cockpit and listened to the wind. It moaned along the frozen shoulder of the towering white peak and across the steep starting ramp, pushing along streamers of snow out against the hard blue sky, and he could hear it cry inside him with the same cold and lonely sound.

He was scared. And what was worse—he knew it.

Forward, under the sleek nose of his sled, the mountain fell away abruptly—straight down, it seemed—and the valley was far below. So very far.

. . . too far this time, buddy-boy, too far for ever . . .

The countdown light on the dash flickered a sudden blood red, then deliberately winked twice. At the same time two red rockets arced out over the valley and exploded into twin crimson fireballs.

Two minutes.

On both sides of the starting ramp, cantilevered gracefully from the mountainside, brightly bannered platforms were crowded with people. He glanced at the hundreds of blankly staring sunglasses, always the same, always turned to the ramp as if trying to see inside the helmets of these men, as if trying to pry into the reasons of their being there waiting to die. He looked back to the deep valley; today he wondered too.

. . . just one last time, wasn't that what you told yourself? One last race and that's the end of it and good-bye to the sleds and thank God! Wasn't that your personal promise?

Then what in hell are you doing here? That 'last race' was last month's race. Why are you in this one?

No answer.

All he could find inside were cold questions and a hollow echo of the wind. He gripped the steering wheel, hard, until cramps began in his hands; he would think about his sled . . .

It was his eleventh sled, and like the others it was a brilliant red, not red for its particular flash, but because of a possible crash far from the course in deep snow. He wanted to be found and found fast. Some of the Kin had never been found in time.

. . . they didn't find Bob Lander until that summer——
He forced himself back.

Empty, the sled weighed 185 pounds and looked very much like the body-shell of a particularly sleek racer but with a full bubble canopy and with runners instead of wheels. It was a mean-looking missile, low and lean, hardly wider than his shoulders, clearing the ice by barely two inches. He sat nearly reclining, the half wheel in his lap, feet braced on the two edging pedals—and this was the feature that made these sleds the awesome things they were. They could tilt their runners—four hollow-ground, chrome-steel 'skis'—edging them against the ice like wide skate blades. This was what had changed bob-sledding into . . . *this*: this special thing with its special brother-hood, this clan apart, this peculiar breed of men set aside for the wonder of other men. The Kin, they called themselves.

. . . someone once, laughing, had said, 'Without peer, we are the world's fastest suicides.'
He snapped himself back again and checked his brakes.

By pulling back on the wheel, two electrically operated flaps—actually halves of the sled's tail section—swung out on either side. Silly to see, perhaps. But quite effective when this twelve and half square feet hit the airstream at eighty m.p.h. A button under his right thumb operated another braking system: with each push it fired forward a solid rocket charge in the nose of the sled. There were seven charges, quite often not enough. But when everything failed, including the man, there was the lever by his left hip. The Final Folly, it was called; a firm pull and, depending on a hundred unknown 'if's' and 'maybe's', he might be lucky enough to find himself hanging from a parachute some 300 feet up. Or it might be the last voluntary act of his life.

He had used it twice. Once streaking into the tall wall of the

Wingover, he had lost a runner . . . and was almost fired into the opposite grandstand, missing the top tier of seats by less than four feet. Another time six sleds suddenly tangled directly in front of him, and he had blasted himself through the overhanging limbs of a large fir tree.

But others had not been so lucky.

Hans Kroger: they finally dug his body out of eighteen feet of snow; he'd gone all the way to the dirt. His sled had been airborne when he blew—and upside-down!

Jarl Yorgensen: his sled tumbling and he ejected directly under the following sleds. No one was certain that all of him was ever found!

Max Conrad: a perfect blow-out! At least 350 feet up and slightly downhill . . . His chute never opened.

Wayne Barley:

He jarred himself hard in the cockpit and felt the sudden seizure of his G-suit. He wanted to hit something. But he could feel the watching eyes and the TV cameras, and there wasn't room in the cockpit to get a decent swing anyway.

His countdown light flickered for attention and blinked once, and a single red rocket flashed into the sky.

One minute—God, had time stopped?

But that was part of it all: the waiting, the God-awful waiting, staring down at the valley over a mile below. And how many men had irrevocably slammed back their canopy in this lifetime of two minutes and stayed behind? A few, yes. And he could too. Simply open his canopy, that was the signal, and when the start came the other sleds would dive down and away and he would be sitting here alone. But, God, so alone! And he would be alone for the rest of his life. He might see some of the Kin again, sometime, somewhere. But they would not see him. It was a kind of death to stay behind.

. . . and a real death to go. Death, the silent rider with every man in every race . . .

He frowned at the other sleds, sixteen in staggered rows of eight. Sixteen bright and beautiful, trim fast projectiles hanging from their starting clamps. He knew them, every one; they were his brothers. They were the Kin—but not here. Not now.

Years ago when he was a novice he had asked old Franz

Cashner, 'Did you see the way I took Basher Bend right beside you?'

And Franz told him, 'Up there I see nobody! Only sleds! Down here you are you, up there you are nothing but another sled. That's all! And don't forget that! That's all! And don't forget that!'

  . . . and it had to be that way. On the course sleds crashed and were no more. . . . Only later, in the valley, were there men missing.

Of these sixteen, chances were that nine would finish. With luck, maybe ten. And chances also said that only fourteen of these men would be alive tonight. Those were the odds, as hard and cold as the ice, the fascinating frosting for this sport. Violent death! Assured, spectacular, magnetic death in a sport such as the world had never known. Incredible men with incredible skills doing an incredible thing.

Back in the Sixties they claimed an empty sled with its steering locked would make a course all by itself. An empty sled here would not last two corners. The Stuka was a cold killer, not a thrill ride. And it was not particular. It killed veterans and novices alike. But there was $20,000 for the man who got to the end of it first, and a whole month before he had to do it again. Money and fame and all the girls in the world. Everything and anything for the men who rode the Stuka.

Was that why they did it?

  . . . yes, always that question: 'Why do you do it?' And before he had died on the Plummet, Sir Robert Brooke had told them, 'Well, why not?'

  And it was an answer as good as any.

  But was it good enough this time?

No answer.

He only knew there was but one way off this mountain for him now and that was straight ahead, and for the first time since his novice runs, his legs were trembling. Twelve and a half miles, call it, and the record was 9 minutes, 1·14 seconds! An average speed of 82·67 m.p.h., and that was *his* record. They would at least remember him by that!

His countdown light flashed, a green rocket rose and burst, and there was a frozen moment . . . the quiet click of the release hook, the lazy, slow-motion start, the sleds sliding forward in formation over the edge . . . then he was looking once again into the terrible top of the Stuka—that 45-degree, quarter-mile straight drop. In six seconds he was doing over 60 m.p.h., and the mouth of the first corner was reaching up.

. . . *Carl's Corner, for Carl Rasch, who went over the top of it nine years ago; and they found him a half-mile down the glacier . . . what was left of him . . .*

He glanced to his right. It was clear. He eased his flap brakes, dropped back slightly and pulled right. The leading sleds were jockeying in front now, lining for this long left. Brakes flapped like quick wings, and they started around, sleds riding up the vertical ice wall and holding there, ice chips spraying back like contrails from those on the lower part of the wall as they edged their runners against the turn. He came in far right and fast, riding high on the wall and diving off with good acceleration.

The ice was a brilliant blue underneath now, and he could feel the trembling rumble of his sled. They rattled into the Chute, a steep traverse, still gaining speed, still bunched and jostling for position. He was in the rear but this was good; he didn't like this early crowding for the corners.

The sheer wall of Basher Bend loomed, a 120-degree right that dropped hard coming out. He was following close in the slipstream of the sled in front of him, overtaking because of the lessened wind resistance. The corner came, and they were on the wall again. With his slightly greater speed he was able to go higher on the wall, nearly to the top and above the other sled. His G-suit tightened. They swarmed out of the corner and into the Strafing Run, a long, steep dive with a hard pull-out.

A roar rose from the mountain now as the sleds reached speed, a dull rumble like that of avalanche . . . and that is actually what they were now—an avalanche of sleds, and just as deadly.

He pulled ahead of the other sled in the dive and hit the savage pull-out right on the tail of another, and the next turn curved up before them: Hell's Left, a double corner, an abrupt left falling into a short straight with another sharp left at the bottom. He was still overtaking, and they went up the wall side by side, he on the inside, under the other. He eased his left pedal, using edges for the first time, holding himself away from the other by a safe six inches. The course dropped away, straight down the mountain to the second half of the corner, and he felt the sickening sudden smoothness of leaving the ice—he had tried it too fast, and the course was falling away under him. . . .

. . . *old Rolfe De Kepler, 'The Flying Dutchman', laughing over his beer and saying, 'Always I am spending more time off the ice than on, hah? So this is more easy to my stomach. Already I have four G-suits to give up on me.'*

. . . . *and he had made his last flight three years ago off the top at the bottom of Hell's Left . . . 400 yards, they claimed.*

He held firm and straight on the wheel and pulled carefully, barely opening his brakes. The sled touched at a slight angle, lurched, but he caught it by edging quickly. The other sled had pulled ahead. He tucked in behind it. The second left was rushing up at them, narrow and filled with sleds. They dived into it less than a foot apart. Ice chips streamed back from edging runners, rattling against his sled like a storm of bullets. There was an abrupt lurching, the quick left-right slam of air turbulence. A sled was braking hard somewhere ahead. Perhaps two or three. Where? He couldn't see. He reacted automatically . . . full air brakes, hard on to his left edges and steer for the inside; the safest area if a wreck was trying to happen. His sled shivered with the strain of coming off the wall, holding against the force of the corner now only with the knifelike edges of its runners. But the force was too great. He began to skid, edges chattering. He eased them off a little, letting the sled drift slightly sideways. Two others had sliced down to the inside too, edges spraying ice. For a moment he was blinded again, but the corner twisted out flat, and he was through and still on the course, and he knew he was too tight, too hard with his control; he was fighting his sled instead of working with it. . . .

. . . *a tourist once asked Erik Sigismund how he controlled his sled, and he answered, 'Barely.' And even that had failed when he flipped it a year ago and four others ran over him.*

An old, lurking thought pounced into him again . . . he couldn't stop this sled now if he wanted to. There was no such thing as stopping, outside of a crash. He had to ride until it ended, and he was suddenly certain that was not going to be at the bottom. Not this time. He had crashed before, too many times, but he had never had this feeling of fear before. Not *this* fear. It was different, and he couldn't say why, and he was letting it affect him. And that was the greatest wrong.

They were thundering into the Jackhammer now, 300 yards of violent dips. Every sled had its brakes out, and there were fast flashes as some fired braking rockets. But where the walls of the course sloped upwards the ice was comparatively smooth. He eased left, to the uphill side, and leaned on his left pedal, holding the sled on the slope with its edges. Then he folded his air brakes and started gaining again. It was necessary; one did not hold back from fear. If that was one's style of life, he would never be a sledder in the first place.

Suddenly from the middle of the leading blurs a sled became airborne from the crest of one of the bumps. It hit once and twisted into the air like something alive. Sleds behind it fired rockets and tried to edge away. One skidded broadside, then rolled. A shattered body panel spun away; the two sleds were demolishing themselves. Someone blewout, streaking into the sky, canopy sparkling high in the sun—and that meant another sled out of control. He pulled full air brakes and fired a rocket, the force slamming him hard against his chest straps. His left arm was ready to fire the charge under the seat. But if he waited too long . . .

. . . *Kurt Schnabel was proud to be the only man who had never ejected . . . but the one time he had tried he had waited the barest fraction of a moment too long, and his chute came down with his shattered corpse.*

The three wild sleds whirled away, spinning out of sight over the low retaining walls. He folded his brakes. There was a trembling in his arms and legs like the slight but solid shuddering of a flywheel out of balance, involuntary and with a threat of getting worse. He cursed himself. He could have blown-out too. No one would have blamed him with that tangle developing in front. But he hadn't . . . and it was too late now.

. . . *only one man had ever blown-out without an apparent reason and got away with it: Shorty Case in his first race. And when he was asked about it afterwards, asked in that over casual, quiet tone, he had answered, 'You bet your sweet, I blew! 'Cause if I hadn't, man, I was gonna pee my pants!'*

But he didn't blow-out that day on the Fallaways, the day his sled somersaulted and sowed its wreckage down the course for a half mile . . . and him too . . .

No, there were no quitters here; only the doers or the dead. And which was he going to be tonight?

. . . drive, don't think . . .

The Jackhammer smoothed out and plunged downwards, and they were hurtling now into the Wingover at over 90 m.p.h. Here were the second biggest grandstands on the course, the second greatest concentration of cameras.

Here two ambulance helicopters stood by, and a priest too. The Wingover. . . .

Imagine an aeroplane peeling off into a dive . . . imagine a sled doing the same on a towering wall of ice, a wall rising like a great, breaking wave, frozen at the moment of its overhanging curl. . . . The Wingover was a monstrous, curving scoop to the right, nearly fifty feet high, rolling the sleds up, over, and hurling them down into a 65 degree pitch then twisted into a 6-G pull-out to the left.

. . . 'Impossible!' When Wilfrid von Gerlach laid out the Stunt that is what they told him about the Wingover. 'It cannot be done!'

But von Gerlach had been a Grand Prix racer and a stunt pilot, and when the Stuka was finished he took the first sled through. At the finish he sat quietly for a moment, staring back at the mountain. 'At the Wingover I was how fast?' he asked thoughtfully. They replied that he'd been radared there at 110 m.p.h. He nodded, then made the statement the sledders had carried with them ever since.

'It's possible.'

He watched the leading sleds line up for that shining, sheer curve and felt the fear freeze through him again. A man was little more than a captive in his sled here. If he was on the right line going in, then it was beautiful; if not, well . . .

. . . the brotherly beers and the late talk . . .

'Remember when Otto Domagk left Cripple's Corner in that snow storm?'

'Ya, und ven him vas digged out—Vas? Two hours?—he vas so sleeping.'

'And not a mark on him, remember?'

. . . Remember, remember . . .

He followed in line barely four feet from the sled in front of him and felt the savage, sickening blow as the wall raised and rolled him. A flicker of shadow, a glimpse of the valley nearly upside down, then the fall and the increasing shriek of wind and runners, and he was pointing perfectly into the pull-out, still lined exactly with the sled ahead—but there was one sled badly out of line . . .

And someone pulled their air brakes full open.

Sleds began weaving in the violent turbulence of those brakes. Rockets flashed. A sled went sideways, rolling lazily above the others, and exploded against the wall of the pull-out. He pulled the ejection lever . . . nothing happened!

He was dead, he knew that. He saw two sleds tumbling into the sky, another shattered to pieces and sliding along the course. All that was necessary was to hit one of those pieces . . . but the corner was suddenly gone behind. The course unwound into a long left traverse. He remembered to breathe. There were tooth chips in his mouth and the taste of blood. He swerved past a piece of wreckage, then another . . .

. . . how many were dead now? Himself and how many others? But it wasn't fear of death—what was it? What was it that he'd walled off inside—that something secret always skirted as carefully as a ship veers from a hidden reef, knowing it is there—what? And now the wall was down, and he was facing . . .

His sled shuddered. He was driving badly, too harsh with his edge control. He narrowly made it through the Boot and Cripple's Corner, spraying ice behind him, but it was not the sled that was out of control. It was him. And he was diving now straight for the gates of hell at over 110 m.p.h.

It was called the Plummet. It began with an innocent, wide left, steeply banked, then the world fell away. It dived over a half mile headlong down a 50-degree slope straight into a ravine and up the other side, then into a full 180-degree uphill hairpin to the right, a steep straight to the bottom of the ravine again, and finally into a sharp left and a long, rolling straight. It had killed more men than any other part of the course.

Here were the biggest grandstands and the most hungry eyes of the cameras. Here there were three clergy, and emergency operating rooms. Here . . .

. . . here he would complete the formality of dying.

He came into the left too low, too fast for the edges to hold. The sled skidded. He reacted automatically, holding slight left edges and steering into the skid. The sled drifted up the wall, arcing towards the top where nothing showed but the cold blue of the sky. He waited, a part of him almost calm now, waiting to see if the corner would straighten before he went over the top. It did, but he was still skidding, close to the retaining wall, plunging into the half-mile drop nearly sideways. He increased his edges. The tail of the sled brushed the wall and it was suddenly swinging the opposite way. He reversed his wheel and edges, anticipating another skid, but he was not quick enough. The sled bucked, careening up on its left runners. It grazed the wall again, completely out of control now—but he kept trying . . .

. . . and that was it; you kept trying. Over and over. No matter how many times you faced yourself it had to be done again. And again. The Self was never satisfied with single victories—you had to keep trying . . .

And he was empty no more.

The hospital. How many times had he awakened here? And it was always wonderfully the same: gentle warmth and his body finally relaxed and he would test it piece by piece to see what was bent and broken this time; and always the newsmen and the writers and the other assorted ghouls, and always the question and answer period. Punchlining, they called it. . . .

'How did it happen?'

'I dozed off.'

'Why didn't you eject?'

'Parachuting is dangerous.'

'When did you realize you were out of control?'

'At the starting line.'

'What will you do now?'

'Heal.'

'Will you race again?'

. . . 'It's possible.'

Outside, the wind was blowing.

What can I say about Samuel 'Chip' Delany? That he is good? The bottom of the next page testifies to the fact that we all think so. He is a story-teller who here has projected something quite different from those three who have preceded him in this volume. I saved his story for this precise moment for a reason. He is a gentleman, an artist. He is gifted with a peculiar insight into the workings of the psyche and the English language. This particular story, however, is very science fiction; i.e. it expands upon, extrapolates, guesses at, a possible thing. In this sense, it follows the rigorous, near-mathematical dicta of science fiction critics, to wit—given this, one day, then this follows, (im)pure and (un)simple.

But enough about the story, since you're about to read it. I am of Polish origin, and therefore the words of the disaffected Polish socialist Czeslaw Milosz occasionally ring in my head. He once said something in his book, The Captive Mind, *which came to me strongly about a year ago when talking to Chip:*

'When, as my friend suggested, I stand before Zeus (whether I die naturally, or under sentence of History) I will repeat all this that I have written as my defence. Many people spend their lives collecting stamps or old coins, or growing tulips. I am sure that Zeus will be merciful towards people who have given themselves entirely to these hobbies, even though they are only amusing and pointless diversions. I shall say to him: "It is not my fault that you made me a poet, and that you gave me the gift of seeing simultaneously what was happening in Omaha and Prague, in the Baltic States and on the shores of the Arctic Ocean. I felt that if I did not use that gift my poetry would be tasteless to me and fame detestable. Forgive me." And perhaps Zeus, who does not call stamp-collectors and tulip-growers silly, will forgive.'*

Any time, anywhere, Chip will write about that which moves him strongly. He is a poet, with the gift of seeing simultaneously what is happening here, today, and there, tomorrow. Whether that tomorrow ever materializes is unimportant. What is important is that he saw it and captured it, today, and not even Zeus can take that away from him.

* 'The Captive Mind', Czeslaw Milosz, Secker & Warburg (London, 1953).

AYE, AND GOMORRAH

Samuel R. Delany

And came down in Paris:

Where we raced along the Rue de Médicis with Bo and Lou and Muse inside the fence, Kelly and me outside, making faces through the bars, making noise, making the Luxembourg Gardens roar at two in the morning. Then climbed out, and down to the square in front of St. Sulpice where Bo tried to knock me into the fountain.

At which point Kelly noticed what was going on around us, got an ash-can cover, and ran into the pissoir, banging the walls. Five guys scooted out; even a big pissoir only holds four.

A very blond young man put his hand on my arm and smiled. 'Don't you think, Spacer, that you . . . people should leave?'

I looked at his hand on my blue uniform. '*Est-ce que tu es un frelk?*'

His eyebrows rose, then he shook his head. 'Une *frelk*,' he corrected. 'No. I am not. Sadly for me. You look as though you may once have been a man. But now . . .' He smiled. 'You have nothing for me now. The police.' He nodded across the street where I noticed the gendarmerie for the first time. 'They don't bother us. You are strangers, though . . .'

But Muse was already yelling, 'Hey, come on! Let's get out of here, huh?' And left. And went up again.

And came down in Houston:

'God damn!' Muse said. 'Gemini Flight Control—you mean this is where it all started? Let's get *out* of here, *please!*'

So took a bus out through Pasadena, then the monoline to Galveston, and were going to take it down the Gulf, but Lou found a couple with a pick-up truck——

 Nebula Award, Best Short Story 1967

'Glad to give you a ride, Spacers. You people up there on them planets and things, doing all that good work for the government.'

—who were going south, them and the baby, so we rode in the back for two hundred and fifty miles of sun and wind.

'You think they're frelks?' Lou asked, elbowing me. 'I bet they're frelks. They're just waiting for us give 'em the come-on.'

'Cut it out. They're a nice, stupid pair of country kids.'

'That don't mean they ain't frelks!'

'You don't trust anybody, do you?'

'No.'

And finally a bus again that rattled us through Brownsville and across the border into Matamoros where we staggered down the steps into the dust and the scorched evening with a lot of Mexicans and chickens and Texas Gulf shrimp fishermen—who smelled worst—and *we* shouted the loudest. Forty-three whores —I counted—had turned out for the shrimp fishermen, and by the time we had broken two of the windows in the bus station they were all laughing. The shrimp fishermen said they wouldn't buy us no food but would get us drunk if we wanted, 'cause that was the custom with shrimp fishermen. But we yelled, broke another window; then, while I was lying on my back on the telegraph office steps, singing, a woman with dark lips bent over and put her hands on my cheeks. 'You are very sweet.' Her rough hair fell forward. 'But the men, they are standing around and watching *you*. And that is taking up *time*. Sadly, their time is our money. Spacer, do you not think you . . . people should leave?'

I grabbed her wrist. '¡*Usted!*' I whispered. '*¿Usted es una frelka?*'

'*Frelko in español.*' She smiled and patted the sunburst that hung from my belt buckle. 'Sorry. But you have nothing that . . . would be useful to me. It is too bad, for you look like you were once a woman, no? And I like women, too . . .'

I rolled off the porch.

'Is this a drag, or is this a drag!' Muse was shouting. 'Come *on*! Let's *go*!'

We managed to get back to Houston before dawn, somehow. And went up.

And came down in Istanbul:

That morning it rained in Istanbul.

At the commissary we drank our tea from pear-shaped glasses, looking out across the Bosphorus. The Princes Islands lay like trash heaps before the prickly city.

'Who knows their way in this town?' Kelly asked.

'Aren't we going around together?' Muse demanded. 'I thought we were going around together.'

'They held up my cheque at the purser's office,' Kelly explained. 'I'm flat broke. I think the purser's got it in for me,' and shrugged. 'Don't want to, but I'm going to have to hunt up a rich frelk and come on friendly,' went back to the tea; *then* noticed how heavy the silence had become. 'Aw, come *on*, now! You gape at me like that and I'll bust every bone in that carefully-conditioned-from-puberty body of yours. Hey you!' meaning me. 'Don't give me that holier-than-thou gawk like you never went with no frelk!'

It was starting.

'I'm not gawking,' I said and got quietly mad.

The longing, the old longing.

Bo laughed to break tensions. 'Say, last time I was in Istanbul —about a year before I joined up with this platoon—I remember we were coming out of Taksim Square down Istiqlal. Just past all the cheap movies we found a little passage lined with flowers. Ahead of us were two other spacers. It's a market in there, and farther down they got fish, and then a courtyard with oranges and candy and sea urchins and cabbage. But flowers in front. Anyway, we noticed something funny about the spacers. It wasn't their uniforms: they were perfect. The haircuts: fine. It wasn't till we heard them talking—They were a man and woman dressed up like spacers, trying *to pick up frelks*! Imagine, queer for frelks!'

'Yeah,' Lou said. 'I seen that before. There were a lot of them in Rio.'

'We beat hell out of them two,' Bo concluded. 'We got them in a side street and went to *town*!'

Muse's tea glass clicked on the counter. 'From Taksim down Istiqlal till you get to the flowers? Now why didn't you say that's where the frelks were, huh?' A smile on Kelly's face would have made that okay. There was no smile.

'Hell,' Lou said, 'nobody ever had to tell me where to look.

I go out in the street and frelks smell me coming. I can spot 'em halfway along Piccadilly. Don't they have nothing but tea in this place? Where can you get a drink?'

Bo grinned. 'Moslem country, remember? But down at the end of the Flower Passage there're a lot of little bars with green doors and marble counters where you can get a litre of beer for about fifteen cents in lira. And there're all these stands selling deep-fat-fried bugs and pig's gut sandwiches——'

'You ever notice how frelks can put it away? I mean liquor, not . . . pig's guts.'

And launched off into a lot of appeasing stories. We ended with the one about the frelk some spacer tried to roll who announced: 'There are two things I go for. One is spacers; the other is a good fight. . . .'

But they only allay. They cure nothing. Even Muse knew we would spend the day apart, now.

The rain had stopped, so we took the ferry up the Golden Horn. Kelly straight off asked for Taksim Square and Istiqlal and was directed to a dolmush, which we discovered was a taxi-cab, only it just goes one place and picks up lots and lots of people on the way. And it's cheap.

Lou headed off over Ataturk Bridge to see the sights of New City. Bo decided to find out what the Dolma Boche really was; and when Muse discovered you could go to Asia for fifteen cents —one lira and fifty krush—well, Muse decided to go to Asia.

I turned through the confusion of traffic at the head of the bridge and up past the grey, dripping walls of Old City, beneath the trolley wires. There are times when yelling and helling won't fill the lack. There are times when you must walk by yourself because it hurts so much to be alone.

I walked up a lot of little streets with wet donkeys and wet camels and women in veils; and down a lot of big streets with buses and trash baskets and men in business suits.

Some people stare at spacers; some people don't. Some people stare or don't stare in a way a spacer gets to recognize within a week after coming out of training school at sixteen. I was walking in the park when I caught her watching. She saw me see and looked away.

I ambled down the wet asphalt. She was standing under the arch of a small, empty mosque shell. As I passed she walked out into the courtyard among the cannons.

'Excuse me.'

I stopped.

'Do you know whether or not this is the shrine of St. Irene?' Her English was charmingly accented. 'I've left my guidebook at home.'

'Sorry. I'm a tourist too.'

'Oh.' She smiled. 'I am Greek. I thought you might be Turkish because you are so dark.'

'American Red Indian.' I nodded. Her turn to curtsy.

'I see. I have just started at the university here in Istanbul. Your uniform, it tells me that you are'—and in the pause, all speculations resolved—'a spacer.'

I was uncomfortable. 'Yeah.' I put my hands in my pockets, moved my feet around on the soles of my boots, licked my third from the rear left molar—did all the things you do when you're uncomfortable. *You're so exciting when you look like that*, a frelk told me once. 'Yeah, I am.' I said it too sharply, too loudly, and she jumped a little.

So now she knew I knew she knew I knew, and I wondered how we would play out the Proust bit.

'I'm Turkish,' she said. 'I'm not Greek. I'm not just starting. I'm a graduate in art history here at the university. These little lies one makes for strangers to protect one's ego . . . why? Sometimes I think my ego is very small.'

That's one strategy.

'How far away do you live?' I asked. 'And what's the going rate in Turkish lira?' That's another.

'I can't pay you.' She pulled her raincoat around her hips. She was very pretty. 'I would like to.' She shrugged and smiled. 'But I am . . . a poor student. Not a rich one. If you want to turn around and walk away, there will be no hard feelings. I shall be sad though.'

I stayed on the path. I thought she'd suggest a price after a little while. She didn't.

And *that's* another.

I was asking myself, *What do you want the damn money for anyway?* when a breeze upset water from one of the park's great cypresses.

'I think the whole business is sad.' She wiped drops from

her face. There had been a break in her voice and for a moment I looked too closely at the water streaks. 'I think it's sad that they have to alter you to make you a spacer. If they hadn't, then *we* . . . If spacers had never been, then we could not be . . . the way we are. Did you start out male or female?'

Another shower. I was looking at the ground and droplets went down my collar.

'Male,' I said. 'It doesn't matter.'

'How old are you? Twenty-three, twenty-four?'

'Twenty-three,' I lied. It's reflex. I'm twenty-five, but the younger they think you are, the more they pay you. But I didn't *want* her *damn* money——

'I guessed right then.' She nodded. 'Most of us are experts on spacers. Do you find that? I suppose we have to be.' She looked at me with wide black eyes. At the end of the stare, she blinked rapidly. 'You would have been a fine man. But now you are a spacer, building water-conservation units on Mars, programming mining computers on Ganymede, servicing communication relay towers on the moon. The alteration . . .' Frelks are the only people I've ever heard say 'the alteration' with so much fascination and regret. 'You'd think they'd have found some other solution. They could have found another way than neutering you, turning you into creatures not even androgynous; things that are——'

I put my hand on her shoulder, and she stopped like I'd hit her. She looked to see if anyone was near. Lightly, so lightly then, she raised her hand to mine.

I pulled my hand away. 'That are what?'

'They could have found another way.' Both hands in her pockets now.

'They could have. Yes. Up beyond the ionosphere, baby, there's too much radiation for those precious gonads to work right anywhere you might want to do something that would keep you there over twenty-four hours, like the moon, or Mars, or the satellites of Jupiter——'

'They could have made protective shields. They could have done more research into biological adjustment——'

'Population Explosion time,' I said. 'No, they were hunting for any excuse to cut down kids back then—especially deformed ones.'

'Ah yes.' She nodded. 'We're still fighting our way up from the neo-puritan reaction to the sex freedom of the twentieth century.'

'It was a fine solution.' I grinned and grabbed my crotch. 'I'm happy with it.' I've never known why that's so much more obscene when a spacer does it.

'Stop it,' she snapped, moving away.

'What's the matter?'

'Stop it,' she repeated. 'Don't do that! You're a child.'

'But they choose us from children whose sexual responses are hopelessly retarded at puberty.'

'And your childish, violent substitutes for love? I suppose that's one of the things that's attractive. Yes, I know you're a child.'

'Yeah? What about frelks?'

She thought a while. 'I think they are the sexually retarded ones they miss. Perhaps it was the right solution. You really don't regret you have no sex?'

'We've got you,' I said.

'Yes.' She looked down. I glanced to see the expression she was hiding. It was a smile. 'You have your glorious, soaring life, *and* you have us.' Her face came up. She glowed. 'You spin in the sky, the world spins under you, and you step from land to land, while we . . .' She turned her head right, left, and her black hair curled and uncurled on the shoulder of her coat. 'We have our dull, circled lives, bound in gravity, *worshipping* you!'

She looked at me. 'Perverted, yes? In love with a bunch of corpses in free fall!' She suddenly hunched her shoulders. 'I don't like having a free-fall-sexual-displacement complex.'

'That always sounded like too much to say.'

She looked away. 'I don't like being a frelk. Better?'

'I wouldn't like it either. Be something else.'

'You don't choose your perversions. *You* have no perversions at all. *You*'re free of the whole business. I love you for that, spacer. My love starts with the fear of love. Isn't that beautiful? A pervert substitutes something unattainable for "normal" love: the homosexual, a mirror, the fetishist, a shoe or a watch or a girdle. Those with free-fall-sexual-dis——'

'Frélks.'

'Frelks substitute'—she looked at me sharply again—'loose,

swinging meat.'

'That doesn't offend me.'

'I wanted it to.'

'Why?'

'You don't have desires. You wouldn't understand.'

'Go on.'

'I want you because you can't want me. That's the pleasure. If someone really had a sexual reaction to . . . us, we'd be scared away. I wonder how many people there were before there were you, waiting for your creation. We're necrophiles. I'm sure grave robbing has fallen off since you started going up. But you don't understand. . . .' She paused. 'If you did, then I wouldn't be scuffing leaves now and trying to think from whom I could borrow sixty lira.' She stepped over the knuckles of a root that had cracked the pavement. 'And that, incidentally, is the going rate in Istanbul.'

I calculated. 'Things still get cheaper as you go east.'

'You know,' and she let her raincoat fall open, 'you're different from the others. You at least *want* to know——'

I said, 'If I spat on you for every time you'd said that to a spacer, you'd drown.'

'Go back to the moon, loose meat.' She closed her eyes. 'Swing on up to Mars. There are satellites around Jupiter where you might do some good. Go up and come down in some other city.'

'Where do you live?'

'You want to come with me?'

'Give me something,' I said. 'Give me something—it doesn't have to be worth sixty lira. Give me something that you like, anything of yours that means something to you.'

'No!'

'Why not?'

'Because I——'

'—don't want to give up part of that ego. None of you frelks do!'

'You really don't understand I just don't want to buy you?'

'You have nothing to buy me with.'

'You are a child,' she said. 'I love you.'

We reached the gate of the park. She stopped, and we stood time enough for a breeze to rise and die in the grass. 'I . . .' she offered tentatively, pointing without taking her hand from her coat pocket. 'I live right down there.'

'All right,' I said. 'Let's go.'

A gas main had once exploded along this street, she explained to me, a gushing road of fire as far as the docks, overhot and over-quick. It had been put out within minutes, no building had fallen, but the charred facias glittered. 'This is sort of an artist and student quarter.' We crossed the cobbles. 'Yuri Pasha, number fourteen. In case you're ever in Istanbul again.' Her door was covered with black scales, the gutter was thick with garbage.

'A lot of artists and professional people are frelks,' I said, trying to be inane.

'So are lots of other people.' She walked inside and held the door. 'We're just more flamboyant about it.'

On the landing there was a portrait of Ataturk. Her room was on the second floor. 'Just a moment while I get my key——'

Mars-scapes! Moonscapes! On her easel was a six-foot canvas showing the sunrise flaring on a crater's rim! There were copies of the original Observer pictures of the moon pinned to the wall, and pictures of every smooth-faced general in the International Spacer Corps.

On one corner of her desk was a pile of those photo magazines about spacers that you can find in most kiosks all over the world: I've seriously heard people say they were printed for adventurous-minded high school children. They've never seen the Danish ones. She had a few of those too. There was a shelf of art books, art history texts. Above them were six feet of cheap paper-covered space operas: *Sin on Space Station No. 12*, *Rocket Rake*, *Savage Orbit*.

'Arrack?' she asked. 'Ouzo or pernod? You've got your choice. But I may pour them all from the same bottle.' She set out glasses on the desk, then opened a waist-high cabinet that turned out to be an icebox. She stood up with a tray of lovelies: fruit puddings, Turkish delight, braised meats.

'What's this?'

'Dolmades. Grape leaves filled with rice and pignolias.'

'Say it again?'

'Dolmades. Comes from the same Turkish word as "dolmush".'

They both mean "stuffed".' She put the tray beside the glasses 'Sit down.'

I sat on the studio-couch-that-becomes-bed. Under the brocade I felt the deep, fluid resilience of a glycogel mattress. They've got the idea that it approximates the feeling of free fall. 'Comfortable? Would you excuse me for a moment? I have some friends down the hall. I want to see them for a moment.' She winked. 'They like spacers.'

'Are you going to take up a collection for me?' I asked. 'Or do you want them to line up outside the door and wait their turn?'

She sucked a breath. 'Actually I was going to suggest both.' Suddenly she shook her head. 'Oh, what do you want?'

'What will you give me? I want something,' I said. 'That's why I came. I'm lonely. Maybe I want to find out how far it goes. I don't know yet.'

'It goes as far as you will. Me? I study, I read, paint, talk with my friends'—she came over to the bed, sat down on the floor—'go to the theatre, look at spacers who pass me in the street, till one looks back; I am lonely too.' She put her head on my knee. 'I want something. But,' and after a minute neither of us had moved, 'you are not the one who will give it to me.'

'You're not going to pay me for it,' I countered. 'You're not, are you?'

On my knee her head shook. After a while she said, all breath and no voice, 'Don't you think you . . . should leave?'

'Okay,' I said, and stood up.

She sat back on the hem of her coat. She hadn't taken it off yet.

I went to the door.

'Incidentally.' She folded her hands in her lap. 'There is a place in New City you might find what you're looking for, called the Flower Passage——'

I turned towards her, angry. 'The frelk hangout? Look, I don't *need* money! I said *any*thing would do! I don't want——'

She had begun to shake her head, laughing quietly. Now she lay her cheek on the wrinkled place where I had sat. 'Do you persist in misunderstanding? It is a spacer hangout. When you leave, I am going to visit my friends and talk about . . . ah, yes, the beautiful one that got away. I thought you might find . . .

perhaps someone you know.'

With anger, it ended.

'Oh,' I said. 'Oh, it's a spacer hangout. Yeah. Well, thanks.'

And went out. And found the Flower Passage, and Kelly and Lou and Bo and Muse. Kelly was buying beer so we all got drunk, and ate fried fish and fried clams and fried sausage, and Kelly was waving the money around, saying. 'You should have seen him! The changes I put that frelk through, you should have *seen* him! Eighty lira is the going rate here, and he gave me a hundred and fifty!' and drank more beer. And went up.

Professor Stythe Thompson spent considerable time and effort in the exploration of myth, legend and folk-motif. After having read something of his works, I thought that I could put my finger on a particular piece and say what it was. Myth, as I understand it, involves the gods, deals with the open end of the human condition. Legend may involve the supernatural, but not in so distinct or religious a fashion as myth. Folklore, basically, is just that: the lore of the folk, passed down, generation to generation, without supernatural overtones.

I'll be damned if I know how to categorize the following story.

Maybe that's why it won a Nebula, however. '. . . The sky was dark, the moon was yellow, the leaves came tumbling down.' I am reminded of Stagalee *and* Red Hanrahan, *and of all the people half of light and half of darkness who pass in the night, fight with the Devil on the banks of the Brazos, crash in their U-2's and cling to coffins while white whales destroy their ships.*

Here is a piece of future myth/legend/folklore—maybe. It is timeless, though, and like all such things, timely.

GONNA ROLL THE BONES

Fritz Leiber

Suddenly Joe Slattermill knew for sure he'd have to get out quick or else blow his top and knock out with the shrapnel of his skull the props and patches holding up his decaying home, that was like a house of big wooden and plaster and wallpaper cards except for the huge fireplace and ovens and chimney across the kitchen from him.

 Nebula Award, Best Novelette 1967

Those were stone-solid enough, though. The fireplace was
chin-high at least twice that long, and filled from end to end
with roaring flames. Above were the square doors of the ovens
in a row—his Wife baked for part of their living. Above the
ovens was the wall-long mantelpiece, too high for his Mother
to reach or Mr. Guts to jump any more, set with all sorts of
ancestral curios, but any of them that weren't stone or glass or
china had been so dried and darkened by decades of heat that
they looked like nothing but shrunken human heads and black
golf balls. At one end were clustered his Wife's square gin
bottles. Above the mantel-piece hung one old chromo, so high
and so darkened by soot and grease that you couldn't tell whether
the swirls and fat cigar shape were a whaleback steamer ploughing through a hurricane or a spaceship plunging through a
storm of light-driven dust motes.

As soon as Joe curled his toes inside his boots, his Mother
knew what he was up to. 'Going bumming,' she mumbled with
conviction. 'Pants pockets full of cartwheels of house money,
too, to spend on sin.' And she went back to munching the long
shreds she stripped fumblingly with her right hand off the turkey
carcass set close to the terrible heat, her left hand ready to fend
off Mr. Guts, who stared at her yellow-eyed, gaunt-flanked,
with long mangy tail a-twitch. In her dirty dress, streaky as the
turkey's sides, Joe's Mother looked like a bent brown bag and
her fingers were lumpy twigs.

Joe's Wife knew as soon or sooner, for she smiled thin-eyed
at him over her shoulder from where she towered at the centre-
most oven. Before she closed its door, Joe glimpsed that she was
baking two long, flat, narrow, fluted loaves and one high, round-
domed one. She was thin as death and disease in her violet
wrapper. Without looking, she reached out a yard-long, skinny
arm for the nearest gin bottle and downed a warm slug and
smiled again. And without word spoken, Joe knew she'd said,
'You're going out and gamble and get drunk and lay a floozy
and come home and beat me and go to jail for it,' and he had a
flash of the last time he'd been in the dark gritty cell and she'd
come by moonlight, which showed the green and yellow lumps
on her narrow skull where he'd hit her, to whisper to him
through the tiny window in the back and slip him a half pint

through the bars.

And Joe knew for certain that this time it would be that bad and worse, but just the same he heaved up himself and his heavy, muffledly clanking pockets and shuffled straight to the door, muttering, 'Guess I'll roll the bones, up the pike a stretch and back,' swinging his bent, knobbly-elbowed arms like paddle-wheels to make a little joke about his words.

When he'd stepped outside, he held the door open a hand's breadth behind him for several seconds. When he finally closed it, a feeling of deep misery struck him. Earlier years, Mr. Guts would have come streaking along to seek fights and females on the roofs and fences, but now the big tom was content to stay home and hiss by the fire and snatch for turkey and dodge a broom, quarrelling and comforting with two house-bound women. Nothing had followed Joe to the door but his Mother's chomping and her gasping breaths and the clink of the gin bottle going back on the mantel and the creaking of the floor boards under his feet.

The night was up-side-down deep among the frosty stars. A few of them seemed to move, like the white-hot jets of spaceships. Down below it looked as if the whole town of Ironmine had blown or buttoned out the light and gone to sleep, leaving the streets and spaces to the equally unseen breezes and ghosts. But Joe was still in the hemisphere of the musty dry odour of the worm-eaten carpentry behind him, and as he felt and heard the dry grass of the lawn brush his calves, it occurred to him that something deep down inside him had for years been planning things so that he and the house and his Wife and Mother and Mr. Guts would all come to an end together. Why the kitchen heat hadn't touched off the tindery place ages ago was a physical miracle.

Hunching his shoulders, Joe stepped out, not up the pike, but down the dirt road that led past Cypress Hollow Cemetery to Night Town.

The breezes were gentle, but unusually restless and variable tonight, like leprechaun squalls. Beyond the drunken, white-washed cemetery fence dim in the starlight, they rustled the scraggly trees of Cypress Hollow and made it seem they were stroking their beards of Spanish moss. Joe sensed that the ghosts were just as restless as the breezes, uncertain where and whom to haunt, or whether to take the night off, drifting together in sorrowfully lecherous companionship. While among the trees the red-green vampire lights pulsed faintly and irregularly, like sick fireflies or a plague-stricken space fleet. The feeling of deep misery stuck with Joe and deepened and he was tempted to turn aside and curl up in any convenient tomb or around some half-toppled head board and cheat his Wife and the other three behind him out of a shared doom. He thought: Gonna roll the bones, gonna roll 'em up and go to sleep. But while he was deciding, he got past the sagged-open gate and the rest of the delirious fence and Shantyville too.

At first Night Town seemed dead as the rest of Ironmine, but then he noticed a faint glow, sick as the vampire lights but more feverish, and with it a jumping music, tiny at first as a jazz for jitterbugging ants. He stepped along the springy sidewalk, wistfully remembering the days when the spring was all in his own legs and he'd bound into a fight like a bobcat or a Martian sand-spider. God, it had been years now since he had fought a real fight, or felt *the power*. Gradually the midget music got raucous as a bunny-hug for grizzly bears and loud as a polka for elephants, while the glow became a riot of gas flares and flambeaux and corpse-blue mercury tubes and jiggling pink neon ones that all jeered at the stars where the spaceships roved. Next thing, he was facing a three-storey false front flaring everywhere like a devil's elbow, with a pale blue topping of St. Elmo's fire. There were wide swinging doors in the centre of it, spilling light above and below. Above the doorway, golden calcium light scrawled over and over again, with wild curlicues and flourishes, 'The Boneyard', while a fiendish red kept printing out, 'Gambling'.

So the new place they'd all been talking about for so long had opened at last! For the first time that night, Joe Slattermill felt a stirring of real life in him and the faintest caress of excitement.

Gonna roll the bones, he thought.

He dusted off his blue-green work clothes with big, careless swipes and slapped his pockets to hear the clank. Then he threw back his shoulders and grinned his lips sneeringly and pushed through the swinging doors as if giving a foe the straight-armed heel of his palm.

Inside, The Boneyard seemed to cover the area of a township

and the bar looked as long as the railroad tracks. Round pools of light on the green poker tables alternated with hourglass shapes of exciting gloom, through which drink girls and change-girls moved like white-legged witches. By the jazz-stand in the distance, belly dancers made *their* white hourglass shapes. The gamblers were thick and hunched down as mushrooms, all bald from agonizing over the fall of a card or a die or the dive of an ivory ball, while the Scarlet Women were like fields of poinsettia.

The calls of the croupiers and the slaps of dealt cards were as softly yet fatefully staccato as the rustle and beat and the jazz drums. Every tight-locked atom of the place was controlledly jumping. Even the dust motes jiggled tensely in the cones of light.

Joe's excitement climbed and he felt sift through him, like a breeze that heralds a gale, the faintest breath of a confidence which he knew could become a tornado. All thoughts of his house and Wife and Mother dropped out of his mind, while Mr. Guts remained only as a crazy young tom walking stiff-legged around the rim of his consciousness. Joe's own leg muscles twitched in sympathy and he felt them grow supplely strong.

He coolly and searchingly looked the place over, his hand going out like it didn't belong to him to separate a drink from a passing, gently bobbing tray. Finally his gaze settled on what he judged to be the Number One Crap Table. All the Big Mushrooms seemed to be there, bald as the rest but standing tall as toadstools. Then through a gap in them Joe saw on the other side of the table a figure still taller, but dressed in a long dark coat with collar turned up and a dark slouch hat pulled low, so that only a triangle of white face showed. A suspicion and a hope rose in Joe and he headed straight for the gap in the Big Mushrooms.

As he got nearer, the white-legged and shiny-topped drifters eddying out of his way, his suspicion received confirmation after confirmation and his hope budded and swelled. Back from one end of the table was the fattest man he'd ever seen, with a long cigar and a silver vest and a gold tie clasp at least eight inches wide that just said in thick script, 'Mr. Bones'. Back a little from the other end was the nakedest change-girl yet and the only one he'd seen whose tray, slung from her bare shoulders, and indenting her belly just below her breasts, was stacked with gold in gleaming little towers and with jet-black chips. While the dice-girl, skinnier and taller and longer armed than his Wife even, didn't seem to be wearing much but a pair of long white gloves. She was all right if you went for the type that isn't much more than pale skin over bones with breasts like china door-knobs.

Beside each gambler was a high round table for his chips. The one by the gap was empty. Snapping his fingers at the near-est silver change-girl, Joe traded all his greasy dollars for an equal number of pale chips and tweaked her left nipple for luck. She playfully snapped her teeth towards his fingers.

Not hurrying but not wasting any time, he advanced and carelessly dropped his modest stacks on the empty table and took his place in the gap. He noted that the second Big Mush-room on his right had the dice. His heart but no other part of him gave an extra jump. Then he steadily lifted his eyes and looked straight across the table.

The coat was a shimmering elegant pillar of black satin with jet buttons, the upturned collar of fine dull plush black as the darkest cellar, as was the slouch hat with down-turned brim and for band only a thin braid of black horse-hair. The arms of the coat were long, lesser satin pillars, ending in slim, long-fingered hands that moved swiftly when they did, but held each position of rest with a statue's poise.

Joe still couldn't see much of the face except for smooth lower forehead with never a bead or trickle of sweat—the eye-brows were like straight snippets of the hat's braid—and gaunt aristocratic cheeks and narrow but somewhat flat nose. The complexion of the face wasn't as white as Joe had first judged. There was a faint touch of brown in it, like ivory that's just begun to age, or Venusian soapstone. Another glance at the hands confirmed this.

Behind the man in black was a knot of just about the flashiest and nastiest customers, male or female, Joe had ever seen. He knew from one look that each bediamonded, pomaded bully had a belly gun beneath the flap of his flowered vest and a blackjack in his hip pocket, and each snake-eyed sporting girl a stiletto in her garter and a pearl-handled silver-plated derringer under the sequinned silk in the hollow between her jutting breasts.

Yet at the same time Joe knew they were just trimmings. It

was the man in black, their master, who was the deadly one, the kind of man you knew at a glance you couldn't touch and live. If without asking you merely laid a finger on his sleeve, no matter how lightly and respectfully, an ivory hand would move faster than thought and you'd be stabbed or shot. Or maybe just the touch would kill you, as if every black article of his clothing were charged from his ivory skin outwards with a high-voltage, high-amperage ivory electricity. Joe looked at the shadowed face again and decided he wouldn't care to try it.

For it was the eyes that were the most impressive feature. All great gamblers have dark-shadowed deep-set eyes. But this one's eyes were sunk so deep you couldn't even be sure you were getting a gleam of them. They were inscrutability incarnate. They were unfathomable. They were like black holes.

But all this didn't disappoint Joe one bit, though it did terrify him considerably. On the contrary, it made him exult. His first suspicion was completely confirmed and his hope spread into full flower.

This must be one of those really big gamblers who hit Iron-mine only once a decade at most, come from the Big City on one of the river boats that ranged the watery dark like luxurious comets, spouting long thick tails of sparks from their sequoia-tall stacks with top foliage of curvy-snipped sheet iron. Or like silver space-liners with dozens of jewel-flamed jets, their portholes a-twinkle like ranks of marshalled asteroids.

For that matter, maybe some of those really big gamblers actually came from other planets where the night-time pace was hotter and the sporting life a delirium of risk and delight.

Yes, this was the kind of man Joe had always yearned to pit his skill against. He felt *the power* begin to tingle in his rock-still fingers, just a little.

Joe lowered his gaze to the crap table. It was almost as wide as a man is tall, at least twice as long, unusually deep, and lined with black, not green, felt, so that it looked like a giant's coffin. There was something familiar about its shape which he couldn't place. Its bottom, though not its sides or ends, had a twinkling iridescence, as if it had been lightly sprinkled with very tiny diamonds. As Joe lowered his gaze all the way and looked directly down, his eyes barely over the table, he got the crazy notion that it went down all the way through the world, so that the

diamonds were the stars on the other side, visible despite the
sunlight there, just as Joe was always able to see the stars by
day up the shaft of the mine he worked in, and so that if a
cleaned-out gambler, dizzy with defeat, toppled forward into it,
he'd fall for ever, towards the bottom-most bottom, be it Hell
or some black galaxy. Joe's thoughts swirled and he felt the
cold, hard-fingered clutch of fear at his crotch. Someone was
crooning beside him, 'Come on, Big Dick.'

Then the dice, which had meanwhile passed to the Big Mushroom immediately on his right, came to rest near the table's
centre, contradicting and wiping out Joe's vision. But instantly
there was another oddity to absorb him. The Ivory dice were
large and unusually round-cornered with dark red spots that
gleamed like real rubies, but the spots were arranged in such a
way that each face looked like a miniature skull. For instance,
the seven thrown just now, by which the Big Mushroom to his
right had lost his point, which had been ten, consisted of a two
with the spots evenly spaced towards one side, like eyes, instead
of towards opposite corners, and of a five with the same red eye-
spots but a central red nose and two spots close together below
that to make teeth.

The long, skinny, white-gloved arm of the dice-girl snaked
out like an albino cobra and scooped up the dice and whisked
them on to the rim of the table right in front of Joe. He inhaled
silently, picked up a single chip from his table and started to lay
it beside the dice, then realized that wasn't the way things were
done here, and put it back. He would have liked to examine the
chip more closely, though. It was curiously lightweight and pale
tan, about the colour of cream with a shot of coffee in it, and it
had embossed on its surface a symbol he could feel, though not
see. He didn't know what the symbol was, that would have taken
more feeling. Yet its touch had been very good, setting the power
tingling full blast in his shooting hand.

Joe looked casually yet swiftly at the faces around the table,
not missing the Big Gambler across from him, and said quietly,
'Roll a penny,' meaning of course one pale chip, or a dollar.

There was a hiss of indignation from all the Big Mushrooms
and the moonface of big-bellied Mr. Bones grew purple as he
started forward to summon his bouncers.

The Big Gambler raised a black-satined forearm and sculptured hand, palm down. Instantly Mr. Bones froze and the hissing stopped faster than that of a meteor prick in self-sealing space steel. Then in a whispery, cultured voice, without the faintest hint of derision, the man in black said, 'Get on him, gamblers.'

Here, Joe thought, was a final confirmation of his suspicion, had it been needed. The really great gamblers were always perfect gentlemen and generous to the poor.

With only the tiny, respectful hint of a guffaw, one of the Big Mushrooms called to Joe, 'You're faded.'

Joe picked up the ruby-featured dice.

Now ever since he had first caught two eggs on one plate, won all the marbles in Ironmine, and juggled six alphabet blocks so they finally fell in a row on the rug spelling 'Mother', Joe Slattermill had been almost incredibly deft at precision throwing. In the mine he could carom a rock off a wall of ore to crack a rat's skull fifty feet away in the dark and he sometimes amused himself by tossing little fragments of rock back into the holes from which they had fallen, so that they stuck there, perfectly fitted in, for at least a second. Sometimes, by fast tossing, he could fit seven or eight fragments into the hole from which they had fallen, like putting together a puzzle block. If he could ever have got into space, Joe would undoubtedly have been able to pilot six Moon-skimmers at once and do figure eights through Saturn's rings blindfold.

Now the only real difference between precision-tossing rocks or alphabet blocks and dice is that you have to bounce the latter off the end wall of a crap table, and that just made it a more interesting test of skill for Joe.

Rattling the dice now, he felt the power in his fingers and palm as never before.

He made a swift low roll, so that the bones ended up exactly in front of the white-gloved dice-girl. His natural seven was made up, as he'd intended, of a four and a three. In red-spot features they were like the five, except that both had only one tooth and the three no nose. Sort of baby-faced skulls. He had won a penny—that is, a dollar.

'Roll two cents,' said Joe Slattermill.

This time, for variety, he made his natural with an eleven. The six was like the five, except it had three teeth, the best-looking skull of the lot.

'Roll a nickel less one.'

Two Big Mushrooms divided that bet with a covert smirk at each other.

Now Joe rolled a three and an ace. His point was four. The ace, with its single spot off centre towards a side, still somehow looked like a skull—maybe of a Lilliputian Cyclops.

He took a while making his point, once absent-mindedly rolling three successive tens the hard way. He wanted to watch the dice-girl scoop up the cubes. Each time it seemed to him that her snake-swift fingers went under the dice while they were still flat on the felt. Finally he decided it couldn't be an illusion. Although the dice couldn't penetrate the felt, her white-gloved fingers somehow could, dipping in a flash through the black, diamond-sparkling material as if it weren't there.

Right away the thought of a crap-table-size hole through the earth came back to Joe. This would mean that the dice were rolling and lying on a perfectly transparent flat surface, impenetrable for them but nothing else. Or maybe it was only the dice-girl's hands that could penetrate the surface, which would turn into a mere fantasy Joe's earlier vision of a cleaned-out gambler taking the Big Dive down that dreadful shaft, which made the deepest mine a mere pin dent.

Joe decided he had to know which was true. Unless absolutely unavoidable, he didn't want to take the chance of being troubled by vertigo at some crucial stage of the game.

He made a few more meaningless throws, from time to time crooning for realism, 'Come on, Little Joe.' Finally he settled on his plan. When he did at last make his point—the hard way, with two twos—he caromed the dice off the far corner so that they landed exactly in front of him. Then, after a minimum pause for his throw to be seen by the table, he shot his left hand down under the cubes, just a flicker ahead of the dice-girl's strike, and snatched them up.

Wow! Joe had never had a harder time in his life making his face and manner conceal what his body felt, not even when the wasp had stung him on the neck just as he had been for the first time putting his hand under the skirt of his prudish, fickle, demanding Wife-to-be. His fingers and the back of his hand were in as much agony as if he'd stuck them into a blast furnace.

No wonder the dice-girl wore white gloves. They must be asbestos. And a good thing he hadn't used his shooting hand, he thought as he ruefully watched the blisters rise.

He remembered he'd been taught in school what Twenty-Mile Mine also demonstrated: that the earth was fearfully hot under its crust. The crap-table-size hole must pipe up that heat, so that any gambler taking the Big Dive would fry before he'd fallen a furlong and come out less than a cinder in China.

As if his blistered hand weren't bad enough, the Big Mushrooms were all hissing at him again and Mr. Bones had purpled once more and was opening his melon-size mouth to shout for his bouncers.

Once again a lift of the Big Gambler's hand saved Joe. The whispery, gentle voice called, 'Tell him, Mr. Bones.'

The latter roared towards Joe, 'No gambler may pick up the dice he or any other gambler has shot. Only my dice-girl may do that. Rule of the house!'

Joe snapped Mr. Bones the barest nod. He said coolly, 'Rolling a dime less two,' and when that still peewee bet was covered, he shot Phoebe for his point and then fooled around for quite a while, throwing anything but a five or a seven, until the throbbing in his left hand should fade and all his nerves feel rock-solid again. There had never been the slightest alteration in the power in his right hand; he felt that strong as ever, or stronger.

Midway of this interlude, the Big Gambler bowed slightly but respectfully towards Joe, hooding those unfathomable eye sockets, before turning around to take a long black cigarette from his prettiest and evilest-looking sporting girl. Courtesy in the smallest matters, Joe thought, another mark of the master devotee of games of chance. The Big Gambler sure had himself a flash crew, all right, though in idly looking them over again as he rolled, Joe noted one bummer towards the back who didn't fit in—a raggedly-elegant chap with the elflocked hair and staring eyes and TB-spotted cheeks of a poet.

As he watched the smoke trickling up from under the black slouch hat, he decided that either the lights across the table had dimmed or else the Big Gambler's complexion was yet a shade darker than he'd thought at first. Or it might even be— wild fantasy—that the Big Gambler's skin was slowly darkening tonight, like a meerschaum pipe being smoked a mile a second. That was almost funny to think of—there was enough heat in this place, all right, to darken meerschaum, as Joe knew from sad experience, but so far as he was aware it was all under the table.

None of Joe's thoughts, either familiar or admiring, about the Big Gambler decreased in the slightest degree his certainty of the supreme menace of the man in black and his conviction that it would be death to touch him. And if any doubts had stirred in Joe's mind, they would have been squelched by the chilling incident which next occurred.

The Big Gambler had just taken into his arms his prettiest-evilest sporting girl and was running an aristocratic hand across her haunch with perfect gentility, when the poet chap, green-eyed from jealousy and lovesickness, came leaping forward like a wildcat and aimed a long gleaming dagger at the black satin back.

Joe couldn't see how the blow could miss, but without taking his genteel right hand off the sporting girl's plush rear end, the Big Gambler shot out his left arm like a steel spring straightening. Joe couldn't tell whether he stabbed the poet chap in the throat, or judo-chopped him there, or gave him the Martian double-finger, or just touched him, but anyhow the fellow stopped as dead as if he'd been shot by a silent elephant gun or an invisible ray pistol and he slammed down on the floor. A couple of darkies came running up to drag off the body and nobody paid the least attention, such episodes apparently being taken for granted at The Boneyard.

It gave Joe quite a turn and he almost shot Phoebe before he intended to.

But by now the waves of pain had stopped running up his left arm and his nerves were like metal-wrapped new guitar strings, so three rolls later he shot a five, making his point, and set in to clean out the table.

He rolled nine successive naturals, seven sevens and two elevens, pyramiding his first wager of a single chip to a stake of over four thousand dollars. None of the Big Mushrooms had dropped out yet, but some of them were beginning to look worried and a couple were sweating. The Big Gambler still hadn't covered any part of Joe's bets, but he seemed to be following the play with interest from the cavernous depths of his eye sockets.

Then Joe got a devilish thought. Nobody could beat him tonight, he knew, but if he held on to the dice until the table was cleaned out, he'd never get a chance to see the Big Gambler exercise *his* skill, and he was truly curious about that. Besides, he thought, he ought to return courtesy for courtesy and have a crack at being a gentleman himself

'Pulling out forty-one dollars less a nickel,' he announced. 'Rolling a penny.'

This time there wasn't any hissing and Mr. Bones's moonface didn't cloud over. But Joe was conscious that the Big Gambler was staring at him disappointedly, or sorrowfully, or maybe just speculatively.

Joe immediately crapped out by throwing boxcars, rather pleased to see the two best-looking tiny skulls grinning ruby-toothed side by side, and the dice passed to the Big Mushroom on his left.

'Knew when his streak was over,' he heard another Big Mushroom mutter with grudging admiration.

The play worked rather rapidly around the table, nobody getting very hot and the stakes never more than medium high. 'Shoot a fin.' 'Rolling a sawbuck.' 'An Andrew Jackson.' 'Rolling thirty bucks.' Now and then Joe covered part of a bet, winning more than he lost. He had over seven thousand dollars, real money, before the bones got around to the Big Gambler.

That one held the dice for a long moment on his statue-steady palm while he looked at them reflectively, though not the hint of a furrow appeared in his almost brownish forehead down which never a bead of sweat trickled. He murmured, 'Rolling a double sawbuck,' and when he had been faded, he closed his fingers, lightly rattled the cubes—the sound was like big seeds inside a small gourd only half dry—and negligently cast the dice towards the end of the table.

It was a throw like none Joe had ever seen before at any crap table. The dice travelled flat through the air without turning over, struck the exact juncture of the table's end and bottom, and stopped there dead, showing a natural seven.

Joe was distinctly disappointed. On one of his own throws he was used to calculating something like, 'Launch three-up, five north, two and a half rolls in the air, hit on the six-five-three corner, three-quarter roll and a one-quarter side-twist right, hit end on the one-two edge, one-half reverse roll and three-quarter side-twist left, land on five face, roll over twice, come up two,' and that would be for just one of the dice, and a really commonplace throw, without extra bounces.

By comparison, the technique of the Big Gambler had been ridiculously, abysmally, horrifyingly simple. Joe could have duplicated it with the greatest ease, of course. It was no more than an elementary form of his old pastime of throwing fallen rocks back into their holes. But Joe had never once thought of pulling such a babyish trick at the crap table. It would make the whole thing too easy and destroy the beauty of the game.

Another reason Joe had never used the trick was that he'd never dreamed he'd be able to get away with it. By all the rules he'd ever heard of, it was a most questionable throw. There was the possibility that one or the other die hadn't completely reached the end of the table, or lay a wee bit cocked against the end. Besides, he reminded himself, weren't both dice supposed to rebound off the end, if only for a fraction of an inch?

However, as far as Joe's very sharp eyes could see, both dice lay perfectly flat and sprang up against the end wall. Moreover, everyone else at the table seemed to accept the throw, the dice-girl had scooped up the cubes, and the Big Mushrooms who had faded the man in black were paying off. As far as the rebound business went, well, The Boneyard appeared to put a slightly different interpretation on that rule, and Joe believed in never questioning House Rules except in dire extremity—both his Mother and Wife had long since taught him it was the least troublesome way.

Besides, there hadn't been any of his own money riding on that roll.

In a voice like wind through Cypress Hollow or on Mars, the Big Gambler announced, 'Roll a century.' It was the biggest bet yet tonight, ten thousand dollars, and the way the Big Gambler said it made it seem something more than that. A hush fell on The Boneyard, they put the mutes on the jazz horns, the croupiers' calls became more confidential, the cards fell softlier, even the roulette balls seemed to be trying to make less noise as they rattled into their cells. The crowd around the Number

One Crap Table quietly thickened. The Big Gambler's flash boys and girls formed a double semicircle around him, ensuring him lots of elbow room.

That century bet, Joe realized, was thirty bucks more than his own entire pile. Three or four of the Big Mushrooms had to signal each other before they'd agreed how to fade it.

The Big Gambler shot another natural seven with exactly the same flat, stop-dead throw.

He bet another century and did it again.

And again.

And again.

Joe was getting mighty concerned and pretty indignant too. It seemed unjust that the Big Gambler should be winning such huge bets with such machinelike, utterly unromantic rolls. Why, you couldn't even call them rolls, the dice never turned over an iota, in the air or after. It was the sort of thing you'd expect from a robot, and a very dully programmed robot at that. Joe hadn't risked any of his own chips fading the Big Gambler, of course, but if things went on like this he'd have to. Two of the Big Mushrooms had already retired sweatingly from the table, confessing defeat, and no one had taken their places. Pretty soon there'd be a bet the remaining Big Mushrooms couldn't entirely cover between them, and then he'd have to risk some of his own chips or else pull out of the game himself—and he couldn't do that, not with the power surging in his right hand like chained lightning.

Joe waited and waited for someone else to question one of the Big Gambler's shots, but no one did. He realized that, despite his efforts to look imperturbable, his face was slowly reddening.

With a little lift of his left hand, the Big Gambler stopped the dice-girl as she was about to snatch at the cubes. The eyes that were like black wells directed themselves at Joe, who forced himself to look back into them steadily. He still couldn't catch the faintest gleam in them. All at once he felt the lightest touch-on-neck of a dreadful suspicion.

With the utmost civility and amiability, the Big Gambler whispered, 'I believe that the fine shooter across from me has doubts about the validity of my last throw, though he is too much of a gentleman to voice them. Lottie, the card test.'

The wraith-tall, ivory dice-girl plucked a playing card from below the table and with a venomous flash of her little white teeth spun it low across the table through the air at Joe. He caught the whirling pasteboard and examined it briefly. It was the thinnest, stiffest, flattest, shiniest playing card Joe had ever handled. It was also the Joker, if that meant anything. He spun it back lazily into her hand and she slid it very gently, letting it descend by its own weight, down the end wall against which the two dice lay. It came to rest in the tiny hollow their rounded edges made against the black felt. She deftly moved it about without force, demonstrating that there was no space between either of the cubes and the table's end at any point.

'Satisfied?' the Big Gambler asked. Rather against his will Joe nodded. The Big Gambler bowed to him. The dice-girl smirked her short, thin lips and drew herself up, flaunting her white-china-doorknob breasts at Joe.

Casually, almost with an air of boredom, the Big Gambler returned to his routine of shooting a century and making a natural seven. The Big Mushrooms wilted fast and one by one tottered away from the table. A particularly pink-faced Toadstool was brought extra cash by a gasping runner, but it was no help, he only lost the additional centuries. While the stacks of pale and black chips beside the Big Gambler grew skyscraper-tall.

Joe got more and more furious and frightened. He watched like a hawk or spy satellite the dice nesting against the end wall, but never could spot justification for calling for another card test, or nerve himself to question the House Rules at this late date. It was maddening, in fact insanitizing, to know that if only he could get the cubes once more he could shoot circles around that black pillar of sporting aristocracy. He damned himself a googelplex of ways for the idiotic, conceited, suicidal impulse that had led him to let go of the bones when he'd had them.

To make matters worse, the Big Gambler had taken to gazing steadily at Joe with those eyes like coal mines. Now he made three rolls running without even glancing at the dice or the end wall, as far as Joe could tell. Why, he was getting as bad as Joe's Wife or Mother—watching, watching, watching Joe.

But the constant staring of those eyes that were not eyes was mostly throwing a terrific scare into him. Supernatural terror added itself to his certainty of the deadliness of the Big Gambler.

Just who, Joe kept asking himself, had he got into a game with tonight? There was curiosity and there was dread—a dreadful curiosity as strong as his desire to get the bones and win. His hair rose and he was all over goose bumps, though the power was still pulsing in his hand like a braked locomotive or a rocket wanting to lift from the pad.

At the same time the Big Gambler stayed just that—a black satin-coated, slouch-hatted elegance, suave, courtly, lethal. In fact, almost the worst thing about the spot Joe found himself in was that, after admiring the Big Gambler's perfect sportsmanship all night, he must now be disenchanted by his machinelike throwing and try to catch him out on any technicality he could.

The remorseless mowing down of the Big Mushrooms went on. The empty spaces outnumbered the Toadstools. Soon there were only three left.

The Boneyard had grown still as Cypress Hollow or the Moon. The jazz had stopped and the gay laughter and the shuffle of feet and the squeak of goosed girls and the clink of drinks and coins. Everybody seemed to be gathered around the Number One Crap Table, rank on silent rank.

Joe was racked by watchfulness, sense of injustice, self-contempt, wild hopes, curiosity and dread. Especially the last two.

The complexion of the Big Gambler, as much as you could see of it, continued to darken. For one wild moment Joe found himself wondering if he'd got into a game with a nigger, maybe a witch-craft-drenched Voodoo Man whose white make-up was wearing off.

Pretty soon there came a century wager which the two remaining Big Mushrooms couldn't fade between them. Joe had to make up a sawbuck from his miserably tiny pile or get out of the game. After a moment's agonizing hesitation, he did the former.

And lost his ten.

The two Big Mushrooms reeled back into the hushed crowd. Pit-black eyes bored into Joe. A whisper: 'Rolling your pile.'

Joe felt well up in him the shameful impulse to confess himself licked and run home. At least his six thousand dollars would make a hit with his Wife and Ma.

But he just couldn't bear to think of the crowd's laughter, or the thought of living with himself knowing that he'd had a final chance, however slim, to challenge the Big Gambler and passed it up.

He nodded.

The Big Gambler shot. Joe leaned out over and down the table, forgetting his vertigo, as he followed the throw with eagle or space-telescope eyes.

'Satisfied?'

Joe knew he ought to say, 'Yes', and slink off with head held as high as he could manage. It was the gentlemanly thing to do. But then he reminded himself that he wasn't a gentleman, but just a dirty, working-stiff miner with a talent for precision hurling.

He also knew that it was probably very dangerous for him to say anything but, 'Yes', surrounded as he was by enemies and strangers. But then he asked himself what right had he, a miserable, mortal, homebound failure, to worry about danger.

Besides, one of the ruby-grinning dice looked just the tiniest hair out of line with the other.

It was the biggest effort yet of Joe's life, but he swallowed and managed to say, 'No. Lottie, the card test.'

The dice-girl fairly snarled and reared up and back as if she were going to spit in his eyes, and Joe had a feeling her spit was cobra venom. But the Big Gambler lifted a finger at her in reproof and she skimmed the card at Joe, yet so low and viciously that it disappeared under the black felt for an instant before flying up into Joe's hand.

It was hot to the touch and singed a pale brown all over, though otherwise unimpaired. Joe gulped and spun it back high.

Sneering poisoned daggers at him, Lottie let it glide down the end wall . . . and after a moment's hesitation, it slithered behind the die Joe had suspected.

A bow and then the whisper: 'You have sharp eyes, sir. Undoubtedly that die failed to reach the wall. My sincerest apologies and . . . your dice, sir.'

Seeing the cubes sitting on the black rim in front of him almost gave Joe apoplexy. All the feelings racking him, including his curiosity, rose to an almost unbelievable pitch of intensity, and when he'd said, 'Rolling my pile', and the Big Gambler had replied, 'You're faded', he yielded to an uncontrollable impulse and cast the two dice straight at the Big Gambler's ungleaming, midnight eyes.

They went right through into the Big Gambler's skull and bounced around inside there, rattling like big seeds in a big gourd not quite yet dry.

Throwing out a hand, palm back, to either side, to indicate that none of his boys or girls or anyone else must make a reprisal on Joe, the Big Gambler dryly gargled the two cubical bones, then spat them out so that they landed in the centre of the table, the one die flat, the other leaning against it.

'Cocked dice, sir,' he whispered as graciously as if no indignity whatever had been done him. 'Roll again.'

Joe shook the dice reflectively, getting over the shock. After a little bit he decided that though he could now guess the Big Gambler's real name, he'd still give him a run for his money.

A little corner of Joe's mind wondered how a live skeleton hung together. Did the bones still have gristle and thews, were they wired, was it done with force-fields, or was each bone a calcium magnet clinging to the next?—this tying in somehow with the generation of the deadly ivory electricity.

In the great hush of The Boneyard, someone cleared his throat, a Scarlet Woman tittered hysterically, a coin fell from the nakedest change-girl's tray with a golden clink and rolled musically across the floor.

'Silence,' the Big Gambler commanded and in a movement almost too fast to follow whipped a hand inside the bosom of his coat and out to the crap table's rim in front of him. A short-barrelled silver revolver lay softly gleaming there. 'Next creature, from the humblest nigger night-girl to you, Mr. Bones, who utters a sound while my worthy opponent rolls, gets a bullet in the head.'

Joe gave him a courtly bow back, it felt funny, and then decided to start his run with a natural seven made up of an ace and a six. He rolled and this time the Big Gambler, judging from the movements of his skull, closely followed the course of the cubes with his eyes that weren't there.

The dice landed, rolled over, and lay still. Incredulously, Joe realized that for the first time in his crap-shooting life he'd made a mistake. Or else there was a power in the Big Gambler's gaze greater than that in his own right hand. The six cube had come down okay, but the ace had taken an extra half roll and come down six too.

'End of the game,' Mr. Bones boomed sepulchrally.

The Big Gambler raised a brown skeletal hand. 'Not necessarily,' he whispered. His black eyepits aimed themselves at Joe like the mouths of siege guns. 'Joe Slattermill, you still have something of value to wager, if you wish. Your life.'

At that a giggling and a hysterical tittering and a guffawing and a braying and a shrieking burst uncontrollably out of the whole Boneyard. Mr. Bones summed up the sentiments when he bellowed over the rest of the racket. 'Now what use or value is there in the life of a bummer like Joe Slattermill? Not two cents, ordinary money.'

The Big Gambler laid a hand on the revolver gleaming before him and all the laughter died.

'I have a use for it,' the Big Gambler whispered. 'Joe Slattermill, on my part I will venture all my winnings of tonight, and throw in the world and everything in it for a side bet. You will wager your life, and on the side your soul. You to roll the dice. What's your pleasure?'

Joe Slattermill quailed, but then the drama of the situation took hold of him. He thought it over and realized he certainly wasn't going to give up being stage centre in a spectacle like this to go home broke to his Wife and Mother and decaying house and the dispirited Mr. Guts. Maybe, he told himself encouragingly, there wasn't a power in the Big Gambler's gaze, maybe Joe had just made his one and only crap-shooting error. Besides, he was more inclined to accept Mr. Bones's assessment of the value of his life than the Big Gambler's.

'It's a bet,' he said.

'Lottie, give him the dice.'

Joe concentrated his mind as never before, the power tingled triumphantly in his hand, and he made his throw.

The dice never hit the felt. They went swooping down, then up, in a crazy curve far out over the end of the table, and then came streaking back like tiny red-glinting meteors towards the face of the Big Gambler, where they suddenly nested and hung in his black eye sockets, each with the single red gleam of an ace showing.

Snake eyes.

The whisper, as those red-glinting dice-eyes stared mockingly at him: 'Joe Slattermill, you've crapped out.'

Using thumb and middle finger—or bone rather—of either hand, the Big Gambler removed the dice from his eye sockets and dropped them in Lottie's white-gloved hand.

'Yes, you've crapped out, Joe Slattermill,' he went on tranquilly. 'And now you can shoot yourself'—he touched the silver gun—'or cut your throat'—he whipped a gold-handled bowie knife out of his coat and laid it beside the revolver—'or poison yourself'—the two weapons were joined by a small black bottle with white skull and crossbones on it—'or Miss Flossie here can kiss you to death.' He drew forward beside him his prettiest, evilest-looking sporting girl. She preened herself and flounced her short violet skirt and gave Joe a provocative, hungry look, lifting her carmine upper lip to show her long white canines.

'Or else,' the Big Gambler added, nodding significantly towards the black-bottomed crap table, 'you can take the Big Dive.'

Joe said evenly, 'I'll take the Big Dive.'

He put his right foot on his empty chip table, his left on the black rim, fell forward . . . and suddenly kicking off from the rim, launched himself in a tiger spring straight across the crap table at the Big Gambler's throat, solacing himself with the thought that certainly the poet chap hadn't seemed to suffer long.

As he flashed across the exact centre of the table he got an instant photograph of what really lay below, but his brain had no time to develop that snapshot, for the next instant he was ploughing into the Big Gambler.

Stiffened brown palm edge caught him in the temple with a lightning-like judo chop . . . and the brown fingers or bones flew all apart like puff paste. Joe's left hand went through the Big Gambler's chest as if there were nothing there but black satin coat, while his right hand, straight-armedly clawing at the slouch-hatted skull, crunched it to pieces. Next instant Joe was sprawled on the floor with some black clothes and brown fragments.

He was on his feet in a flash and snatching at the Big Gambler's tall stacks. He had time for one left-handed grab. He couldn't see any gold or silver or any black chips, so he stuffed his left pants pocket with a handful of the pale chips and ran.

Then the whole population of The Boneyard was on him and after him. Teeth, knives and brass knuckles flashed. He was punched, clawed, kicked, tripped and stamped on with spike heels. A gold-plated trumpet with a bloodshot-eyed black face behind it bopped him on the head. He got a white flash of the golden dice-girl and made a grab for her, but she got away. Someone tried to mash a lighted cigar in his eye. Lottie, writhing and flailing like a white boa constrictor, almost got a simultaneous strangle hold and scissors on him. From a squat wide-mouth bottle Flossie, snarling like a feline fiend, threw what smelt like acid past his face. Mr. Bones peppered shots around him from the silver revolver. He was stabbed at, gouged, rabbit-punched, scragmauled, slugged, kneed, bitten, bearhugged, butted, beaten and had his toes trampled.

But somehow none of the blows or grabs had much real force. It was like fighting ghosts. In the end it turned out that the whole population of The Boneyard, working together, had just a little more strength than Joe. He felt himself being lifted by a multitude of hands and pitched out through the swinging doors so that he thudded down on his rear end on the board sidewalk. Even that didn't hurt much. It was more like a kick of encouragement.

He took a deep breath and felt himself over and worked his bones. He didn't seem to have suffered any serious damage. He stood up and looked around. The Boneyard was dark and silent as the grave, or the planet Pluto, or all the rest of Ironmine. As his eyes got accustomed to the starlight and occasional roving spaceship-gleam, he saw a padlocked sheet-iron door where the swinging ones had been.

He found he was chewing on something crusty that he'd somehow carried in his right hand all the way through the final fracas. Mighty tasty, like the bread his Wife baked for best customers. At that instant his brain developed the photograph it had taken when he had glanced down as he flashed across the centre of the crap table. It was a thin wall of flames moving sideways across the table and just beyond the flames the faces of his Wife, Mother, and Mr. Guts, all looking very surprised. He realized that what he was chewing was a fragment of the

Big Gambler's skull, and he remembered the shape of the three loaves his Wife had started to bake when he left the house. And he understood the magic she'd made to let him get a little ways away and feel half a man, and then come diving home with his fingers burned.

He spat out what was in his mouth and pegged the rest of the bit of giant-popover skull across the street.

He fished in his left pocket. Most of the pale poker chips had been mashed in the fight, but he found a whole one and explored its surface with his fingertips. The symbol embossed on it was a cross. He lifted it to his lips and took a bite. It tasted delicate, but delicious. He ate it and felt his strength revive. He patted his bulging left pocket. At least he'd started out well provisioned.

Then he turned and headed straight for home, but he took the long way, around the world.

Anybody who has read The Passover Plot *will see what is going on here quickly enough. This story won the Nebula award in its category. It deals with a man who travels through Time in search of the Christ. He is, in a very strange way, successful in his quest. On first reading, if you're of the Christian persuasion, this story may seem blasphemous and irreverent. Well, maybe it is. Maybe the author is an iconoclast. Say that. Then again, maybe you're an atheist, and a sophisticated one, and you might say that the author is kicking a dead dog. Say that. Christian or atheist, though, if these be your initial reactions, consider the story a bit more closely. It may just be that both reactions are wrong.*

Michael Moorcock is a wonderous man, twice the size of any of us, with a beard like Father Time and the ability to practically kill himself for that which he loves and believes in. He edits the British periodical New Worlds, *which has been the vehicle for some very fine tellings since he took it over. He is a good editor, and a man who would literally give you his shirt, if you were to stop him on the street and demonstrate that you really needed it. He is a professional human being. What more can I say? Plenty. I've met Michael Moorcock a couple of times, and because of this I know what I am saying when I say that there are very few people who could spend an afternoon with him and not come away liking him.*

Read his story carefully, please.

BEHOLD THE MAN*

Michael Moorcock

He has no material power as the god-emperors had; he has only a following of desert people and fishermen. They tell him he is a god; he believes them. The followers of Alexander said: 'He is unconquerable, therefore he is a god.' The followers of this man do not think at all; he was their act of spontaneous creation. Now he leads them, this madman called Jesus of Nazareth.

And he spoke, saying unto them: Yeah verily I *was* Karl Glogauer and now I am Jesus the Messiah, the Christ.

And it was so.

I

The time machine was a sphere full of milky fluid in which the traveller floated, enclosed in a rubber suit, breathing through a mask attached to a hose leading to the wall of the machine. The sphere cracked as it landed and the fluid spilled into the dust and was soaked up. Instinctively, Glogauer curled himself into a ball as the level of the liquid fell and he sank to the yielding plastic of the sphere's inner lining. The instruments, cryptographic, unconventional, were still and silent. The sphere shifted and rolled as the last of the liquid dripped from the great gash in its side.

Momentarily, Glogauer's eyes opened and closed, then his mouth stretched in a kind of yawn and his tongue fluttered and he uttered a groan that turned into a ululation.

 Nebula Award, Best Novella 1967

* The expanded book-length version of this award-winning story is published in paperback by Mayflower Books.

He heard himself. The Voice of Tongues, he thought. The language of the unconscious. But he could not guess what he was saying.

His body became numb and he shivered. His passage through time had not been easy and even the thick fluid had not wholly protected him, though it had doubtless saved his life. Some ribs were certainly broken. Painfully, he straightened his arms and legs and began to crawl over the slippery plastic towards the crack in the machine. He could see harsh sunlight, a sky like shimmering steel. He pulled himself halfway through the crack, closing his eyes as the full strength of the sunlight struck them. He lost consciousness.

Christmas term, 1949. He was nine years old, born two years after his father had reached England from Austria.

The other children were screaming with laughter in the gravel of the playground. The game had begun earnestly enough and somewhat nervously Karl had joined in in the same spirit. Now he was crying.

'Let me *down*! Please, Mervyn, stop it!'

They had tied him with his arms spreadeagled against the wire-netting of the playground fence. It bulged outwards under his weight and one of the posts threatened to come loose. Mervyn Williams, the boy who had proposed the game, began to shake the post so that Karl was swung heavily back and forth on the netting.

'Stop it!'

He saw that his cries only encouraged them and he clenched his teeth, becoming silent.

He slumped, pretending unconsciousness; the school ties they had used as bonds cut into his wrists. He heard the children's voices drop.

'Is he all right?' Molly Turner was whispering.

'He's only kidding,' Williams replied uncertainly.

He felt them untying him, their fingers fumbling with the knots. Deliberately, he sagged, then fell to his knees, grazing them on the gravel, and dropped face down to the ground.

Distantly, for he was half-convinced by his own deception, he heard their worried voices.

Williams shook him.

'Wake up, Karl. Stop mucking about.'

He stayed where he was, losing his sense of time until he heard Mr. Matson's voice over the general babble.

'What on earth were you doing, Williams?'

'It was a play, sir, about Jesus. Karl was being Jesus. We tied him to the fence. It was his idea, sir. It was only a game, sir.'

Karl's body was stiff, but he managed to stay still, breathing shallowly.

'He's not a strong boy like you, Williams. You should have known better.'

'I'm sorry, sir. I'm really sorry.' Williams sounded as if he were crying.

Karl felt himself lifted; felt the triumph. . . .

He was being carried along. His head and side were so painful that he felt sick. He had had no chance to discover where exactly the time machine had brought him, but, turning his head now, he could see by the way the man on his right was dressed that he was at least in the Middle East.

He had meant to land in the year A.D. 29 in the wilderness beyond Jerusalem, near Bethlehem. Were they taking him to Jerusalem now?

He was on a stretcher that was apparently made of animal skins; this indicated that he was probably in the past, at any rate. Two men were carrying the stretcher on their shoulders. Others walked on both sides. There was a smell of sweat and animal fat and a musty smell he could not identify. They were walking towards a line of hills in the distance.

He winced as the stretcher lurched and the pain in his side increased. For the second time he passed out.

He woke up briefly, hearing voices. They were speaking what was evidently some form of Aramaic. It was night, perhaps, for it seemed very dark. They were no longer moving. There was straw beneath him. He was relieved. He slept.

'In those days came John the Baptist preaching in the wilderness of Judaea, And saying, Repent ye: for the kingdom of heaven is at hand. For this is he that was spoken of by the prophet Esaias, saying, The voice of one crying in the wlderness. Prepare ye the way of the Lord, make his paths straight. And the same John had

his raiment of camel's hair, and a leathern girdle about his loins;
and his meat was locusts and wild honey. Then went out to him
Jerusalem, and all Judaea, and all the region round about Jordan.
And were baptized of him in Jordan, confessing their sins.'

(Matthew 3: 1–6)

They were washing him. He felt the cold water running over
his naked body. They had managed to strip off his protective
suit. There were now thick layers of cloth against his ribs on
the right, and bands of leather bound them to him.

He felt very weak now, and hot, but there was less pain.

He was in a building—or perhaps a cave; it was too gloomy
to tell—lying on a heap of straw that was saturated by the water.
Above him, two men continued to sluice water down on him
from their earthenware pots. They were stern-faced, heavily-
bearded men, in cotton robes.

He wondered if he could form a sentence they might understand. His knowledge of written Aramaic was good, but he was
not sure of certain pronunciations.

He cleared his throat. 'Where—be—this—place?'

They frowned, shaking their heads and lowering their water
jars.

'I—seek—a—Nazarene—Jesus. . . .'

'Nazarene. Jesus.' One of the men repeated the words, but
they did not seem to mean anything to him. He shrugged.

The other, however, only repeated the word Nazarene,
speaking it slowly as if it had some special significance for him.
He muttered a few words to the other man and went towards
the entrance of the room.

Karl Glogauer continued to try to say something the remaining
man would understand.

'What—year—doth—the Roman Emperor—sit—in Rome?'

It was a confusing question to ask, he realized. He knew
Christ had been crucified in the fifteenth year of Tiberius' reign,
and that was why he had asked the question. He tried to phrase
it better.

'How many—year—doth Tiberius rule?'

'Tiberius?' The man frowned.

Glogauer's ear was adjusting to the accent now and he tried
to simulate it better. 'Tiberius. The emperor of the Romans.

How many years has he ruled?'

'How many?' The man shook his head. 'I know not.'

At least Glogauer had managed to make himself understood.
'Where is this place?' he asked.

'It is the wilderness beyond Machaerus,' the man replied.
'Know you not that?'

Machaerus lay to the south-east of Jerusalem, on the other
side of the Dead Sea. There was no doubt that he was in the
past and that the period was some time in the reign of Tiberius,
for the man had recognized the name easily enough.

His companion was now returning, bringing with him a huge
fellow with heavily muscled hairy arms and a great barrel chest.
He carried a big staff in one hand. He was dressed in animal
skins and was well over six feet tall. His black, curly hair was
long and he had a black, bushy beard that covered the upper half
of his chest. He moved like an animal and his large, piercing
brown eyes looked reflectively at Glogauer.

When he spoke, it was in a deep voice, but too rapidly for
Glogauer to follow. It was Glogauer's turn to shake his head.

The big man squatted down beside him. 'Who art thou?'

Glogauer paused. He had not planned to be found in this
way. He had intended to disguise himself as a traveller from
Syria, hoping that the local accents would be different enough
to explain his own unfamiliarity with the language. He decided
that it was best to stick to this story and hope for the best.

'I am from the north,' he said.

'Not from Egypt?' the big man asked. It was as if he had
expected Glogauer to be from there. Glogauer decided that if
this was what the big man thought, he might just as well agree
to it.

'I came out of Egypt two years since,' he said.

The big man nodded, apparently satisfied. 'So you are a
magus from Egypt. That is what we thought. And your name
is Jesus, and you are the Nazarene.'

'I *seek* Jesus, the Nazarene,' Glogauer said.

'Then what is your name?' The man seemed disappointed.

Glogauer could not give his own name. It would sound too
strange to them. On impulse, he gave his father's first name.
'Emmanuel,' he said.

The man nodded, again satisfied. 'Emmanuel.'

Glogauer realized belatedly that the choice of name had been an unfortunate one in the circumstances, for Emmanuel meant in Hebrew 'God with us' and doubtless had a mystic significance for his questioner.

'And what is your name?' he asked.

The man straightened up, looking broodingly down on Glogauer. 'You do not know me? You have not heard of' John, called the Baptist?'

Glogauer tried to hide his surprise, but evidently John the Baptist saw that his name was familiar. He nodded his shaggy head. 'You do know of me, I see. Well magus, now I must decide, eh?'

'What must you decide?' Glogauer asked nervously.

'If you be the friend of the prophecies or the false one we have been warned against by Adonai. The Romans would deliver me into the hands of mine enemies, the children of Herod.'

'Why is that?'

'You must know why, for I speak against the Romans who enslave Judaea, and I speak against the unlawful things that Herod does, and I prophesy the time when all those who are not righteous shall be destroyed and Adonai's kingdom will be restored on Earth as the old prophets said it would be. I say to the people, "Be ready for that day when ye shall take up the sword to do Adonai's will." The unrighteous know that they will perish on this day, and they would destroy me.'

Despite the intensity of his words, John's tone was matter of fact. There was no hint of insanity or fanaticism in his face or bearing. He sounded most of all like an Anglican vicar reading a sermon whose meaning for him had lost its edge.

The essence of what he said, Karl Glogauer realized, was that he was arousing the people to throw out the Romans and their puppet Herod and establish a more 'righteous' regime. The attributing of this plan to 'Adonai' (one of the spoken names of Jahweh and meaning The Lord) seemed, as many scholars had guessed in the twentieth century, a means of giving the plan extra weight. In a world where politics and religion, even in the west, were inextricably bound together, it was necessary to ascribe a supernatural origin to the plan.

Indeed, Glogauer thought, it was more than likely that John believed his idea had been inspired by God, for the Greeks on the other side of the Mediterranean had not yet stopped arguing about the origins of inspiration—whether it originated in a man's head or was placed there by the gods. That John accepted him as an Egyptian magician of some kind did not surprise Glogauer particularly, either. The circumstances of his arrival must have seemed extraordinarily miraculous and at the same time acceptable, particularly to a sect like the Essenes who practised self-mortification and starvation and must be quite used to seeing visions in this hot wilderness. There was no doubt now that these people were the neurotic Essenes, whose ritual washing—baptism—and self-deprivation, coupled with the almost paranoiac mysticism that led them to invent secret languages and the like, was a sure indication of their mentally unbalanced condition. All this occurred to Glogauer the psychiatrist manqué, but Glogauer the man was torn between the poles of extreme rationalism and the desire to be convinced by the mysticism itself.

'I must meditate,' John said, turning towards the cave entrance. 'I must pray. You will remain here until guidance is sent to me.'

He left the cave, striding rapidly away.

Glogauer sank back on the wet straw. He was without doubt in a limestone cave, and the atmosphere in the cave was surprisingly humid. It must be very hot outside. He felt drowsy.

II

Five years in the past. Nearly two thousand in the future. Lying in the hot, sweaty bed with Monica. Once again, another attempt to make normal love had metamorphosed into the performance of minor aberrations which seemed to satisfy her better than anything else.

Their real courtship and fulfilment was yet to come. As usual, it would be verbal. As usual, it would find its climax in argumentative anger.

'I suppose you're going to tell me you're not satisfied again.' She accepted the lighted cigarette he handed to her in the darkness.

'I'm all right,' he said.

There was silence for a while as they smoked.

Eventually, and in spite of knowing what the result would be if he did so, he found himself talking.

'It's ironic, isn't it?' he began.

He waited for her reply. She would delay for a little while yet.

'What is?' she said at last.

'All this. You spend all day trying to help sexual neurotics to become normal. You spend your nights doing what they do.'

'Not to the same extent. You know it's all a matter of degree.'

'So you say.'

He turned his head and looked at her face in the starlight from the window. She was a gaunt-featured redhead, with the calm, professional seducer's voice of the psychiatric social worker that she was. It was a voice that was soft, reasonable and insincere. Only occasionally, when she became particularly agitated, did her voice seem to indicate her real character. Her features never seemed to be in repose, even when she slept. Her eyes were for ever wary, her movements rarely spontaneous. Every inch of her was protected, which was probably why she got so little pleasure from ordinary lovemaking.

'You just can't let yourself go, can you?' he said.

'Oh, shut up, Karl. Have a look at yourself if you're looking for a neurotic mess.'

Both were amateur psychiatrists—she a psychiatric social worker, he merely a reader, a dabbler, though he had done a year's study some time ago when he had planned to become a psychiatrist. They used the terminology of psychiatry freely. They felt happier if they could name something.

He rolled away from her groping for the ashtray on the bedside table, catching a glance of himself in the dressing table mirror. He was a sallow, intense, moody Jewish bookseller, with a head full of images and unresolved obsessions, a body full of emotions. He always lost these arguments with Monica. Verbally, she was the dominant one. This kind of exchange often seemed to him more perverse than their lovemaking, where usually at least his role was masculine. Essentially, he realized, he was passive, masochistic, indecisive. Even his anger, which came frequently, was impotent. Monica was ten years older than he was, ten years more bitter. As an individual, of course, she had far more dynamism than he had; but as a psychiatric social worker she had had just as many failures. She plugged on, becoming increasingly cynical on the surface but still, perhaps, hoping for a few spectacular successes with patients. They tried to do too much, that was the trouble, he thought. The priests in the confessional supplied a panacea; the psychiatrists tried to cure, and most of the time they failed. But at least they tried, he thought, and then wondered, if that was, after all, a virtue.

'I did look at myself,' he said.

Was she sleeping? He turned. Her wary eyes were still open, looking out of the window.

'I did look at myself,' he repeated. 'The way Jung did. "How can I help those persons if I am myself a fugitive and perhaps also suffer from the *morbus sacer* of a neurosis?" That's what Jung asked himself. . . .'

'That old sensationalist. That old rationalizer of his own mysticism. No wonder you never became a psychiatrist.'

'I wouldn't have been any good. It was nothing to do with Jung. . . .'

'Don't take it out on me. . . .'

'You've told me yourself that you feel the same—you think it's useless. . . .'

'After a hard week's work, I might say that. Give me another fag.'

He opened the packet on the bedside table and put two cigarettes in his mouth, lighting them and handing one to her.

Almost abstractedly, he noticed that the tension was increasing. The argument was, as ever, pointless. But it was not the argument that was the important thing; it was simply the expression of the essential relationship. He wondered if that was in any way important, either.

'You're not telling the truth.' He realized that there was no stopping now that the ritual was in full swing.

'I'm telling the practical truth. I've no compulsion to give up my work. I've no wish to be a failure. . . .'

'Failure? You're more melodramatic than I am.'

'You're too earnest, Karl. You want to get out of yourself a bit.'

He sneered. 'If I were you, I'd give up my work, Monica. You're no more suited for it than I was.'

She shrugged. 'You're a petty bastard.'

'I'm not jealous of you, if that's what you think. You'll never understand what I'm looking for.'

Her laugh was artificial, brittle. 'Modern man in search of a soul, eh? Modern man in search of a crutch, I'd say. And you can take that any way you like.'

'We're destroying the myths that make the world go round.'

'Now you say "And what are we putting in their place?" You're stale and stupid, Karl. You've never looked rationally at anything—including yourself.'

'What of it? You say the myth is unimportant.'

'The reality that creates it is important.'

'Jung knew that the myth can also create the reality.'

'Which shows what a muddled old fool he was.'

He stretched his legs. In doing so, he touched hers and he recoiled. He scratched his head. She still lay there smoking, but she was smiling now.

'Come on,' she said. 'Let's have some stuff about Christ.'

He said nothing. She handed him the stub of her cigarette and he put it in the ashtray. He looked at his watch. It was two o'clock in the morning.

'Why do we do it?' he said.

'Because we must.' She put her hand to the back of his head and pulled it towards her breast. 'What else can we do?'

'*We Protestants must sooner or later face this question: Are we to understand the "imitation of Christ" in the sense that we should copy his life and, if I may use the expression, ape his stigmata; or in the deeper sense that we are to live our own proper lives as truly as he lived his in all its implications? It is no easy matter to live a life that is modelled on Christ's, but it is unspeakably harder to live one's own life as truly as Christ lived his. Anyone who did this would . . . be misjudged, derided, tortured and crucified . . . A neurosis is a dissociation of personality.*'

(Jung: *Modern Man in Search of a Soul*)

For a month, John the Baptist was away and Glogauer lived with the Essenes, finding it surprisingly easy, as his ribs mended, to join in their daily life. The Essenes' township consisted of a mixture of single-storey houses, built of limestone and clay brick, and the caves that were to be found on both sides of the shallow valley. The Essenes shared their goods in common and this particular sect had wives, though many Essenes led completely monastic lives. The Essenes were also pacifists, refusing to own or to make weapons—yet this sect plainly tolerated the warlike Baptist. Perhaps their hatred of the Romans overcame their principles. Perhaps they were not sure of John's entire intention. Whatever the reason for their toleration, there was little doubt that John the Baptist was virtually their leader.

The life of the Essenes consisted of ritual bathing three times a day, of prayer and of work. The work was not difficult. Sometimes Glogauer guided a plough pulled by two other members of the sect; sometimes he looked after the goats that were allowed to graze on the hillsides. It was a peaceful, ordered life, and even the unhealthy aspects were so much a matter of routine that Glogauer hardly noticed them for anything else after a while.

Tending the goats, he would lie on a hilltop, looking out over the wilderness which was not a desert, but rocky scrubland sufficient to feed animals like goats or sheep. The scrubland was broken by low-lying bushes and a few small trees growing along the banks of the river that doubtless ran into the Dead Sea. It was uneven ground. In outline, it had the appearance of a stormy lake, frozen and turned yellow and brown. Beyond the Dead Sea lay Jerusalem. Obviously Christ had not entered the city for the last time yet. John the Baptist would have to die before that happened.

The Essenes' way of life was comfortable enough, for all its simplicity. They had given him a goatskin loincloth and a staff and, except for the fact that he was watched by day and night, he appeared to be accepted as a kind of lay member of the sect.

Sometimes they questioned him casually about his chariot—the time machine they intended soon to bring in from the desert—and he told them that it had borne him from Egypt to Syria and then to here. They accepted the miracle calmly. As he had suspected, they were used to miracles.

The Essenes had seen stranger things than his time machine. They had seen men walk on water and angels descend to and from heaven; they had heard the voice of God and His archangels as well as the tempting voice of Satan and his minions. They wrote all these things down in their vellum scrolls. They were merely a record of the supernatural as their other scrolls were records of their daily lives and of the news that travelling members of their sect brought to them.

They lived constantly in the presence of God and spoke to God and were answered by God when they had sufficiently mortified their flesh and starved themselves and chanted their prayers beneath the blazing sun of Judaea.

Karl Glogauer grew his hair long and let his beard come unchecked. He mortified his flesh and starved himself and chanted his prayers beneath the sun, as they did. But he rarely heard God and only once thought he saw an archangel with wings of fire.

In spite of his willingness to experience the Essenes' hallucinations, Glogauer was disappointed, but he was surprised that he felt so well considering all the self-inflicted hardships he had to undergo, and he also felt relaxed in the company of these men and women who were undoubtedly insane. Perhaps it was because their insanity was not so very different from his own that after a while he stopped wondering about it.

John the Baptist returned one evening, striding over the hills followed by twenty or so of his closest disciples. Glogauer saw him as he prepared to drive the goats into their cave for the night. He waited for John to get closer.

The Baptist's face was grim, but his expression softened as he saw Glogauer. He smiled and grasped him by the upper arm in the Roman fashion.

'Well, Emmanuel, you are our friend, as I thought you were. Sent by Adonai to help us accomplish His will. You shall baptize me on the morrow, to show all the people that He is with us.'

Glogauer was tired. He had eaten very little and had spent most of the day in the sun, tending the goats. He yawned, finding it hard to reply. However, he was relieved. John had plainly been in Jerusalem trying to discover if the Romans had sent him as a spy. John now seemed reassured and trusted him.

He was worried, however, by the Baptist's faith in his powers.

'John,' he began. 'I'm no seer. . . .'

The Baptist's face clouded for a moment, then he laughed awkwardly. 'Say nothing. Eat with me tonight. I have wild-honey and locusts.'

Glogauer had not eaten this food, which was the staple of travellers who did not carry provisions but lived off the food they could find on the journey. Some regarded it as a delicacy.

He tried it later, as he sat in John's house. There were only two rooms in the house. One was for eating in, the other for sleeping in. The honey and locusts was too sweet for his taste, but it was a welcome change from barley or goat-meat.

He sat cross-legged, opposite John the Baptist, who ate with relish. Night had fallen. From outside came low murmurs and the moans and cries of those at prayer.

Glogauer dipped another locust into the bowl of honey that rested between them. 'Do you plan to lead the people of Judaea in revolt against the Romans?' he asked.

The Baptist seemed disturbed by the direct question. It was the first of its nature that Glogauer had put to him.

'If it be Adonai's will,' he said, not looking up as he leant towards the bowl of honey.

'The Romans know this?'

'I do not know, Emmanuel, but Herod the incestuous has doubtless told them I speak against the unrighteous.'

'Yet the Romans do not arrest you.'

'Pilate dare not—not since the petition was sent to the Emperor Tiberius.'

'Petition?'

'Aye, the one that Herod and the Pharisees signed when Pilate the procurator did place votive shields in the palace at Jerusalem and seek to violate the Temple. Tiberius rebuked Pilate and since then, though he still hates the Jews, the procurator is more careful in his treatment of us.'

'Tell me, John, do you know how long Tiberius has ruled in Rome?' He had not had the chance to ask that question again until now.

'Fourteen years.'

It was A.D. 28—something less than a year before the crucifixion would take place, and his time machine was smashed.

Now John the Baptist planned armed rebellion against the occupying Romans, but, if the Gospels were to be believed, would soon be decapitated by Herod. Certainly no large-scale rebellion had taken place at this time. Even those who claimed that the entry of Jesus and his disciples into Jerusalem and the invasion of the Temple were plainly the actions of armed rebels had found no records to suggest that John had led a similar revolt.

Glogauer had come to like the Baptist very much. The man was plainly a hardened revolutionary who had been planning revolt against the Romans for years and had slowly been building up enough followers to make the attempt successful. He reminded Glogauer strongly of the resistance leaders of the Second World War. He had a similar toughness and understanding of the realities of his position. He knew that he would only have one chance to smash the cohorts garrisoned in the country. If the revolt became protracted, Rome would have ample time to send more troops to Jerusalem.

'When do you think Adonai intends to destroy the unrighteous through your agency?' Glogauer said tactfully.

John glanced at him with some amusement. He smiled. 'The Passover is a time when the people are restless and resent the strangers most,' he said.

'When is the next Passover?'

'Not for many months.'

'How can I help you?'

'You are a magus.'

'I can work no miracles.'

John wiped the honey from his beard. 'I cannot believe that, Emmanuel. The manner of your coming was miraculous. The Essenes did not know if you were a devil or a messenger from Adonai.'

'I am neither.'

'Why do you confuse me, Emmanuel? I know that you are Adonai's messenger. You are the sign that the Essenes sought. The time is almost ready. The kingdom of heaven shall soon be established on earth. Come with me. Tell the people that you speak with Adonai's voice. Work mighty miracles.'

'Your power is waning, is that it?' Glogauer looked sharply at John. 'You need me to renew your rebels' hopes?'

'You speak like a Roman, with such lack of subtlety.' John got up angrily. Evidently, like the Essenes he lived with, he preferred less direct conversation. There was a practical reason for this, Glogauer realized, in that John and his men feared betrayal all the time. Even the Essenes' records were partially written in cipher, with one innocent-seeming word or phrase meaning something else entirely.

'I am sorry, John. But tell me if I am right.' Glogauer spoke softly.

'Are you not a magus, coming in that chariot from nowhere?' The Baptist waved his hands and shrugged his shoulders. 'My men saw you! They saw the shining thing take shape in air, crack and let you enter out of it. Is that not magical? The clothing you wore—was that earthly raiment? The talismans within the chariot—did they not speak of powerful magic? The prophet said that a magus would come from Egypt and be called Emmanuel. So it is written in the Book of Micah! Are none of these things true?'

'Most of them. But there are explanations——' He broke off, unable to think of the nearest word to 'rational'. 'I am an ordinary man, like you. I have no power to work miracles! I am just a man!'

John glowered. 'You mean you refuse to help us?'

'I'm grateful to you and the Essenes. You saved my life almost certainly. If I can repay that . . .'

John nodded his head deliberately. 'You can repay it, Emmanuel.'

'How?'

'Be the great magus I need. Let me present you to all those who become impatient and would turn away from Adonai's will. Let me tell them the manner of your coming to us. Then you can say that all is Adonai's will and that they must prepare to accomplish it.'

John stared at him intensely.

'Will you, Emmanuel?'

'For your sake, John. And in turn, will you send men to bring my chariot here as soon as possible? I wish to see if it may be mended.'

'I will.'

Glogauer felt exhilarated. He began to laugh. The Baptist looked at him with slight bewilderment. Then he began to join in.

Glogauer laughed on. History would not mention it, but he,

with John the Baptist, would prepare the way for Christ.

Christ was not born yet. Perhaps Glogauer knew it, one year before the crucifixion.

'And the Word was made flesh and dwelt among us (and we beheld his glory, the glory as of the only begotten of the Father) full of grace and truth. John bare witness of him, and cried, saying. This was he of whom I spake, He that cometh after me is preferred before me: for he was before me.'

(John 1 : 14–15)

Even when he had first met Monica they had had long arguments. His father had not then died and left him the money to buy an occult bookshop in Great Russell Street, opposite the British Museum. He was doing all sorts of temporary work and his spirits were very low. At that time Monica had seemed a great help, a great guide through the mental darkness engulfing him. They had both lived close to Holland Park and went there for walks almost every Sunday of the summer of 1962. At twenty-two, he was already obsessed with Jung's strange brand of Christian mysticism. She, who despised Jung, had soon begun to denigrate all his ideas. She never really convinced him. But, after a while, she had succeeded in confusing him. It would be another six months before they went to bed together.

It was uncomfortably hot.

They sat in the shade of the cafeteria, watching a distant cricket match. Nearer to them, two girls and a boy sat on the grass, drinking orange squash from plastic cups. One of the girls had a guitar across her lap and she set the cup down and began to play, singing a folksong in a high, gentle voice. Glogauer tried to listen to the words. As a student, he had always liked traditional folk music.

'Christianity is dead.' Monica sipped her tea. 'Religion is dying. God was killed in 1945.'

'There may yet be a resurrection,' he said.

'Let us hope not. Religion was the creation of fear. Knowledge destroys fear. Without fear, religion can't survive.'

'You think there's no fear about these days?'

'Not the same kind, Karl.'

'Haven't you ever considered the *idea* of Christ?' he asked her, changing his tack. 'What that means to Christians?'

'The idea of the tractor means as much to a Marxist,' she replied.

'But what came first? The idea or the actuality of Christ?'

She shrugged. 'The actuality, if it matters. Jesus was a Jewish troublemaker organizing a revolt against the Romans. He was crucified for his pains. That's all we know and all we need to know.'

'A great religion couldn't have begun so simply.'

'When people need one, they'll make a great religion out of the most unlikely beginnings.'

'That's my point, Monica.' He gesticulated at her and she drew away slightly. 'The *idea* preceded the *actuality* of Christ.'

'Oh, Karl, don't go on. The actuality of *Jesus* preceded the idea of *Christ*.'

A couple walked past, glancing at them as they argued.

Monica noticed them and fell silent. She got up and he rose as well, but she shook her head. 'I'm going home, Karl. You stay here. I'll see you in a few days.'

He watched her walk down the wide path towards the park gates.

The next day, when he got home from work, he found a letter. She must have written it after she had left him and posted it the same day.

'*Dear Karl,*

'*Conversation doesn't seem to have much effect on you, you know. It's as if you listen to the tone of the voice, the rhythm of the words, without ever hearing what is trying to be communicated. You're a bit like a sensitive animal who can't understand what's being said to it, but can tell if the person talking is pleased or angry and so on. That's why I'm writing to you—to try go get my idea across. You respond too emotionally when we're together.*

'*You make the mistake of considering Christianity as something that developed over the course of a few years, from the death of Jesus to the time the Gospels were written. But Christianity wasn't new. Only the name was new. Christianity was merely a stage in the meeting, cross-fertilization metamorphosis of Western logic and Eastern mysticism. Look how the religion itself changed over the centuries, re-interpreting itself to meet changing times. Christianity is just a new name for a conglomeration of old myths and philosophies. All the Gospels do is retell the sun myth and garble some of the ideas from the Greeks and Romans. Even in the second century, Jewish scholars were showing it up for the mish-mash it was! They pointed out the strong similarities between the various sun myths and the Christ myth. The miracles didn't happen—they were invented later, borrowed from here and there.*

'*Remember the old Victorians who used to say that Plato was really a Christian because he anticipated Christian thought? Christian thought! Christianity was a vehicle for ideas in circulation for centuries before Christ. Was Marcus Aurelius a Christian? He was writing in the direct tradition of Western philosophy. That's why Christianity caught on in Europe and not in the East! You should have been a theologian with your bias, not a psychiatrist. The same goes for your friend Jung.*

'*Try to clear your head of all this morbid nonsense and you'll be a lot better at your job.*

'*Yours,*

Monica.'

He screwed the letter up and threw it away. Later that evening he was tempted to look at it again, but he resisted the temptation.

III

John stood up to his waist in the river. Most of the Essenes stood on the banks watching him. Glogauer looked down at him.

'I cannot, John. It is not for me to do it.'

The Baptist muttered, 'You must.'

Glogauer shivered as he lowered himself into the river beside the Baptist. He felt light-headed. He stood there trembling, unable to move.

His foot slipped on the rocks of the river and John reached out and gripped his arm, steadying him.

In the clear sky, the sun was at zenith, beating down on his unprotected head.

'Emmanuel!' John cried suddenly. 'The spirit of Adonai is within you!'

Glogauer still found it hard to speak. He shook his head slightly. It was aching and he could hardly see. Today he was having his first migraine attack since he had come here. He wanted to vomit. John's voice sounded distant.

He swayed in the water.

As he began to fall towards the Baptist, the whole scene around him shimmered. He felt John catch him and heard himself say desperately: 'John baptize *me*!' And then there was water in his mouth and throat and he was coughing.

John's voice was crying something. Whatever the words were, they drew a response from the people on both banks. The roaring in his ears increased, its quality changing. He thrashed in the water, then felt himself lifted to his feet.

The Essenes were swaying in unison, every face lifted upwards towards the glaring sun.

Glogauer began to vomit into the water, stumbling as John's hands gripped his arms painfully and guided him up the bank.

A peculiar, rhythmic humming came from the mouths of the Essenes as they swayed; it rose as they swayed to one side, fell as they swayed to the other.

Glogauer covered his ears as John released him. He was still retching, but it was dry now, and worse than before.

He began to stagger away, barely keeping his balance, running, with his ears still covered; running over the rocky scrubland; running as the sun throbbed in the sky and its head pounded at his head; running away.

'But John forbade him, saying, I have need to be baptized of thee, and comest thou to me? And Jesus answering said unto him, Suffer it to be so now: for thus it becometh us to fulfil all righteousness. Then he suffered him. And Jesus, when he was baptized, went up straight-way out of the water: and, lo, the heavens were opened unto him, and he saw the Spirit of God descending like a dove, and lighting upon him: And lo a voice from heaven, saying, This is my beloved Son, in whom I am well pleased.'

(Matthew 3: 14–17)

He had been fifteen, doing well at the grammar school. He

had read in the newspapers about the Teddy Boy gangs that roamed South London, but the odd youth he had seen in pseudo-Edwardian clothes had seemed harmless and stupid enough.

He had gone to the pictures in Brixton Hill and decided to walk home to Streatham because he had spent most of the bus money on an ice cream. They came out of the cinema at the same time. He hardly noticed them as they followed him down the hill.

Then, quite suddenly, they had surrounded him. Pale, mean-faced boys, most of them a year or two older than he was. He realized that he knew two of them vaguely. They were at the big council school in the same street as the grammar school. They used the same football ground.

'Hello,' he said weakly.

'Hello, son,' said the oldest Teddy Boy. He was chewing gum, standing with one knee bent, grinning at him. 'Where you going, then?'

'Home.'

'Heouwm,' said the biggest one, imitating his accent. 'What are you going to do when you get there?'

'Go to bed.' Karl tried to get through the ring, but they wouldn't let him. They pressed him back into a shop doorway. Beyond them, cars droned by on the main road. The street was brightly lit, with street lamps and neon from the shops. Several people passed, but none of them stopped. Karl began to feel panic.

'Got no homework to do, son?' said the boy next to the leader. He was redheaded and freckled and his eyes were a hard grey.

'Want to fight one of us?' another boy asked. It was one of the boys he knew.

'No. I don't fight. Let me go.'

'You scared, son?' said the leader, grinning. Ostentatiously, he pulled a streamer of gum from his mouth and then replaced it. He began chewing again.

'No. Why should I want to fight you?'

'You reckon you're better than us, is that it, son?'

'No.' He was beginning to tremble. Tears were coming into his eyes. ''Course not.'

''Course not, son.'

He moved forward again, but they pushed him back into the doorway.

'You're the bloke with the kraut name, ain't you?' said the other boy he knew. 'Glow-worm or somethink.'

'Glogauer. Let me go.'

'Won't your mummy like it if you're back late?'

'More a yid name than a kraut name.'

'You a yid, son?'

'He looks like a yid.'

'You a yid, son?'

'You a Jewish boy, son?'

'You a yid, son?'

'Shut up!' Karl screamed. He pushed into them. One of them punched him in the stomach. He grunted with pain. Another pushed him and he staggered.

People were still hurrying by on the pavement. They glanced at the group as they went past. One man stopped but his wife pulled him on. 'Just some kids larking about,' she said.

'Get his trousers down,' one of the boys suggested with a laugh. 'That'll prove it.'

Karl pushed through them and this time they didn't resist. He began to run down the hill.

'Give him a start,' he heard one of the boys say.

He ran on.

They began to follow him, laughing.

They did not catch up with him by the time he turned into the avenue where he lived. He reached the house and ran along the dark passage beside it. He opened the back door. His stepmother was in the kitchen.

'What's the matter with you?' she said.

She was a tall, thin woman, nervous and hysterical. Her dark hair was untidy.

He went past her into the breakfast-room.

'What's the matter, Karl?' she called. Her voice was high-pitched.

'Nothing,' he said.

He didn't want a scene.

It was cold when he woke up. The false dawn was grey and he could see nothing but barren country in all directions. He could not remember a great deal about the previous day, except that he had run a long way.

Dew had gathered on his loincloth. He wet his lips and rubbed the skin over his face. As he always did after a migraine attack he felt weak and completely drained. Looking down at his naked body, he noticed how skinny he had become. Life with the Essenes had caused that, of course.

He wondered why he had panicked so much when John had asked him to baptize him. Was it simply honesty—something in him which resisted deceiving the Essenes into thinking he was a prophet of some kind? It was hard to know.

He wrapped the goatskin about his hips and tied it tightly just above his left thigh. He supposed he had better try to get back to the camp and find John and apologize, see if he could make amends.

The time machine was there now, too. They had dragged it there, using only rawhide ropes.

If a good blacksmith could be found, or some other metal-worker, there was just a chance that it could be repaired. The journey back would be dangerous.

He wondered if he ought to go back right away, or try to shift to a time nearer to the actual crucifixion. He had not gone back specifically to witness the crucifixion, but to get the mood of Jerusalem during the Feast of the Passover, when Jesus was supposed to have entered the city. Monica had thought Jesus had stormed the city with an armed band. She had said that all the evidence pointed to that. All the evidence of one sort did point to it, but he could not accept the evidence. There was more to it, he was sure. If only he could meet Jesus. John had apparently never heard of him, though he had told Glogauer that there was a prophecy that the Messiah would be a Nazarene. There were many prophecies, and many of them conflicted.

He began to walk back in the general direction of the Essene camp. He could not have come so far. He would soon recognize the hills where they had their caves.

Soon it was very hot and the ground more barren. The air wavered before his eyes. The feeling of exhaustion with which he had awakened increased. His mouth was dry and his legs were weak. He was hungry and there was nothing to eat. There was no sign of the range of hills where the Essenes had their camp.

There was one hill, about two miles away to the south. He decided to make for it. From there he would probably be able to get his bearings, perhaps even see a township where they would give him food.

The sandy soil turned to floating dust around him as his feet disturbed it. A few primitive shrubs clung to the ground and jutting rocks tripped him.

He was bleeding and bruised by the time he began, painfully, to clamber up the hillside.

The journey to the summit (which was much farther away than he had originally judged) was difficult. He would slide on the loose stones of the hillside, falling on his face, bracing his torn hands and feet to stop himself from sliding down to the bottom, clinging to tufts of grass and lichen that grew here and there, embracing larger projections of rock when he could, resting frequently, his mind and body both numb with pain and weariness.

He sweated beneath the sun. The dust stuck to the moisture on his half-naked body, caking him from head to foot. The goatskin was in shreds.

The barren world reeled around him, sky somehow merging with land, yellow rock with white clouds. Nothing seemed still.

He reached the summit and lay there gasping. Everything had become unreal.

He heard Monica's voice, thought he glanced her for a moment from the corner of his eye.

Don't be melodramatic, Karl. . . .

She had said that many times. His own voice replied now.

I'm born out of my time, Monica. This age of reason has no place for me. It will kill me in the end.

Her voice replied.

Guilt and fear and your own masochism. You could be a brilliant psychiatrist, but you've given in to all your own neuroses so completely. . . .

'Shut up!'

He rolled over on his back. The sun blazed down on his tattered body.

'Shut up!'

The whole Christian syndrome, Karl. You'll become a Catholic convert next I shouldn't doubt. Where's your strength of mind?

'Shut up! Go away, Monica.'

Fear shapes your thoughts. You're not searching for a soul or even a meaning for life. You're searching for comforts.

'Leave me alone, Monica!'

His grimy hands covered his ears. His hair and beard were matted with dust. Blood had congealed on the minor wounds that were now on every part of his body. Above, the sun seemed to pound in unison with his heartbeats.

You're going downhill, Karl, don't you realize that? Downhill. Pull yourself together. You're not entirely incapable of rational thought. . . .

'Oh, Monica! Shut up!'

His voice was harsh and cracked. A few ravens circled the sky above him now. He heard them calling back at him in a voice not unlike his own.

God died in 1945. . . .

'It isn't 1945—it's A.D. 28. God is alive!'

How you can bother to wonder about an obvious syncretistic religion like Christianity—Rabbinic Judaism, Stoic ethics, Greek mystery cults, Oriental ritual. . . .

'It doesn't matter!'

Not to win in your present state of mind.

'I need God!'

That's what it boils down to, doesn't it? Okay, Karl, carve your own crutches. Just think what you could have been if you'd have come to terms with yourself. . . .

Glogauer pulled his ruined body to its feet and stood on the summit of the hill and screamed.

The ravens were startled. They wheeled in the sky and flew away.

The sky was darkening now.

'Then was Jesus led up of the Spirit into the wilderness to be tempted of the devil. And when he had fasted forty days and forty nights, he was afterward an hungred.'

(Matthew 4: 1–2)

IV

The madman came stumbling into the town. His feet stirred the dust and made it dance and dogs barked around him as he walked mechanically, his head turned upwards to face the sun, his arms limp at his sides, his lips moving.

To the townspeople, the words they heard were in no familiar language; yet they were uttered with such intensity and conviction that God himself might be using this emaciated, naked creature as his spokesman.

They wondered where the madman had come from.

The white town consisted primarily of double- and single-storeyed houses of stone and clay-brick, built around a market place that was fronted by an ancient, simple synagogue outside which old men sat and talked, dressed in dark robes. The town was prosperous and clean, thriving on Roman commerce. Only one or two beggars were in the streets and these were well-fed. The streets followed the rise and fall of the hillside on which they were built. They were winding streets, shady and peaceful: country streets. There was a smell of newly-cut timber everywhere in the air, and the sound of carpentry, for the town was chiefly famous for its skilled carpenters. It lay on the edge of the Plain of Jezreel, close to the trade route between Damascus and Egypt, and wagons were always leaving it, laden with the work of the town's craftsmen. The town was called Nazareth.

The madman had found it by asking every traveller he saw where it was. He had passed through other towns—Philadelphia, Gerasa, Pella and Scythopolis, following the Roman roads—asking the same question in his outlandish accent: 'Where lies Nazareth?'

Some had given him food on the way. Some had asked for his blessing and he had laid hands on them, speaking in that strange tongue. Some had pelted him with stones and driven him away.

He had crossed the Jordan by the Roman viaduct and continued northwards towards Nazareth.

There had been no difficulty in finding the town, but it had been difficult for him to force himself towards it. He had lost a great deal of blood and had eaten very little on the journey. He would walk until he collapsed and lie there until he could go on, or, as had happened increasingly, until someone found him and had given him a little sour wine or bread to revive him.

Once some Roman legionaries had stopped and with brusque kindness asked him if he had any relatives they could take him to. They had addressed him in pidgin-Aramaic and had been surprised when he replied in a strangely-accented Latin that was purer than the language they spoke themselves.

They asked him if he was a Rabbi or a scholar. He told them he was neither. The officer of the legionaries had offered him some dried meat and wine. The men were part of a patrol that passed this way once a month. They were stocky, brown-faced men, with hard, clean-shaven faces. They were dressed in stained leather kilts and breast-plates and sandals, and had iron helmets on their heads, scabbarded short swords at their hips. Even as they stood around him in the evening sunlight they did not seem relaxed. The officer, softer-voiced than his men but otherwise much like them save that he wore a metal breastplate and a long cloak, asked the madman what his name was.

For a moment the madman had paused, his mouth opening and closing, as if he could not remember what he was called.

'Karl,' he said at length, doubtfully. It was more a suggestion than a statement.

'Sounds almost like a Roman name,' said one of the legionaries.

'Are you a citizen?' the officer asked.

But the madman's mind was wandering, evidently. He looked away from them, muttering to himself.

All at once, he looked back at them and said: 'Nazareth?'

'That way.' The officer pointed down the road that cut between the hills. 'Are you a Jew?'

This seemed to startle the madman. He sprang to his feet and tried to push through the soldiers. They let him through, laughing. He was a harmless madman.

They watched him run down the road.

'One of their prophets, perhaps,' said the officer, walking towards his horse. The country was full of them. Every other man you met claimed to be spreading the message of their god. They didn't make much trouble and religion seemed to keep their minds off rebellion. *We should be grateful*, thought the officer.

His men were still laughing.

They began to march down the road in the opposite direction to the one the madman had taken.

Now the madman was in Nazareth and the townspeople looked at him with curiosity and more than a little suspicion as he staggered into the market square. He could be a wandering prophet or he could be possessed by devils. It was often hard to tell. The rabbis would know.

As he passed the knots of people standing by the merchants' stalls, they fell silent until he had gone by. Women pulled their heavy woollen shawls about their well-fed bodies and men tucked in their cotton robes so that he would not touch them. Normally their instinct would have been to have taxed him with his business in the town, but there was an intensity about his gaze, a quickness and vitality about his face, in spite of his emaciated appearance, that made them treat him with some respect and they kept their distance.

When he reached the centre of the market place, he stopped and looked around him. He seemed slow to notice the people. He blinked and licked his lips.

A woman passed, eyeing him warily. He spoke to her, his voice soft, the words carefully formed. 'Is this Nazareth?'

'It is.' She nodded and increased her pace.

A man was crossing the square. He was dressed in a woollen robe of red and brown stripes. There was a red skull cap on his curly, black hair. His face was plump and cheerful. The madman walked across the man's path and stopped him. 'I seek a carpenter.'

'There are many carpenters in Nazareth. The town is famous for its carpenters. I am a carpenter myself. Can I help you?' The man's voice was good-humoured, patronizing.

'Do you know a carpenter called Joseph? A descendant of David. He has a wife called Mary and several children. One is named Jesus.'

The cheerful man screwed his face into a mock frown and scratched the back of his neck. 'I know more than one Joseph. There is one poor fellow in yonder street.' He pointed. 'He has a wife called Mary. Try there. You should soon find him. Look for a man who never laughs.'

The madman looked in the direction in which the man pointed. As soon as he saw the street, he seemed to forget everything else and strode towards it.

In the narrow street he entered the smell of cut timber was even stronger. He walked ankle-deep in wood-shavings. From every building came the thud of hammers, the scrape of saws. There were planks of all sizes resting against the pale, shaded walls of the houses and there was hardly room to pass between them. Many of the carpenters had their benches just outside their doors. They were carving bowls, operating simple lathes, shaping wood into everything imaginable. They looked up as the madman entered the street and approached one old carpenter in a leather apron who sat at his bench carving a figurine. The man had grey hair and seemed short-sighted. He peered up at the madman.

'What do you want?'

'I seek a carpenter called Joseph. He has a wife—Mary.'

The old man gestured with his hand that held the half-completed figurine. 'Two houses along on the other side of the street.'

The house the madman came to had very few planks leaning against it, and the quality of the timber seemed poorer than the other wood he had seen. The bench near the entrance was warped on one side and the man who sat hunched over it repairing a stool seemed misshapen also. He straightened up as the madman touched his shoulder. His face was lined and pouched with misery. His eyes were tired and this thin beard had premature streaks of grey. He coughed slightly, perhaps in surprise at being disturbed.

'Are you Joseph?' asked the madman.

'I've no money.'

'I want nothing—just to ask a few questions.'

'I'm Joseph. Why do you want to know?'

'Have you a son?'

'Several, and daughters, too.'

'Your wife is called Mary? You are of David's line.'

The man waved his hand impatiently. 'Yes, for what good either have done me. . . .'

'I wish to meet one of your sons. Jesus. Can you tell me where he is?'

'That good for nothing. What has he done now?'

'Where is he?'

Joseph's eyes became more calculating as he stared at the madman. 'Are you a seer of some kind? Have you come to cure my son?'

'I am a prophet of sorts. I can foretell the future.'

Joseph got up with a sigh. 'You can see him. Come.' He led the madman through the gateway into the cramped courtyard of the house. It was crowded with pieces of wood, broken furniture and implements, rotting sacks of shavings. They entered the darkened house. In the first room—evidently a kitchen—a woman stood by a large clay stove. She was tall and bulging with fat. Her long, black hair was unbound and greasy, falling over large, lustrous eyes that still had the heat of sensuality. She looked the madman over.

'There's no food for beggars,' she grunted. 'He eats enough as it is.' She gestured with a wooden spoon at a small figure sitting in the shadow of a corner. The figure shifted as she spoke.

'He seeks our Jesus,' said Joseph to the woman. 'Perhaps he comes to ease our burden.'

The woman gave the madman a sidelong look and shrugged. She licked her red lips with a fat tongue. 'Jesus!'

The figure in the corner stood up.

'That's him,' said the woman with a certain satisfaction.

The madman frowned, shaking his head rapidly. 'No.'

The figure was misshapen. It had a pronounced hunched back and a cast in its left eye. The face was vacant and foolish. There was a little spittle on the lips. It giggled as its name was repeated. It took a crooked step forward. 'Jesus,' it said. The word was slurred and thick. 'Jesus.'

'That's all he can say.' The woman sneered. 'He's always been like that.'

'God's judgment,' said Joseph bitterly.

'What is wrong with him?' There was a pathetic, desperate note in the madman's voice.

'He's always been like that.' The woman turned back to the stove. 'You can have him if you want him. Addled inside and outside. I was carrying him when my parents married me off to that half-man. . . .'

'You shameless——' Joseph stopped as his wife glared at him. He turned to the madman. 'What's your business with our son?'

'I wished to talk to him. I . . .'

'He's no oracle—no seer—we used to think he might be. There are still people in Nazareth who come to him to cure them or tell their fortunes, but he only giggles at them and speaks his name over and over again. . . .'

'Are—you sure—there is not—something about him—you have not noticed?'

'Sure!' Mary snorted sardonically. 'We need money badly enough. If he had any magical powers, we'd know.'

Jesus giggled again and limped away into another room.

'It is impossible,' the madman murmured. Could history itself have changed? Could he be in some other dimension of time where Christ had never been?

Joseph appeared to notice the look of agony in the madman's eyes.

'What is it?' he said. 'What do you see? You said you foretold the future. Tell us how we will fare?'

'Not *now*,' said the prophet, turning away. 'Not *now*.'

He ran from the house and down the street with its smell of planed oak, cedar and cypress. He ran back to the market place and stopped, looking wildly about him. He saw the synagogue directly ahead of him. He began to walk towards it.

The man he had spoken to earlier was still in the market place, buying cooking pots to give to his daughter as a wedding gift. He nodded towards the strange man as he entered the synagogue. 'He's a relative of Joseph the carpenter,' he told the man beside him. 'A prophet, I shouldn't wonder.'

The madman, the prophet, Karl Glogauer, the time-traveller, the neurotic psychiatrist manqué, the searcher for meaning, the masochist, the man with a death-wish and the messiah-complex, the anachronism, made his way into the synagogue gasping for breath. He had seen the man he had sought. He had seen Jesus, the son of Joseph and Mary. He had seen a man he recognized without any doubt as a congenital imbecile.

'All men have a messiah-complex, Karl,' Monica had said.

The memories were less complete now. His sense of time and identity was becoming confused.

'There were dozens of messiahs in Galilee at the time. That Jesus should have been the one to carry the myth and the philosophy was a coincidence of history. . . .'

'There must have been more to it than that, Monica.'

Every Tuesday in the room above the occult bookshop, the Jungian discussion group would meet for purposes of group analysis and therapy. Glogauer had not organized the group, but he had willingly lent his premises to it and had joined it eagerly. It was a great relief to talk with like-minded people once a week. One of his reasons for buying the occult bookshop was so that he would meet interesting people like those who attended the Jungian discussion group.

An obsession with Jung brought them together, but everyone had special obsessions of his own. Mrs. Rita Blen charted the courses of flying saucers, though it was not clear if she believed in them or not. Hugh Joyce believed that all Jungian archetypes derived from the original race of Atlanteans who had perished millennia before. Alan Cheddar, the youngest of the group, was interested in Indian mysticism, and Sandra Peterson, the organizer, was a great witchcraft specialist. James Headington was interested in time. He was the group's pride; he was Sir James Headington, war-time inventor, very rich and with all sorts of decorations for his contribution to the Allied victory. He had had the reputation of being a great improviser during the war, but after it had become something of an embarrassment to the War Office. He was a crank, they thought, and what was worse, he aired his crankiness in public.

Every so often, Sir James would tell the other members of the group about his time machine. They humoured him. Most of them were liable to exaggerate their own experiences connected with their different interests.

One Tuesday evening, after everyone else had left, Headington told Glogauer that his machine was ready.

'I can't believe it,' Glogauer said truthfully.

'You're the first person I've told.'

'Why me?'

'I don't know. I like you—and the shop.'

'You haven't told the government.'

Headington had chuckled. 'Why should I? Not until I've

tested it fully, anyway. Serves them right for putting me out to pasture.'

'You don't know it works?'

'I'm sure it does. Would you like to see it?'

'A time machine.' Glogauer smiled weakly.

'Come and see it.'

'Why me?'

'I thought you might be interested. I know you don't hold with the orthodox view of science. . . .'

Glogauer felt sorry for him.

'Come and see,' said Headington.

He went down to Banbury the next day. The same day he left 1976 and arrived in A.D. 28.

The synagogue was cool and quiet with a subtle scent of incense. The rabbis guided him into the courtyard. They, like the townspeople, did not know what to make of him, but they were sure it was not a devil that possessed him. It was their custom to give shelter to the roaming prophets who were now everywhere in Galilee, though this one was stranger than the rest. His face was immobile and his body was stiff, and there were tears running down his dirty cheeks. They had never seen such agony in a man's eyes before.

'Science can say how, but it never asks why,' he had told Monica. 'It can't answer.'

'Who wants to know?' she'd replied.

'I do.'

'Well, you'll never find out, will you?

'Sit down, my son,' said the rabbi. 'What do you wish to ask of us?'

'Where is Christ?' he said. 'Where is Christ?'

They did not understand the language.

'Is it Greek?' asked one, but another shook his head.

Kyrios: The Lord.

Adonai: The Lord.

Where was the Lord?

He frowned, looking vaguely about him.

'I must rest,' he said in their language.

'Where are you from?'

He could not think what to answer.

'Where are you from?' a rabbi repeated.

'*Ha-Olam Hab-Bah* . . .' he murmured at length.

They looked at one another. '*Ha-Olam Hab-Bah*,' they said. *Ha-Olam Hab-Bah; Ha-Olam Haz-Zeh:* The world to come and the world that is.

'Do you bring us a message?' said one of the rabbis. They were used to prophets, certainly, but none like this one. 'A message?'

'I do not know,' said the prophet hoarsely. 'I must rest. I am hungry.'

'Come. We will give you food and a place to sleep.'

He could only eat a little of the rich food and the bed with its straw-stuffed mattress was too soft for him. He was not used to it.

He slept badly, shouting as he dreamed, and, outside the room, the rabbis listened, but could understand little of what he said.

Karl Glogauer stayed in the synagogue for several weeks. He would spend most of his time reading in the library, searching through the long scrolls for some answer to his dilemma. The words of the Testaments, in many cases capable of a dozen interpretations, only confused him further. There was nothing to grasp, nothing to tell him what had gone wrong.

The rabbis kept their distance for the most part. They had accepted him as a holy man. They were proud to have him in their synagogue. They were sure that he was one of the special chosen of God and they waited patiently for him to speak to them.

But the prophet said little, muttering only to himself in snatches of their own language and snatches of the incomprehensible language he often used, even when he addressed them directly.

In Nazareth, the townsfolk talked of little else but the mysterious prophet in the synagogue, but the rabbis would not answer their questions. They would tell the people to go about their business, that there were things they were not yet meant to know. In this way, as priests had always done, they avoided questions they could not answer while at the same time appearing to have much more knowledge than they actually possessed.

Then, one sabbath, he appeared in the public part of the synagogue and took his place with the others who had come to worship.

The man who was reading from the scroll on his left stumbled over the words, glancing at the prophet from the corner of his eye.

The prophet sat and listened, his expression remote.

The Chief Rabbi looked uncertainly at him, then signed that the scroll should be passed to the prophet. This was done hesitantly by a boy who placed the scroll into the prophet's hands.

The prophet looked at the words for a long time and then began to read. The prophet read without comprehending at first what he read. It was the book of Esaias.

'The Spirit of the Lord is upon me, because he hath anointed me to preach the gospel to the poor; he hath sent me to heal the broken-hearted, to preach deliverance to the captives, and recovering of sight to the blind, to set at liberty them that are bruised, to preach the acceptable year of the Lord. And he closed the book, and gave it again to the minister, and sat down. And the eyes of all of them that were in the synagogue were fastened on him.'

(Luke 4: 18–20)

v

They followed him now, as he walked away from Nazareth towards the Lake of Galilee. He was dressed in the white linen robe they had given him and though they thought he led them, they, in fact, drove him before them.

'He is our messiah,' they said to those that inquired. And there were already rumours of miracles.

When he saw the sick, he pitied them and tried to do what he could because they expected something of him. Many he could do nothing for, but others, obviously in psychosomatic conditions, he could help. They believed in his power more strongly than they believed in their sickness. So he cured them.

When he came to Capernaum, some fifty people followed him into the streets of the city. It was already known that he was in some way associated with John the Baptist, who enjoyed huge prestige in Galilee and had been declared a true prophet by many Pharisees. Yet this man had a power greater, in some ways, than John's. He was not the orator that the Baptist was, but he had worked miracles.

Capernaum was a sprawling town beside the crystal lake of Galilee, its houses separated by large market gardens. Fishing boats were moored at the white quayside, as well as trading ships that plied the lakeside towns. Though the green hills came down from all sides to the lake, Capernaum itself was built on flat ground, sheltered by the hills. It was a quiet town and, like most others in Galilee, had a large population of gentiles. Greek, Roman and Egyptian traders walked its streets and many had made permanent homes there. There was a prosperous middle-class of merchants, artisans and ship-owners, as well as doctors, lawyers and scholars, for Capernaum was on the borders of the provinces of Galilee, Trachonitis and Syria and though a comparatively small town was a useful junction for trade and travel.

The strange, mad prophet in his swirling linen robes, followed by the heterogeneous crowd that was primarily composed of poor folk but also could be seen to contain men of some distinction, swept into Capernaum. The news spread that this man really could foretell the future, that he had already predicted the arrest of John by Herod Antipas and soon after Herod had imprisoned the Baptist at Peraea. He did not make the predictions in general terms, using vague words the way other prophets did. He spoke of things that were to happen in the near future and he spoke of them in detail.

None knew his name. He was simply the prophet from Nazareth, or the Nazarene. Some said he was a relative, perhaps the son, of a carpenter in Nazareth, but this could be because the written words for 'son of a carpenter' and 'magus' were almost the same and the confusion had come about in that way. There was even a very faint rumour that his name was Jesus. The name had been used once or twice, but when they asked him if that was, indeed, his name, he denied it or else, in his abstracted way, refused to answer at all.

His actual preaching tended to lack the fire of John's. This man spoke gently, rather vaguely, and smiled often. He spoke of God in a strange way, too, and he appeared to be connected, as John was, with the Essenes, for he preached against the accumulation of personal wealth and spoke of mankind as a brotherhood, as they did.

But it was the miracles that they watched for as he was guided to the graceful synagogue of Capernaum. No prophet before him had healed the sick and seemed to understand the troubles that people rarely spoke of. It was his sympathy that they responded to, rather than the words he spoke.

For the first time in his life, Karl Glogauer had forgotten about Karl Glogauer. For the first time in his life he was doing what he had always sought to do as a psychiatrist.

But it was not his life. He was bringing a myth to life—a generation before that myth would be born. He was completing a certain kind of psychic circuit. He was not changing history, but he was giving history more substance.

He could not bear to think that Jesus had been nothing more than a myth. It was in his power to make Jesus a physical reality rather than the creation of a process of mythogenesis.

So he spoke in the synagogues and he spoke of a gentler God than most of them had heard of, and where he could remember them, he told them parables.

And gradually the need to justify what he was doing faded and his sense of identity grew increasingly more tenuous and was replaced by a different sense of identity, where he gave greater and greater substance to the role he had chosen. It was an archetypal role. It was a role to appeal to a disciple of Jung. It was a role that went beyond a mere imitation. It was a role that he must now play out to the very last grand detail. Karl Glogauer had discovered the reality he had been seeking.

'And in the synagogue there was a man, which had a spirit of an unclean devil, and cried out with a loud voice, saying, Let us alone; what have we to do with thee, thou Jesus of Nazareth? art thou come to destroy us? I know thee who thou art; the Holy One of God. And Jesus rebuked him, saying, Hold thy peace, and come out of him. And when the devil had thrown him in the midst, he came out of him, and hurt him not. And they were all amazed, and spake

*among themselves, saying, What a word is this! for with authority
and power he commandeth the unclean spirits, and they come out.
And the fame of him went out into every place of the country
round about.'*

(Luke 4: 33–37)

'Mass hallucination. Miracles, flying saucers, ghosts, it's all
the same,' Monica had said.

'Very likely,' he had replied. 'But *why* did they see them?'

'Because they wanted to.'

'Why did they want to?'

'Because they were afraid.'

'You think that's all there is to it?'

'Isn't it enough?'

When he left Capernaum for the first time, many more
people accompanied him. It had become impractical to stay in
the town, for the business of the town had been brought almost
to a standstill by the crowds that sought to see him work his
simple miracles.

He spoke to them in the spaces beyond the towns. He talked
with intelligent, literate men who appeared to have something
in common with him. Some of them were the owners of fishing
fleets—Simon, James and John among them. Another was a
doctor, another a civil servant who had first heard him speak in
Capernaum.

'There must be twelve,' he said to them one day. 'There must
be a zodiac.'

He was not careful in what he said. Many of his ideas were
strange. Many of the things he talked about were unfamiliar to
them. Some Pharisees thought he blasphemed.

One day he met a man he recognized as an Essene from the
colony near Machaerus.

'John would speak with you,' said the Essene.

'Is John not dead yet?' he asked the man.

'He is confined at Paraea. I would think Herod is too frightened to kill him. He lets John walk about within the walls and
gardens of the palace, lets him speak with his men, but John
fears that Herod will find the courage soon to have him stoned
or decapitated. He needs your help.'

'How can I help him? He is to die. There is no hope for him.'

The Essene looked uncomprehendingly into the mad eyes of the prophet.

'But, master, there is no one else who can help him.'

'I have done all that he wished me to do,' said the prophet. 'I have healed the sick and preached to the poor.'

'I did not know he wished this. Now he needs help master. You could save his life.'

The prophet had drawn the Essene away from the crowd.

'His life cannot be saved.'

'But if it is not the unrighteous will prosper and the Kingdom of Heaven will not be restored.'

'His life cannot be saved.'

'Is it God's will?'

'If I am God, then it is God's will.'

'Hopelessly, the Essene turned and began to walk away from the crowd.

John the Baptist would have to die. Glogauer had no wish to change history, only to strengthen it.

He moved on, with his following, through Galilee. He had selected his twelve educated men, and the rest who followed him were still primarily poor people. To them he offered their only hope of fortune. Many were those who had been ready to follow John against the Romans, but now John was imprisoned. Perhaps this man would lead them in revolt, to loot the riches of Jerusalem and Jericho and Caesarea. Tired and hungry, their eyes glazed by the burning sun, they followed the man in the white robe. They needed to hope and they found reasons for their hope. They saw him work greater miracles.

Once he preached to them from a boat, as was often his custom, and as he walked back to the shore through the shallows, it seemed to them that he walked over the water.

All through Galilee in the autumn they wandered, hearing from everyone the news of John's beheading. Despair at the Baptist's death turned to renewed hope in this new prophet who had known him.

In Caesarea they were driven from the city by Roman guards used to the wildmen with their prophecies who roamed the country.

They were banned from other cities as the prophet's fame

grew. Not only the Roman authorities, but the Jewish ones as well seemed unwilling to tolerate the new prophet as they had tolerated John. The political climate was changing.

It became hard to find food. They lived on what they could find, hungering like starved animals.

He taught them how to pretend to eat and take their minds off their hunger.

Karl Glogauer, witch-doctor, psychiatrist, hypnotist, messiah.

Sometimes his conviction in his chosen role wavered and those that followed him would be disturbed when he contradicted himself. Often, now, they called him the name they had heard, Jesus the Nazarene. Most of the time he did not stop them from using the name, but at others he became angry and cried a peculiar, guttural name.

'Karl Glogauer! Karl Glogauer!'

And they said, Behold, he speaks with the voice of Adonai.

'Call me not by that name!' he would shout, and they would become disturbed and leave him by himself until his anger had subsided.

When the weather changed and the winter came, they went back to Capernaum, which had become a stronghold of his followers.

In Capernaum he waited the winter through, making prophecies.

Many of these prophecies concerned himself and the fate of those that followed him.

'*Then charged he his disciples that they should tell no man that he was Jesus the Christ. From that time forth began Jesus to shew unto his disciples, how that he must go into Jerusalem and suffer many things of the elders and chief priests and scribes, and be killed, and be raised again the third day.*'

(Matthew 16: 20–21)

They were watching television at her flat. Monica was eating an apple. It was between six and seven on a warm Sunday evening. Monica gestured at the screen with her half-eaten apple.

'Look at that nonsense,' she said. 'You can't honestly tell me it means anything to you.'

The programme was a religious one, about a pop-opera in a Hampstead Church. The opera told the story of the crucifixion.

'Pop-groups in the pulpit,' she said. 'What a come-down.'

He didn't reply. The programme seemed obscene to him, in an obscure way. He couldn't argue with her.

'God's corpse is really beginning to rot now,' she jeered. 'Whew! The stink!'

'Turn it off, then,' he said quietly.

'What's the pop-group called? The Maggots?'

'Very funny. I'll turn it off, shall I?'

'No, I want to watch. It's funny.'

'Oh, turn it off!'

'Imitation of Christ!' she snorted. 'It's a bloody caricature.'

A Negro singer, who was playing Christ and singing flat to a banal accompaniment, began to drone out lifeless lyrics about the brotherhood of man.

'If he sounded like that, no wonder they nailed him up,' said Monica.

He reached forward and switched the picture off.

'I was enjoying it.' She spoke with mock disappointment. 'It was a lovely swan-song.'

Later, she said with a trace of affection that worried him, 'You old fogey. What a pity. You could have been John Wesley or Calvin or someone. You can't be a messiah these days, not in your terms. There's nobody to listen.'

VI

The prophet was living in the house of a man called Simon, though the prophet preferred to call him Peter. Simon was grateful to the prophet because he had cured his wife of a complaint which she had suffered from for some time. It had been a mysterious complaint, but the prophet had cured her almost effortlessly.

There were a great many strangers in Capernaum at that time, many of them coming to see the prophet. Simon warned the prophet that some were known agents of the Romans or the Pharisees. The Pharisees had not, on the whole, been anti-pathetic towards the prophet, though they distrusted the talk of miracles that they heard. However, the whole political atmosphere was disturbed and the Roman occupation troops, from Pilate, through his officers, down to the troops, were tense, expecting an outbreak but unable to see any tangible signs that one was coming.

Pilate himself hoped for trouble on a large scale. It would prove to Tiberius that the emperor had been too lenient with the Jews over the matter of the votive shields. Pilate would be vindicated and his power over the Jews increased. At present he was on bad terms with all the Tetrarchs of the provinces— particularly the unstable Herod Antipas who had seemed at one time his only supporter. Aside from the political situation, his own domestic situation was upset in that his neurotic wife was having her nightmares again and was demanding far more attention from him than he could afford to give her.

There might be a possibility, he thought, of provoking an incident, but he would have to be careful that Tiberius never learnt of it. This new prophet might provide a focus, but so far the man had done nothing against the laws of either the Jews or the Romans. There was no law that forbade a man to claim he was a messiah, as some said this one had done, and he was hardly inciting the people to revolt—rather the contrary.

Looking through the window of his chamber, with a view of the minarets and spires of Jerusalem, Pilate considered the information his spies had brought him.

Soon after the festival that the Romans called Saturnalia, the prophet and his followers left Capernaum again and began to travel through the country.

There were fewer miracles now that the hot weather had passed, but his prophecies were eagerly asked. He warned them of all the mistakes that would be made in the future, and of all the crimes that would be committed in his name.

Through Galilee he wandered, and through Samaria, following the good Roman roads towards Jerusalem.

The time of the Passover was coming close now.

In Jerusalem, the Roman officials discussed the coming festival. It was always a time of the worst disturbances. There had been riots before during the Feast of the Passover, and doubtless there would be trouble of some kind this year, too.

Pilate spoke to the Pharisees, asking for their co-operation.

The Pharisees said they would do what they could, but they could not help it if the people acted foolishly.

Scowling, Pilate dismissed them.

His agents brought him reports from all over the territory. Some of the reports mentioned the new prophet, but said that he was harmless.

Pilate thought privately that he might be harmless now, but if he reached Jerusalem during the Passover, he might not be so harmless.

Two weeks before the Feast of the Passover, the prophet reached the town of Bethany near Jerusalem. Some of his Galilean followers had friends in Bethany and these friends were more than willing to shelter the man they had heard of from other pilgrims on their way to Jerusalem and the Great Temple.

The reason they had come to Bethany was that the prophet had become disturbed at the number of the people following him.

'There are too many,' he had said to Simon. 'Too many, Peter.'

Glogauer's face was haggard now. His eyes were set deeper into their sockets and he said little.

Sometimes he would look around him vaguely, as if unsure where he was.

News came to the house in Bethany that Roman agents had been making inquiries about him. It did not seem to disturb him. On the contrary, he nodded thoughtfully, as if satisfied.

Once he walked with two of his followers across country to look at Jerusalem. The bright yellow walls of the city looked splendid in the afternoon light. The towers and tall buildings, many of them decorated in mosaic reds, blues and yellows, could be seen from several miles away.

The prophet turned back towards Bethany.

'When shall we go into Jerusalem?' one of his followers asked him.

'Not yet,' said Glogauer. His shoulders were hunched and he grasped his chest with his arms and hands as if cold.

Two days before the Feast of the Passover in Jerusalem, the prophet took his men towards the Mount of Olives and a suburb of Jerusalem that was built on its side and called Beth-phage.

'Get me a donkey,' he told them. 'A colt. I must fulfil the prophecy now.'

'Then all will know you are the Messiah,' said Andrew.

'Yes.'

Glogauer sighed. He felt afraid again, but this time it was not physical fear. It was the fear of an actor who was about to make his final, most dramatic scene and who was not sure he could do it well.

There was cold sweat on Glogauer's upper lip. He wiped it off.

In the poor light he peered at the men around him. He was still uncertain of some of their names. He was not interested in their names, particularly, only in their number. There were ten here. The other two were looking for the donkey.

They stood on the grassy slope of the Mount of Olives, looking towards Jerusalem and the great Temple which lay below. There was a light, warm breeze blowing.

'Judas?' said Glogauer inquiringly.

There was one called Judas.

'Yes, master,' he said. He was tall and good looking, with curly red hair and neurotic intelligent eyes. Glogauer believed he was an epileptic.

Glogauer looked thoughtful at Judas Iscariot. 'I will want you to help me later,' he said, 'when we have entered Jerusalem.'

'How, master?'

'You must take a message to the Romans.'

'The Romans?' Iscariot looked troubled. 'Why?'

'It must be the Romans. It can't be the Jews—they would use a stake or an axe. I'll tell you more when the time comes.'

The sky was dark now, and the stars were out over the Mount of Olives. It had become cold. Glogauer shivered.

> *Rejoice greatly O daughter of Zion,*
> *Shout, O daughter of Jerusalem:*
> *Behold, thy King cometh unto thee!*
> *He is just and having salvation;*
> *Lowly and riding upon an ass,*
> *And upon a colt, the foal of an ass.*
>   (Zechariah 9: 9)

'*Osha'na! Osha'na! Osha'na!*'

As Glogauer rode the donkey into the city, his followers ran ahead, throwing down palm branches. On both sides of the street were crowds, forewarned by the followers of his coming.

Now the new prophet could be seen to be fulfilling the prophecies of the ancient prophets and many believed that he had come to lead them against the Romans. Even now, possibly, he was on his way to Pilate's house to confront the procurator.

'*Osha'na! Osha'na!*'

Glogauer looked around distractedly. The back of the donkey, though softened by the coats of his followers, was uncomfortable. He swayed and clung to the beast's mane. He heard the words, but could not make them out clearly.

'*Osha'na! Osha'na!*'

It sounded like 'hosanna' at first, before he realized that they were shouting the Aramaic for 'Free us.'

'Free us! Free us!'

John had planned to rise in arms against the Romans this Passover. Many had expected to take part in the rebellion.

They believed that he was taking John's place as a rebel leader.

'No,' he muttered at them as he looked around at their expectant faces. 'No, I am the messiah. I cannot free you. I can't. . . .'

They did not hear him above their own shouts.

Karl Glogauer entered Christ. Christ entered Jerusalem. The story was approaching its climax.

'*Osha'na!*'

It was not in the story. He could not help them.

'*Verily, verily, I say unto you, that one of you shall betray me. Then the disciples looked at one another, doubting of whom he spake. Now there was leaning on Jesus's bosom one of his disciples, whom Jesus loved. Simon Peter therefore beckoned to him, that he should ask who it should be of whom he spake. He then lying on Jesus' breast saith unto him, Lord, who is it? Jesus answered, He it is, to whom I shall give a sop, when I have dipped it. And when he had dipped the sop, he gave it to Judas Iscariot, the son of Simon. And after the sop Satan entered into him. Then said Jesus unto him, that thou doest, do quickly.*'

(John 13: 20–27)

Judas Iscariot frowned with some uncertainty as he left the room and went out into the crowded street, making his way towards the governor's palace. Doubtless he was to perform a part in a plan to deceive the Romans and have the people rise up in Jesus' defence, but he thought the scheme foolhardy. The mood among the jostling men, women and children in the streets was tense. Many more Roman soldiers than usual patrolled the city.

Pilate was a stout man. His face was self-indulgent and his eyes were hard and shallow. He looked disdainfully at the Jew.

'We do not pay informers whose information is proved to be false,' he warned.

'I do not seek money, lord,' said Judas, feigning the ingratiating manner that the Romans seemed to expect of the Jews. 'I am a loyal subject of the Emperor.'

'Who is this rebel?'

'Jesus of Nazareth, lord. He entered the city today . . .'

'I know. I saw him. But I heard he preached of peace and obeying the law.'

'To deceive you, lord.'

Pilate frowned. It was likely. It smacked of the kind of deceit he had grown to anticipate in these soft-spoken people.

'Have you proof?'

'I am one of his lieutenants, lord. I will testify to his guilt.'

Pilate pursed his heavy lips. He could not afford to offend the Pharisees at this moment. They had given him enough trouble. Caiaphas, in particular, would be quick to cry 'injustice' if he arrested the man.

'He claims to be the rightful king of the Jews, the descendant of David,' said Judas, repeating what his master had told him to say.

'Does he?' Pilate looked thoughtfully out of the window.

'As for the Pharisees, lord . . .'

'What of them?'

'The Pharisees distrust him. They would see him dead. He speaks against them.'

Pilate nodded. His eyes were hooded as he considered this information. The Pharisees might hate the madman, but they would be quick to make political capital out of his arrest.

'The Pharisees want him arrested,' Judas continued. 'The people flock to listen to the prophet and today many of them rioted in the Temple in his name.'

'Is this true?'

'It is true, lord.' It was true. Some half-a-dozen people had attacked the money-changers in the Temple and tried to rob them. When they had been arrested, they had said they had been carrying out the will of the Nazarene.

'I cannot make the arrest,' Pilate said musingly. The situation in Jerusalem was already dangerous, but if they were to arrest this 'king', they might find that they precipitated a revolt. Tiberius would blame him, not the Jews. The Pharisees must be won over. They must make the arrest. 'Wait here,' he said to Judas. 'I will send a message to Caiaphas.'

'And they came to a place which was called Gethsemane: and he saith to his disciples, Sit ye here, while I shall pray. And he taketh with him Peter and James and John, and began to be sore amazed, and to be very heavy; And saith unto them, My soul is exceeding sorrowful unto death: tarry ye here, and watch.'

(Mark 14: 32–34)

Glogauer could see the mob approaching now. For the first time since Nazareth he felt physically weak and exhausted. They were going to kill him. He had to die; he accepted that, but he was afraid of the pain that was to come. He sat down on the ground of the hillside, watching the torches as they came closer.

'The ideal of martyrdom only ever existed in the minds of a few ascetics,' Monica had said. 'Otherwise it was morbid masochism, an easy way to forgo ordinary responsibility, a method of keeping repressed people under control. . . .'

'It isn't as simple as that. . . .'

'It is, Karl.'

He could show Monica now. His regret was that she was unlikely ever to know. He had meant to write everything down and put it into the time machine and hope that it would be recovered. It was strange. He was not a religious man in the usual sense. He was an agnostic. It was not conviction that had led him to defend religion against Monica's cynical contempt for it; it was rather *lack* of conviction in the ideal in which she had set her own faith, the ideal of science as a solver of all problems. He could not share her faith and there was nothing else but religion, though he could not believe in the kind of God of Christianity. The God seen as a mystical force of the mysteries of Christianity and other great religions had not been personal enough for him. His rational mind had told him that God did not exist in any personal form. His unconscious had told him that faith in science was not enough.

'*Science is basically opposed to religion,*' Monica had once said harshly. '*No matter how many Jesuits get together and rationalize their views of science, the fact remains that religion cannot accept the fundamental attitudes of science and it is implicit to science to attack the fundamental principles of religion. The only area in which there is no difference and need be no war is in the ultimate assumption. One may or may not assume there is a supernatural being called God. But as soon as one begins to defend one's assumption, there must be strife.*'

'*You're talking about organized religion. . . .*'

'*I'm talking about religion as opposed to a belief. Who needs the ritual of religion when we have the far superior ritual of science to replace it? Religion is a reasonable substitute for knowledge. But there is no longer any need for substitutes, Karl. Science offers a sounder basis on which to formulate systems of thought and ethics. We don't need the carrot of heaven and the big stick of hell any more when science can show the consequences of actions and men can judge easily for themselves whether those actions are right or wrong.*'

'*I can't accept it.*'

'*That's because you're sick. I'm sick, too, but at least I can see the promise of health.*'

'*I can only see the threat of death. . . .*'

As they had agreed, Judas kissed him on the cheek and the mixed force of Temple guards and Roman soldiers surrounded him.

To the Romans he said, with some difficulty, 'I am the King

of the Jews.' To the Pharisees' servants he said: 'I am the
messiah who has come to destroy your masters.' Now he was
committed and the final ritual was to begin.

VII

It was an untidy trial, an arbitrary mixture of Roman and
Jewish law which did not altogether satisfy anyone. The object
was accomplished after several conferences between Pontius
Pilate and Caiaphas and three attempts to bend and merge their
separate legal systems in order to fit the expediencies of the
situation. Both needed a scapegoat for their different purposes
and so at last the result was achieved and the madman convicted,
on the one hand of rebellion against Rome and on the other of
heresy.

A peculiar feature of the trial was that the witnesses were all
followers of the man and yet had seemed eager to see him
convicted.

The Pharisees agreed that the Roman method of execution
would fit the time and the situation best in this case and it was
decided to crucify him. The man had prestige, however, so that
it would be necessary to use some of the tried Roman methods
of humiliation in order to make him into a pathetic and ludicrous
figure in the eyes of the pilgrims. Pilate assured the Pharisees
that he would see to it, but he made sure that they signed
documents that gave their approval to his actions.

*'And the soldiers led him away into the hall, called Praetorium;
and they call together the whole band. And they clothed him with
purple, and platted a crown of thorns, and put it about his head,
And began to salute him, Hail, King of the Jews! And they smote
him on the head with a reed, and did spit upon him, and bowing
their knees worshipped him. And when they had mocked him, they
took off the purple from him, and put his own clothes on him, and
led him out to crucify him.'*

(Mark 15: 16–20)

His brain was clouded now, by pain and by the ritual of
humiliation; by his having completely given himself up to his
role.

He was too weak to bear the heavy wooden cross and he walked behind it as it was dragged towards Golgotha by a Cyrenian whom the Romans had press-ganged for the purpose.

As he staggered through the crowded, silent streets, watched by those who had thought he would lead them against the Roman overlords, his eyes filled with tears so that his sight was blurred and he occasionally staggered off the road and was nudged back on to it by one of the Roman guards.

'You are too emotional, Karl. Why don't you use that brain of yours and pull yourself together? . . .'

He remembered the words, but it was difficult to remember who had said them or who Karl was.

The road that led up the side of the hill was stony and he slipped sometimes, remembering another hill he had climbed long ago. It seemed to him that he had been a child, but the memory merged with others and it was impossible to tell.

He was breathing heavily and with some difficulty. The pain of the thorns in his head was barely felt, but his whole body seemed to throb in unison with his heartbeat. It was like a drum.

It was evening. The sun was setting. He fell on his face, cutting his head on a sharp stone, just as he reached the top of the hill. He fainted.

'And they bring him unto the place Golgotha, which is being interpreted, The place of the skull. And they gave him to drink wine mingled with myrrh: but he received it not.'

(Mark 15: 22–23)

He knocked the cup aside. The soldier shrugged and reached out for one of his arms. Another soldier already held the other arm.

As he recovered consciousness Glogauer began to tremble violently. He felt the pain intensely as the ropes bit into the flesh of his wrists and ankles. He struggled.

He felt something cold placed against his palm. Although it only covered a small area in the centre of his hand it seemed very heavy. He heard a sound that also was in rhythm with his heartbeats. He turned his head to look at the hand.

The large iron peg was being driven into his hand by a soldier swinging a mallet as he lay on the cross which was at this moment horizontal on the ground. He watched, wondering why there was no pain. The soldier swung the mallet higher as the peg met the resistance of the wood. Twice he missed the peg and struck Glogauer's fingers.

Glogauer looked to the other side and saw that the second soldier was also hammering a peg. Evidently he missed the peg a great many times because the fingers of the hand were bloody and crushed.

The first soldier finished hammering in his peg and turned his attention to the feet. Glogauer felt the iron slide through his flesh, heard it hammered home.

Using a pulley, they began to haul the cross into a vertical position. Glogauer noticed that he was alone. There were no others being crucified that day.

He got a clear view of the lights of Jerusalem below him. There was still a little light in the sky but not much. Soon it would be completely dark. There was a small crowd looking on. One of the women reminded him of Monica. He called to her. 'Monica?'

But his voice was cracked and the word was a whisper. The woman did not look up.

He felt his body dragging at the nails which supported it. He thought he felt a twinge of pain in his left hand. He seemed to be bleeding very heavily.

It was odd, he reflected, that it should be him hanging here. He supposed that it was the event he had originally come to witness. There was little doubt, really. Everything had gone perfectly.

The pain in his left hand increased.

He glanced down at the Roman guards who were playing dice at the foot of his cross. They seemed absorbed in their game. He could not see the markings of the dice from this distance.

He sighed. The movement of his chest seemed to throw extra strain on his hands. The pain was quite bad now. He winced and tried somehow to ease himself back against the wood.

The pain began to spread through his body. He gritted his teeth. It was dreadful. He gasped and shouted. He writhed.

There was no longer any light in the sky. Heavy clouds

obscured stars and moon.

From below came whispered voices.

'Let me down,' he called. 'Oh, please let me down!'

The pain filled him. He slumped forward, but nobody released him.

A little while later he raised his head. The movement caused a return of the agony and again he began to writhe on the cross.

'Let me down. Please. Please stop it!'

Every part of his flesh, every muscle and tendon and bone of him, was filled with an almost impossible degree of pain.

He knew he would not survive until the next day as he had thought he might. He had not realized the extent of his pain.

'And at the ninth hour Jesus cried with a loud voice, saying, "Eloi, Eloi, lama sabachthani?" which is, being interpreted, My God, my God, why hast thou forsaken me?'

(Mark 15: 34)

Glogauer coughed. It was a dry, barely heard sound. The soldiers below the cross heard it because the night was now so quiet.

'It's funny,' one said. 'Yesterday they were worshipping him. Today they seemed to want us to kill him—even the ones who were closest to him.'

'I'll be glad when we get out of this country,' said another.

He heard Monica's voice again. 'It's weakness and fear, Karl, that's driven you to this. Martyrdom is a conceit. Can't you see that?'

Weakness and fear.

He coughed once more and the pain returned, but it was duller now.

Just before he died he began to talk again, muttering the words until his breath was gone. 'It's a lie. It's a lie. It's a lie.'

Later, after his body was stolen by the servants of some doctors who believed it to have special properties, there were rumours that he had not died. But the corpse was already rotting in the doctors' dissecting rooms and would soon be destroyed.

Anne McCaffrey is a lovely lady, and she writes the way she looks. This story, calculated to end the book on a romantic note, may contain a universe only Jack Vance, Andre Norton or Anne McCaffrey could have dreamed up, but the afflatus is that which only this dear lady is capable of providing. For all that, much modern writing is pretty dreary. This piece, though, serves to show that, as Dante noted in at least three places, at the end of everything there are always stars. If her husband won't punch me in the nose, I'd like to confess that I'm in love with her, and that I hope she writes at least a thousand more stories like this one, which was good enough to come in second for the Nebula in this category. This book needs das ewig Weibliche to zieht uns hinan, and this is the place for the feminine spirit to take over and tell Messrs. Ballard, Ellison, Wright, Delany, Leiber, Moorcock (me?) the way a woman sees the Game we've been playing. Ergo, I won't tell you a bloody thing about the following tale, save that I like it, I chose it, and it, too, occurs in another time and another place.

WEYR SEARCH

Anne McCaffrey

When is a legend legend? Why is a myth a myth? How old and disused must a fact be for it to be relegated to the category: Fairy tale? And why do certain facts remain incontrovertible; while others lose their validity to assume a shabby, unstable character?

Rukbat, in the Sagittarian sector, was golden G-type star. It had five planets, plus one stray it had attracted and held in recent millennia. Its third planet was enveloped by air man could breathe, boasted water he could drink, and possessed a gravity which permitted man to walk confidently erect. Men discovered it, and promptly colonized it, as they did every habitable planet they came to and then—whether callously or through collapse of empire, the colonists never discovered, and eventually forgot to ask —left the colonies to fend for themselves.

*When men first settled on Rukbat's third world, and named it
Pern, they had taken little notice of the stranger-planet, swinging
around its primary in a wildly erratic elliptical orbit. Within a
few generations they had forgotten its existence. The desperate
path the wanderer pursued brought it close to its stepsister every
two hundred [Terran] years at perihelion.*

*When the aspects were harmonious and the conjunction with its
sister-planet close enough, as it often was, the indigenous life of the
wanderer sought to bridge the space gap to the more temperate
and hospitable planet.*

*It was during the frantic struggle to combat this menace dropping
through Pern's skies like silver threads, that Pern's contact with
the mother-planet weakened and broke. Recollections of Earth
receded further from Pernese history with each successive generation
until memory of their origins degenerated past legend or myth, into
oblivion.*

*To forestall the incursions of the dreaded Threads, the Pernese
with the ingenuity of their forgotten Terran forebears and between
first onslaught and return, developed a highly specialized variety
of life form indigenous to their adopted planet—the winged, tailed,
and fire-breathing dragons, named for the Earth legend they resembled. Such humans as had a high empathy rating and some
innate telepathic ability were trained to make use of and preserve
this unusual animal whose ability to teleport was of immense value
in the fierce struggle to keep Pern bare of Threads.*

*The dragons and their dragon-men, a breed apart, and the shortly
renewed menace they battled, created a whole new group of legends
and myths.*

*As the menace was conquered the populace in the Holds of Pern
settled into a more comfortable way of life. Most of the dragon
Weyrs eventually were abandoned, and the descendants of heroes
fell into disfavour, as the legends fell into disrepute.*

*This, then, is a tale of legends disbelieved and their restoration.
Yet—how goes a legend? When is myth?*

> *Drummer, beat, and piper, blow,*
> *Harper, strike, and soldier, go.*
> *Free the flame and sear the grasses*
> *Till the dawning Red Star passes.*

Lessa woke, cold. Cold with more than the chill of the everlastingly clammy stone walls. Cold with the prescience of a danger greater than when, ten full Turns ago, she had run, whimpering, to hide in the watch-wher's odorous lair.

Rigid with concentration, Lessa lay in the straw of the redolent cheese room, sleeping quarters shared with the other kitchen drudges. There was an urgency in the ominous portent unlike any other forewarning. She touched the awareness of the watch-wher, slithering on its rounds in the courtyard. It circled at the choke-limit of its chain. It was restless, but oblivious to anything unusual in the pre-dawn darkness.

The danger was definitely not within the walls of Hold Ruath. Nor approaching the paved perimeter without the Hold where relentless grass had forced new growth through the ancient mortar, green witness to the deterioration of the once stone-clean Hold. The danger was not advancing up the now little used causeway from the valley, nor lurking in the craftsmen's stony holdings at the foot of the Hold's cliff. It did not scent the wind that blew from Tillek's cold shores. But still it twanged sharply through her senses, vibrating every nerve in Lessa's slender frame. Fully roused, she sought to identify it before the prescient mood dissolved. She cast outward, towards the Pass, farther than she had ever pressed. Whatever threatened was not in Ruatha . . . yet. Nor did it have a familiar flavour. It was not, then, Fax.

Lessa had been cautiously pleased that Fax had not shown himself at Hold Ruath in three full Turns. The apathy of the craftsmen, the decaying farmholds, even the green-etched stones of the Hold infuriated Fax, self-styled Lord of the High Reaches, to the point where he preferred to forget the reason why he had subjugated the once proud and profitable Hold.

Lessa picked her way among the sleeping drudges, huddled together for warmth, and glided up the worn steps to the kitchen-proper. She slipped across the cavernous kitchen to the stable-yard door. The cobbles of the yard were icy through the thin soles of her sandals and she shivered as the pre-dawn air penetrated her patched garment.

The watch-wher slithered across the yard to greet her, pleading, as it always did, for release. Glancing fondly down at the awesome head, she promised it a good rub presently. It

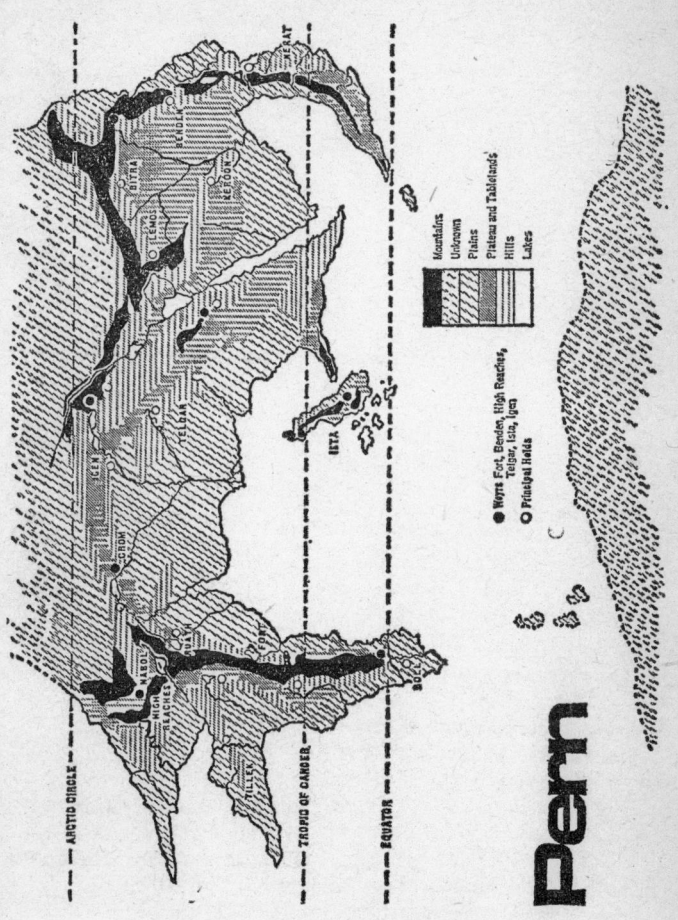

crouched, groaning, at the end of its chain as she continued to
the grooved steps that led to the rampart over the Hold's
massive gate. Atop the tower, Lessa stared towards the east
where the stony breasts of the Pass rose in black relief against
the gathering day.

Indecisively she swung to her left, for the sense of danger
issued from that direction as well. She glanced upwards, her
eyes drawn to the red star which had recently begun to dominate
the dawn sky. As she stared, the star radiated a final ruby
pulsation before its magnificence was lost in the brightness of
Pern's rising sun.

For the first time in many Turns, Lessa gave thought to
matters beyond Pern, beyond her dedication to vengeance on the
murderer Fax for the annihilation of her family. Let him but
come within Ruath Hold now and he would never leave.

But the brilliant ruby sparkle of the Red Star recalled the
Disaster Ballads—grim narratives of the heroism of the dragonriders as they braved the dangers of *between* to breathe fiery
death on the silver Threads that dropped through Pern's skies.
Not one Thread must fall to the rich soil, to burrow deep and
multiply, leaching the earth of minerals and fertility. Straining her
eyes as if vision would bridge the gap between peril and person,
she stared intently eastward. The watch-wher's thin, whistled
question reached her just as the prescience waned.

Dawnlight illumined the tumbled landscape, the unploughed
fields in the valley below. Dawnlight fell on twisted orchards,
where the sparse herds of milchbeasts hunted stray blades of
spring grass. Grass in Ruatha grew where it should not, died
where it should flourish. An odd brooding smile curved Lessa's
lips. Fax realized no profit from his conquest of Ruatha . . . nor
would he, while she, Lessa, lived. And he had not the slightest
suspicion of the source of this undoing.

Or had he? Lessa wondered, her mind still reverberating from
the savage prescience of danger. East lay Fax's ancestral and
only legitimate Hold. North-east lay little but bare and stony
mountains and Benden, the remaining Weyr, which protected
Pern.

Lessa stretched, arching her back, inhaling the sweet, un-
tainted wind of morning.

A cock crowed in the stableyard. Lessa whirled, her face

alert, eyes darting around the outer Hold lest she be observed in such an uncharacteristic pose. She unbound her hair, letting it fall about her face concealingly. Her body drooped into the sloppy posture she affected. Quickly she thudded down the stairs, crossing to the watch-wher. It lurred piteously, its great eyes blinking against the growing daylight. Oblivious to the stench of its rank breath, she hugged the scaly head to her, scratching its ears and eye ridges. The watch-wher was ecstatic with pleasure, its long body trembling, its clipped wings rustling. It alone knew who she was or cared. And it was the only creature in all Pern she trusted since the day she had blindly sought refuge in its dark stinking lair to escape Fax's thirty swords that had drunk so deeply of Ruathan blood.

Slowly she rose, cautioning it to remember to be as vicious to her as to all should anyone be near. It promised to obey her, swaying back and forth to emphasize its reluctance.

The first rays of the sun glanced over the Hold's outer wall. Crying out, the watch-wher darted into its dark nest. Lessa crept back to the kitchen and into the cheese room.

> From the Weyr and from the Bowl
> Bronze and brown and blue and green
> Rise the dragonmen of Pern,
> Aloft, on wing, seen, then unseen.

F'lar on bronze Mnementh's great neck appeared first in the skies above the chief Hold of Fax, so-called Lord of the High Reaches. Behind him, in proper wedge formation, the wingmen came into sight. F'lar checked the formation automatically; as precise as at the moment of entry to *between*.

As Mnementh curved in an arc that would bring them to the perimeter of the Hold, consonant with the friendly nature of this visitation, F'lar surveyed with mounting aversion the disrepair of the ridge defences. The firestone pits were empty and the rock cut gutters radiating from the pits were green-tinged with a mossy growth.

Was there even one lord in Pern who maintained his Hold rocky in observance of the ancient Laws? F'lar's lips tightened to a thinner line. When this Search was over and the Impression made, there would have to be a solemn, punitive Council held at the Weyr. And by the golden shell of the queen, he, F'lar, meant to be its moderator. He would replace lethargy with industry. He would scour the green and dangerous scum from the heights of Pern, the grass blades from its stone-works. No verdant skirt would be condoned in any farmhold. And the tithings which had been so miserly, so grudgingly presented would, under pain of firestoning, flow with decent generosity into the Dragonweyr.

Mnementh rumbled approvingly as he vaned his pinions to land lightly on the grass-etched flagstones of Fax's Hold. The bronze dragon furled his great wings, and F'lar heard the warning klaxon in the Hold's Great Tower. Mnementh dropped to his knees as F'lar indicated he wished to dismount. The bronze rider stood by Mnementh's huge wedge-shaped head, politely awaiting the arrival of the Hold lord. F'lar idly gazed down the valley, hazy with warm spring sunlight. He ignored the furtive heads that peered at the dragonman from the parapet slits and the cliff windows.

F'lar did not turn as a rush of air announced the arrival of the rest of the wing. He knew, however, when F'nor, the brown rider, his half-brother, took the customary position on his left, a dragon-length to the rear. F'lar caught a glimpse of F'nor's boot-heel twisting to death the grass crowding up between the stones.

An order, muffled to an intense whisper, issued from within the great court, beyond the open gates. Almost immediately a group of men marched into sight, led by a heavy-set man of medium height.

Mnementh arched his neck, angling his head so that his chin rested on the ground. Mnementh's many faceted eyes, on a level with F'lar's head, fastened with disconcerting interest on the approaching party. The dragons could never understand why they generated such abject fear in common folk. At only one point in his life span would a dragon attack a human and that could be excused on the grounds of simple ignorance. F'lar could not explain to the dragon the politics behind the necessity of inspiring awe in the holders, lord and craftsmen alike. He could only observe that the fear and apprehension showing in the faces of the advancing squad which troubled Mnementh was oddly pleasing to him, F'lar.

'Welcome, Bronze Rider, to the Hold of Fax, Lord of the High Reaches. He is at your service,' and the man made an adequately respectful salute.

The use of the third person pronoun could be construed, by the meticulous, to be a veiled insult. This fitted in with the information F'lar had on Fax; so he ignored it. His information was also correct in describing Fax as a greedy man. It showed in the restless eyes which flicked at every detail of F'lar's clothing, at the slight frown when the intricately etched sword-hilt was noticed.

F'lar noticed, in his own turn, the several rich rings which flashed on Fax's left hand. The overlord's right hand remained slightly cocked after the habit of the professional swordsman. His tunic, of rich fabric, was stained and none too fresh. The man's feet, in heavy wher-hide boots, were solidly planted, weight balanced forward on his toes. A man to be treated cautiously, F'lar decided, as one should the conqueror of five neighbouring Holds. Such greedy audacity was in itself a revelation. Fax had married into a sixth . . . and had legally inherited, however unusual the circumstances, the seventh. He was a lecherous man by reputation.

Within these seven Holds, F'lar anticipated a profitable Search. Let R'gul go southerly to pursue Search among the indolent, if lovely, women there. The Weyr needed a strong woman this time; Jora had been worse than useless with Nemorth. Adversity, uncertainty: those were the conditions that bred the qualities F'lar wanted in a weyrwoman.

'We ride in Search,' F'lar drawled softly, 'and request the hospitality of your Hold, Lord Fax.'

Fax's eyes widened imperceptibly at mention of Search.

'I had heard Jora was dead,' Fax replied, dropping the third person abruptly as if F'lar had passed some sort of test by ignoring it. 'So Nemorth has a new queen, hm-m-m?' he continued, his eyes darting across the rank of the ring, noting the disciplined stance of the riders, the healthy colour of the dragons.

F'lar did not dignify the obvious with an answer.

'And, my Lord——?' Fax hesitated, expectantly inclining his head slightly towards the dragonman.

For a pulse beat, F'lar wondered if the man were deliberately provoking him with such subtle insults. The name of bronze riders should be as well known throughout Pern as the name of the Dragonqueen and her Weyrwoman. F'lar kept his face composed, his eyes on Fax's.

Leisurely, with the proper touch of arrogance, F'nor stepped forward, stopping slightly behind Mnementh's head, one hand negligently touching the jaw hinge of the huge beast.

'The Bronze Rider of Mnementh, Lord F'lar, will require quarters for himself. I, F'nor, brown rider, prefer to be lodged with the wingmen. We are, in number, twelve.'

F'lar liked that touch of F'nor's, totting up the wing strength, as if Fax were incapable of counting. F'nor had phrased it so adroitly as to make it impossible for Fax to protest the insult.

'Lord F'lar,' Fax said through teeth fixed in a smile, 'the High Reaches are honoured with your Search.'

'It will be to the credit of the High Reaches,' F'lar replied smoothly, 'if one of its own supplies the Weyr.'

'To our everlasting credit,' Fax replied as suavely. 'In the old days, many notable weyrwomen came from my Holds.'

'Your Holds?' asked F'lar, politely smiling as he emphasized the plural. 'Ah, yes, you are now overlord of Ruatha, are you not? There have been many from that Hold.'

A strange tense look crossed Fax's face. 'Nothing good comes from Ruath Hold.' Then he stepped aside, gesturing F'lar to enter the Hold.

Fax's troop leader barked a hasty order and the men formed two lines, their metal-edged boots flicking sparks from the stones.

At unspoken orders, all the dragons rose with a great churning of air and dust. F'lar strode nonchalantly past the welcoming files. The men were rolling their eyes in alarm as the beasts glided above to the inner courts. Someone on the high tower uttered a frightened yelp as Mnementh took his position on that vantage point. His great wings drove phosphoric-scented air across the inner court as he manoeuvred his great frame on to the inadequate landing space.

Outwardly oblivious to the consternation, fear and awe the dragons inspired, F'lar was secretly amused and rather pleased by the effect. Lords of the Holds needed this reminder that they must deal with dragons, not just with riders, who were men, mortal and murderable. The ancient respect for dragonmen as well as dragonkind must be reinstilled in modern breasts.

'The Hold has just risen from table, Lord F'lar, if . . .' Fax suggested. His voice trailed off at F'lar's smiling refusal.

'Convey my duty to your lady, Lord Fax,' F'lar rejoined, noticing with inward satisfaction the tightening of Fax's jaw muscles at the ceremonial request.

'You would prefer to see your quarters first?' Fax countered.

F'lar flicked an imaginary speck from his soft wher-hide sleeve and shook his head. Was the man buying time to sequester his ladies as the old time lords had?

'Duty first,' he said with a rueful shrug.

'Of course,' Fax all but snapped and strode smartly ahead, his heels pounding out the anger he could not express otherwise. F'lar decided he had guessed correctly.

F'lar and F'nor followed at a slower pace through the double-doored entry with its massive metal panels, into the great hall, carved into the cliffside.

'They eat not badly,' F'nor remarked casually to F'lar, appraising the remnants still on the table.

'Better than the Weyr, it would seem,' F'lar replied dryly.

'Young roasts and tender,' F'nor said in a bitter undertone, 'while the stringy, barren beasts are delivered up to us.'

'The change is overdue,' F'lar murmured, then raised his voice to conversational level. 'A well-favoured hall,' he was saying amiably as they reached Fax. Their reluctant host stood in the portal to the inner Hold, which, like all such Holds, burrowed deep into stone, traditional refuge of all in time of peril.

Deliberately, F'lar turned back to the banner-hung Hall. 'Tell me, Lord Fax, do you adhere to the old practices and mount a dawn guard?'

Fax frowned, trying to grasp F'lar's meaning.

'There is always a guard at the Tower.'

'An easterly guard?'

Fax's eyes jerked towards F'lar, then to F'nor.

'There are always guards,' he answered sharply, 'on all the approaches.'

'Oh, just the approaches,' and F'lar nodded wisely to F'nor.

'Where else?' demanded Fax, concerned, glancing from one dragonman to the other.

'I must ask that of your harper. You do keep a trained harper in your Hold?'

'Of course. I have several trained harpers,' and Fax jerked his shoulders straighter.

F'lar affected not to understand.

'Lord Fax is the overlord of six other holds,' F'nor reminded his wingleader.

'Of course,' F'lar assented, with exactly the same inflection Fax had used a moment before.

The mimicry did not go unnoticed by Fax but as he was unable to construe deliberate insult out of an innocent affirmative, he stalked into the glow-lit corridors. The dragonmen followed.

The women's quarters in Fax's Hold had been moved from the traditional innermost corridors to those at cliff-face. Sunlight poured down from three double-shuttered, deep-casement windows in the outside wall. F'lar noted that the bronze hinges were well oiled, and the sills regulation spear-length. Fax had not, at least, diminished the protective wall.

The chamber was richly hung with appropriately gentle scenes of women occupied in all manner of feminine tasks. Doors gave off the main chamber on both sides into smaller sleeping alcoves and from these, at Fax's bidding, his women hesitantly emerged. Fax sternly gestured to a blue-gowned woman, her hair white-streaked, her face lined with disappointments and bitterness, her body swollen with pregnancy. She advanced awkwardly, stopping several feet from her lord. From her attitude, F'lar deduced that she came no closer to Fax than was absolutely necessary.

'The Lady of Crom, mother of my heirs,' Fax said without pride or cordiality.

'My Lady——' F'lar hesitated, waiting for her name to be supplied.

She glanced warily at her lord.

'Gemma,' Fax snapped curtly.

F'lar bowed deeply. 'My Lady Gemma, the Weyr is on Search and requests the Hold's hospitality.'

'My Lord F'lar,' the Lady Gemma replied in a low voice, 'you are most welcome.'

F'lar did not miss the slight blur on the adverb nor the fact that Gemma had no trouble naming him. His smile was warmer than courtesy demanded, warm with gratitude and sympathy. Looking at the number of women in these quarters, F'lar thought there might be one or two Lady Gemma could bid farewell without regret.

Fax preferred his women plump and small. There wasn't a saucy one in the lot. If there once had been, the spirit had been beaten out of her. Fax, no doubt, was stud, not lover. Some of the covey had not all winter long made much use of water, judging by the amount of sweet oil gone rancid in their hair. Of them all, if these were all, the Lady Gemma was the only wilful one; and she, too old.

The amenities over, Fax ushered his unwelcome guests outside, and led the way to the quarters he had assigned the bronze rider.

'A pleasant room,' F'lar acknowledged, stripping off gloves and wher-hide tunic, throwing them carelessly to the table. 'I shall see to my men and the beasts. They have been fed recently,' he commented, pointing up Fax's omission in inquiring. 'I request liberty to wander through the crafthold.'

Fax sourly granted what was a dragonman's traditional privilege.

'I shall not further disrupt your routine, Lord Fax, for you must have many demands on you, with seven Holds to supervise.' F'lar inclined his body slightly to the overlord, turning away as a gesture of dismissal. He could imagine the infuriated expression on Fax's face from the stamping retreat.

F'nor and the men had settled themselves in a hastily vacated barrack-room. The dragons were perched comfortably on the rocky ridges above the Hold. Each rider kept his dragon in light, but alert, charge. There were to be no incidents on a Search.

As a group, the dragonmen rose at F'lar's entrance.

'No tricks, no troubles, but look around closely,' he said laconically. 'Return by sundown with the names of any likely prospects.' He caught F'nor's grin, remembering how Fax had slurred over some names. 'Descriptions are in order and craft affiliation.'

The men nodded, their eyes glinting with understanding. They were flatteringly confident of a successful Search even as F'lar's doubts grew now that he had seen Fax's women. By all logic, the pick of the High Reaches should be in Fax's chief Hold—but they were not. Still, there were many large craftholds not to mention the six other High Holds to visit. All the same . . .

In unspoken accord F'lar and F'nor left the barracks. The men would follow, unobtrusively, in pairs or singly, to reconnoitre the crafthold and the nearer farmholds. The men were as overtly eager to be abroad as F'lar was privately. There had been a time when dragonmen were frequent and favoured guests in all the great Holds throughout Pern, from southern Fort to high north Igen. This pleasant custom, too, had died along with other observances, evidence of the low regard in which the Weyr was presently held. F'lar vowed to correct this.

He forced himself to trace in memory the insidious changes. The Records, which each Weyrwoman kept, were proof of the gradual, but perceptible, decline, traceable through the past two hundred full Turns. Knowing the facts did not alleviate the condition. And F'lar was of that scant handful in the Weyr itself who did credit Records and Ballad alike. The situation might shortly reverse itself radically if the old tales were to be believed.

There was a reason, an explanation, a purpose, F'lar felt, for every one of the Weyr laws from First Impression to the Firestones: from the grass-free heights to ridge-running gutters. For elements as minor as controlling the appetite of a dragon to limiting the inhabitants of the Weyr. Although why the other five Weyrs had been abandoned, F'lar did not know. Idly he wondered if there were records, dusty and crumbling, lodged in the disused Weyrs. He must contrive to check when next his wings flew patrol. Certainly there was no explanation in Benden Weyr.

'There is industry but no enthusiasm,' F'nor was saying, drawing F'lar's attention back to their tour of the crafthold.

They had descended the guttered ramp from the Hold into the crafthold proper, the broad roadway lined with cottages up to the imposing stone crafthalls. Silently F'lar noted moss-clogged gutters on the roofs, the vines clasping the walls. It was painful for one of his calling to witness the flagrant disregard of simple safety precautions. Growing things were forbidden near the habitations of mankind.

'News travels fast,' F'nor chuckled, nodding at a hurrying craftsman, in the smock of a baker, who gave them a mumbled good day. 'Not a female in sight.'

His observation was accurate. Women should be abroad at this hour, bringing in supplies from the storehouses, washing in the river on such a bright warm day, or going out to the farmholds to help with planting. Not a gowned figure in sight.

'We used to be preferred mates,' F'nor remarked caustically.

'We'll visit the Clothmen's Hall first. If my memory serves me right . . .'

'As it always does . . .' F'nor interjected wryly. He took no advantage of their blood relationship but he was more at ease with the bronze rider than most of the dragonmen, the other bronze riders included. F'lar was reserved in a close-knit society of easy equality. He flew a tightly disciplined wing but men manoeuvred to serve under him. His wing always excelled in the Games. None ever floundered in *between* to disappear for ever and no beast in his wing sickened, leaving a man in dragonless exile from the Weyr, a part of him numb for ever.

'L'tol came this way and settled in one of the High Reaches,' F'lar continued.

'L'tol?'

'Yes, a green rider from S'lel's wing. You remember.'

An ill-timed swerve during the Spring Games had brought L'tol and his beast into the full blast of a phosphene emission from S'lel's bronze Tuenth. L'tol had been thrown from his beast's neck as the dragon tried to evade the blast. Another wingmate had swooped to catch the rider but the green dragon, his left wing crisped, his body scorched, had died of shock and phosphene poisoning.

'L'tol would aid our Search,' F'nor agreed as the two dragonmen walked up to the bronze doors of the Clothmen's Hall. They paused on the threshold, adjusting their eyes to the dimmer light within. Glows punctuated the wall recesses and hung in clusters above the larger looms where the finer tapestries and fabrics were woven by master craftsmen. The pervading mood was one of quiet, purposeful industry.

Before their eyes had adapted, however, a figure glided to them, with a polite, if curt, request for them to follow him.

They were led to the right of the entrance, to a small office, curtained from the main hall. Their guide turned to them, his face visible in the wallglows. There was that air about him that marked him indefinably as a dragonman. But his face was lined deeply, one side seamed with old burnmarks. His eyes, sick with a hungry yearning, dominated his face. He blinked constantly.

'I am now Lytol,' he said in a harsh voice.

F'lar nodded acknowledgment.

'You would be F'lar,' Lytol said 'and you F'nor. You've both the look of your sire.'

F'lar nodded again.

Lytol swallowed convulsively, the muscles of his face twitching as the presence of dragonmen revived his awareness of exile. He essayed a smile.

'Dragons in the sky! The news spread faster than Threads.'

'Nemorth has a new queen.'

'Jora dead?' Lytol asked concernedly, his face cleared of its nervous movement for a second.

F'lar nodded.

Lytol grimaced bitterly. 'R'gul again, huh.' He stared off in the middle distance, his eyelids quiet but the muscles along his jaw took up the constant movement. 'You've the High Reaches? All of them?' Lytol asked, turning back to the dragonman, a slight emphasis on 'all'.

F'lar gave an affirmative nod again.

'You've seen the women.' Lytol's disgust showed through the words. It was a statement, not a question, for he hurried on. 'Well, there are no better in all the High Reaches,' and his tone expressed utmost disdain.

'Fax likes his women comfortably fleshed and docile,' Lytol rattled on. 'Even the Lady Gemma has learned. It'd be different if he didn't need her family's support. Ah, it would be different indeed. So he keeps her pregnant, hoping to kill her in childbed one day. And he will. He will.'

Lytol drew himself up, squaring his shoulders, turning full to the two dragonmen. His expression was vindictive, his voice low and tense.

'Kill that tyrant, for the sake and safety of Pern. Of the Weyr. Of the queen. He only bides his time. He spreads discontent among the other lords. He'—Lytol's laughter had an hysterical edge to it now—'he fancies himself as good as dragonmen.'

'There are no candidates then in this Hold?' F'lar said, his voice sharp enough to cut through the man's pre-occupation with his curious theory.

Lytol stared at the bronze rider. 'Did I not say it?'

'What of Ruath Hold?'

Lytol stopped shaking his head and looked sharply at F'lar, his lips curling in a cunning smile. He laughed mirthlessly.

'You think to find a Torene, or a Moreta, hidden at Ruath Hold in these times? Well, all of that Blood are dead. Fax's blade was thirsty that day. He knew the truth of those harper's tales, that Ruathan lords gave full measure of hospitality to dragonmen and the Ruathan were a breed apart. There were, you know,' Lytol's voice dropped to a confiding whisper, 'exiled Weyrmen like myself in that Line.'

F'lar nodded gravely, unwilling to deprive the man of such a sop to his self-esteem.

'No,' and Lytol chuckled softly. 'Fax gets nothing from that Hold but trouble. And the women Fax used to take . . .' his laugh turned nasty in tone. 'It is rumoured he was impotent for months afterwards.'

'Any families in the holdings with Weyr blood?'

Lytol frowned, glanced surprised at F'lar. He rubbed the scarred side of his face thoughtfully.

'There were,' he admitted slowly. 'There were. But I doubt if any live on.' He thought a moment longer, then shook his head emphatically.

F'lar shrugged.

'I wish I had better news for you,' Lytol murmured.

'No matter.' F'lar reassured him, one hand poised to part the hanging in the doorway.

Lytol came up to him swiftly, his voice urgent.

'Heed what I say, Fax is ambitious. Force R'gul, or whoever is Weyrleader next, to keep watch on the High Reaches.'

Lytol jabbed a finger in the direction of the Hold. 'He scoffs openly at tales of the Threads. He taunts the harpers for the stupid nonsense of the old ballads and has banned from their repertoire all dragonlore. The new generation will grow up totally ignorant of duty, tradition and precaution.'

F'lar was not surprised to hear that on top of Lytol's other disclosures. Yet the Red Star pulsed in the sky and the time was drawing near when they would hysterically re-avow the old allegiances in fear for their very lives.

'Have you been abroad in the early morning of late?' asked F'nor, grinning maliciously.

'I have,' Lytol breathed out in a hushed, choked whisper. 'I have . . .' A groan was wrenched from his guts and he whirled away from the dragonmen, his head bowed between hunched shoulders. 'Go,' he said, gritting his teeth. And, as they hesitated, he pleaded, '*Go!*'

F'lar walked quickly from the room, followed by F'nor. The bronze rider crossed the quiet dim Hall with long strides and exploded into the startling sunlight. His momentum took him into the centre of the square. There he stopped so abruptly that F'nor, hard on his heels, nearly collided with him.

'We will spend exactly the same time within the other Halls,' he announced in a tight voice, his face averted from F'nor's eyes. F'lar's throat was constricted. It was difficult, suddenly, for him to speak. He swallowed hard, several times.

'To be dragonless . . .' murmured F'nor, pityingly. The encounter with Lytol had roiled his depths in a mournful way to which he was unaccustomed. That F'lar appeared equally shaken went far to dispel F'nor's private opinion that his half-brother was incapable of emotion.

'There is no other way once First Impression has been made. You know that,' F'lar roused himself to say curtly. He strode off to the Hall bearing the Leathermen's device.

> *The Hold is barred*
> *The Hall is bare.*
> > *And men vanish.*
> *The soil is barren,*
> *The rock is bald.*
> > *All hope banish.*

Lessa was shovelling ashes from the hearth when the agitated messenger staggered into the Great Hall. She made herself as inconspicuous as possible so the Warder would not dismiss her. She had contrived to be sent to the Great Hall that morning, knowing that the Warder intended to brutalize the Head Clothman for the shoddy quality of the goods readied for shipment to Fax.

'Fax is coming! With dragonmen!' the man gasped out as he plunged into the dim Great Hall.

The Warder, who had been about to lash the Head Clothman, turned, stunned, from his victim. The courier, a farmholder from the edge of Ruatha, stumbled up to the Warder, so excited with his message that he grabbed the Warder's arm.

'How dare you leave your Hold?' and the Warder aimed his lash at the astonished holder. The force of the first blow knocked the man from his feet. Yelping, he scrambled out of reach of a second lashing. 'Dragonmen indeed! Fax? Ha! He shuns Ruatha. There!' The Warder punctuated each denial with another blow, kicking the helpless wretch for good measure, before he turned breathless to glare at the clothman and the two under-warders. 'How did he get in here with such a threadbare lie?' The Warder stalked to the great door. It was flung open just as he reached out for the iron handle. The ashen-faced guard officer rushed in, nearly toppling the Warder.

'Dragonmen! Dragons! All over Ruatha!' the man gibbered, arms flailing wildly. He, too, pulled at the Warder's arm, dragging the stupefied official towards the outer courtyard, to bear out the truth of his statement.

Lessa scooped up the last pile of ashes. Picking up her equipment, she slipped out of the Great Hall. There was a very pleased smile on her face under the screen of matted hair.

A dragonman at Ruatha! She must somehow contrive to get Fax so humiliated, or so infuriated, that he would renounce his claim to the Hold, in the presence of a dragonman. Then she could claim her birthright.

But she would have to be extraordinarily wary. Dragonriders were men apart. Anger did not cloud their intelligence. Greed did not sully their judgment. Fear did not dull their reactions. Let the dense-witted believe human sacrifice, unnatural lusts, insane revel. She was not so gullible. And those stories went against her grain. Dragonmen were still human and there was Weyr blood in *her* veins. It was the same colour as that of anyone else; enough of hers had been spilled to prove that.

She halted for a moment, catching a sudden shallow breath. Was this the danger she had sensed four days ago at dawn? The final encounter in her struggle to regain the Hold?—No—there had been more to that portent than revenge.

The ash bucket banged against her shins as she shuffled down the low ceilinged corridor to the stable door. Fax would find a cold welcome. She had laid no new fire on the hearth. Her laugh echoed back unpleasantly from the damp walls. She rested her bucket and propped her broom and shovel as she wrestled with the heavy bronze door that gave into the new stables.

They had been built outside the cliff of Ruatha by Fax's first Warder, a subtler man than all eight of his successors. He had achieved more than all the others and Lessa had honestly regretted the necessity of his death. But he would have made her revenge impossible. He would have caught her out before she had learned how to camouflage herself and her little interferences. What had his name been? She could not recall. Well, she regretted his death.

The second man had been properly greedy and it had been easy to set up a pattern of misunderstanding between Warder and craftsmen. That one had been determined to squeeze all profit from Ruathan goods so that some of it would drop into his pocket before Fax suspected a shortage. The craftsmen who had begun to accept the skilful diplomacy of the first Warder bitterly resented the second's grasping, high-handed ways. They resented the passing of the Old Line and, even more so, the way of its passing. They were unforgiving of the insult to Ruatha; its now secondary position in the High Reaches; and they resented the individual indignities that holders, craftsmen and farmers alike, suffered under the second Warder. It took little manipulation to arrange for matters at Ruatha to go from bad to worse.

The second was replaced and his successor fared no better. He was caught diverting goods, the best of the goods at that. Fax had had him executed. His bony head still hung in the main firepit above the great Tower.

The present incumbent had not been able to maintain the Hold in even the sorry condition in which he had assumed its management. Seemingly simple matters developed rapidly into disasters. Like the production of cloth . . . Contrary to his boasts to Fax, the quality had not improved, and the quantity had fallen off.

Now Fax was here. And the dragonmen! Why dragonmen? The import of the question froze Lessa, and the heavy door closing behind her barked her heels painfully. Dragonmen used to be frequent visitors at Ruatha, that she knew, and even vaguely remembered. Those memories were like a harper's tale, told of someone else, not something within her own experience. She had limited her fierce attention to Ruatha only. She could not even recall the name of Queen or Weyrwoman from the instructions of her childhood, nor could she recall hearing mention of any queen or weyrwoman by anyone in the Hold these past ten Turns.

Perhaps the dragonmen were finally going to call the lords of the Holds to ask for the disgraceful show of greenery about the Holds. Well, Lessa was to blame for much of that in Ruatha but she defied even a dragonman to confront her with her guilt. Did all Ruatha fall to the Threads it would be better than remaining dependent to Fax! The heresy shocked Lessa even as she thought it.

Wishing she could as easily unburden her conscience of such blasphemy, she ditched the ashes on the stable midden. There was a sudden change in air pressure around her. Then a fleeting shadow caused her to glance up.

From behind the cliff above glided a dragon, its enormous wings spread to their fullest as he caught the morning updraught. Turning effortlessly, he descended. A second, a third, a full wing of dragons followed in soundless flight and patterned descent, graceful and awesome. The klaxon rang belatedly from the Tower and from within the kitchen there issued the screams and shrieks of the terrified drudges.

Lessa took cover. She ducked into the kitchen where she was instantly seized by the assistant cook and thrust with a buffet and a kick towards the sinks. There she was put to scrubbing grease-encrusted serving bowls with cleansing sand.

The yelping canines were already lashed to the spitrun,

turning a scrawny herdbeast that had been set to roast. The cook was ladling seasonings on the carcass, swearing at having to offer so poor a meal to so many guests, and some of them high-rank. Winter-dried fruits from the last scanty harvest had been set to soak and two of the oldest drudges were scraping roots.

An apprentice cook was kneading bread; another, carefully spicing a sauce. Looking fixedly at him, she diverted his hand from one spice box to a less appropriate one as he gave a final shake to the concoction. She added too much wood to the wall oven, insuring ruin for the breads. She controlled the canines deftly, slowing one and speeding the other so that the meat would be underdone on one side, burned on the other. That the feast should be a fast, the food presented found inedible, was her whole intention.

Above in the Hold, she had no doubt that certain other measures, undertaken at different times for this exact contingency, were being discovered.

Her fingers bloodied from a beating, one of the Warder's women came shrieking into the kitchen, hopeful of refuge there.

'Insects have eaten the best blankets to shreds! And a canine who had littered on the best linens snarled at me as she gave suck! And the rushes are noxious, the best chamber's full of debris driven in by the winter wind. Somebody left the shutters ajar. Just a tiny bit, but it was enough . . .' the woman wailed, clutching her hand to her breast and rocking back and forth.

Lessa bent with great industry to shine the plates.

> *Watch-wher, watch-wher,*
> *In your lair,*
> *Watch well, watch-wher!*
> *Who goes there?*

'The watch-wher is hiding something,' F'lar told F'nor as they consulted in the hastily cleaned Great Hall. The room delighted to hold the wintry chill although a generous fire now burned on the hearth.

'It was but gibbering when Canth spoke to it,' F'nor remarked. He was leaning against the mantel, turning slightly from side to side to gather some warmth. He watched his wingleader's impatient pacing.

'Mnementh is calming it down,' F'lar replied. 'He may be able to sort out the nightmare. The creature may be more senile than aware, but . . .'

'I doubt it,' F'nor concurred helpfully. He glanced with apprehension up at the web-hung ceiling. He was certain he'd found most of the crawlers, but he didn't fancy their sting. Not on top of the discomforts already experienced in this forsaken Hold. If the night stayed mild, he intended curling up with Canth on the heights. 'That would be more reasonable than anything Fax or his Warder have suggested.'

'Hm-m-m,' F'lar muttered, frowning at the brown rider.

'Well, it's unbelievable that Ruatha could have fallen to such disrepair in ten short Turns. Every dragon caught the feeling of power and it's obvious the watch-wher has been tampered with. That takes a good deal of control.'

'From someone of the Blood,' F'lar reminded him.

F'nor shot his wingleader a quick look, wondering if he could possibly be serious in the light of all information to the contrary.

'I grant you there is power here, F'lar,' F'nor conceded. 'It could easily be a hidden male of the old Blood. But we need a female. And Fax made it plain, in his inimitable fashion, that he left none of the old Blood alive in the Hold the day he took it. No, no.' The brown rider shook his head, as if he could dispel the lack of faith in his wingleader's curious insistence that the Search would end in Ruath with Ruathan blood.

'That watch-wher is hiding something and only someone of the Blood of its Hold can arrange that,' F'lar said emphatically. He gestured around the Hall and towards the walls, bare of hangings. 'Ruatha has been overcome. But she resists . . . Subtly. I say it points to the old Blood, *and* power. Not power alone.'

The obstinate expression in F'lar's eyes, the set of his jaw, suggested that F'nor seek another topic.

'The pattern was well-flown today,' F'nor suggested tentatively. 'Does a dragonman good to ride a flaming beast. Does the beast good, too. Keeps the digestive process in order.'

F'lar nodded sober agreement. 'Let R'gul temporize as he chooses. It is fitting and proper to ride a fire-spouting beast and these holders need to be reminded of Weyr power.'

'Right now, anything would help our prestige,' F'nor commented sourly. 'What had Fax to say when he hailed you in the Pass?' F'nor knew his question was almost impertinent but if it were, F'lar would ignore it.

F'lar's slight smile was unpleasant and there was an ominous glint in his amber eyes.

'We talked of rule and resistance.'

'Did he not also draw on you?' F'nor asked.

F'lar's smile deepened. 'Until he remembered I was dragon-mounted.'

'He's considered a vicious fighter,' F'nor said.

'I am at some disadvantage?' F'lar asked, turning sharply to his brown rider, his face too controlled.

'To my knowledge, no,' F'nor reassured his leader quickly. F'lar had tumbled every man in the Weyr, efficiently and easily. 'But Fax kills often and without cause.'

'And because we dragonmen do not seek blood, we are not to be feared as fighters?' snapped F'lar. 'Are you ashamed of your heritage?'

'I? No!' F'nor sucked in his breath. 'Nor any of our wing!' he added proudly. 'But there is that in the attitude of the men in this progression of Fax's that . . . that makes me wish some excuse to fight.'

'As you observed today, Fax seeks some excuse. And,' F'lar added thoughtfully, 'there is something here in Ruatha that unnerves our noble overlord.'

He caught sight of Lady Tela, whom Fax had so courteously assigned him for comfort during the progression, waving to him from the inner Hold portal.

'A case in point. Fax's Lady Tela is some three months gone.' F'nor frowned at that insult to his leader.

'She giggles incessantly and appears so addlepated that one cannot decide whether she babbles out of ignorance or at Fax's suggestion. As she has apparently not bathed all winter, and is not, in any case, my ideal, I have'—F'lar grinned maliciously—'deprived myself of her kind offices.'

F'nor hastily cleared his throat and his expression as Lady Tela approached them. He caught the unappealing odour from the scarf or handkerchief she waved constantly. Dragonmen endured a great deal for the Weyr. He moved away, with apparent courtesy, to join the rest of the dragonmen entering the Hall.

F'lar turned with equal courtesy to Lady Tela as she jabbered away about the terrible condition of the rooms which Lady Gemma and the other ladies had been assigned.

'The shutters, both sets, were ajar all winter long and you should have seen the trash on the floors. We finally got two of the drudges to sweep it all into the fireplace. And then that smoked something fearful 'til a man was sent up.' Lady Tela giggled. 'He found the access blocked by a chimney stone fallen aslant. The rest of the chimney, for a wonder, was in good repair.'

She waved her handkerchief. F'lar held his breath as the gesture wafted an unappealing odour in his direction.

He glanced up the Hall towards the inner Hold door and saw Lady Gemma descending, her steps slow and awkward. Some subtle difference about her gait attracted him and he stared at her, trying to identify it.

'Oh, yes, poor Lady Gemma,' Lady Tela babbled, sighing deeply. 'We are so concerned. Why Lord Fax insisted on her coming, I do not know. She is not near her time and yet . . .' The lighthead's concern sounded sincere.

F'lar's incipient hatred for Fax and his brutality matured abruptly. He left his partner chattering to thin air and courteously extended his arm to Lady Gemma to support her down the steps and to the table. Only the brief tightening of her fingers on his forearm betrayed her gratitude. Her face was very white and drawn, the lines deeply etched around mouth and eyes, showing the effort she was expending.

'Some attempt has been made, I see, to restore order to the Hall,' she remarked in a conversational tone.

'Some,' F'lar admitted dryly, glancing around the grandly proportioned Hall, its rafters festooned with the webs of many Turns. The inhabitants of those gossamer nests dropped from time to time, with ripe splats, to the floor, on to the table and into the serving platters. Nothing replaced the old banners of the Ruathan Blood, which had been removed from the stark brown stone walls. Fresh rushes did obscure the greasy flagstones. The trestle tables appeared recently sanded and scraped, and the platters gleamed dully in the refreshed glows. Unfortunately, the brighter light was a mistake for it was much too unflattering.

'This was such a graceful Hall,' Lady Gemma murmured for F'lar's ears alone.

'You were a friend?' he asked, politely.

'Yes, in my youth,' her voice dropped expressively on the last word, evoking for F'lar a happier girlhood. 'It was a noble line!'

'Think you *one* might have escaped the sword?'

Lady Gemma flashed him a startled look, then quickly composed her features, lest the exchange be noted. She gave a barely perceptible shake of her head and then shifted her awkward weight to take her place at the table. Graciously she inclined her head towards F'lar, both dismissing and thanking him.

F'lar returned to his own partner and placed her at the table on his left. As the only person of rank who would dine that night at Ruatha Hold, Lady Gemma was seated on his right; Fax would be beyond her. The dragonmen and Fax's upper soldiery would sit at the lower tables. No guildmen had been invited to Ruatha. Fax arrived just then with his current lady and two underleaders, the Warder bowing them effusively into the Hall. The man, F'lar noticed, kept a good distance from his overlord— as well a Warder might whose responsibility was in this sorry condition. F'lar flicked a crawler away. Out of the corner of his eye, he saw Lady Gemma wince and shudder.

Fax stamped up to the raised table, his face black with suppressed rage. He pulled back his chair roughly, slamming it into Lady Gemma's before he seated himself. He pulled the chair to the table with a force that threatened to rock the none too stable trestle-top from its supporting legs. Scowling, he inspected his goblet and plate, fingering the surface, ready to throw them aside if they displeased him.

'A roast and fresh bread, Lord Fax, and such fruits and roots as are left. Had I but known of your arrival, I could have sent to Crom for . . .'

'Sent to Crom?' roared Fax, slamming the plate he was inspecting on to the table so forcefully the rim bent under his hands. The Warder winced again as if he himself had been maimed.

'The day one of my Holds cannot support itself *or* the visit of its rightful overlord. I shall renounce it.'

Lady Gemma gasped. Simultaneously the dragons roared.

F'lar felt the unmistakable surge of power. His eyes instinctively sought F'nor at the lower table. The brown rider—all the dragonmen—had experienced that inexplicable shaft of exultation.

'What's wrong, Dragonman?' snapped Fax.

F'lar, affecting unconcern, stretched his legs under the table and assumed an indolent posture in the heavy chair.

'Wrong?'

'The dragons!'

'Oh, nothing. They often roar . . . at the sunset, at a flock of passing wherries, at mealtimes,' and F'lar smiled amiably at the Lord of the High Reaches. Beside him his tablemate gave a squeak.

'Mealtimes? Have they not been fed?'

'Oh, yes. Five days ago.'

'Oh. Five . . . days ago? And are they hungry . . . now?' Her voice trailed into a whisper of fear, her eyes grew round.

'In a few days,' F'lar assured her. Under cover of his detached amusement, F'lar scanned the Hall. That surge had come from nearby. Either in the Hall or just outside. It must have been from within. It came so soon upon Fax's speech that his words must have triggered it. And the power had had an indefinably feminine touch to it.

One of Fax's women? F'lar found that hard to credit. Mnementh had been close to all of them and none had shown a vestige of power. Much less, with the exception of Lady Gemma, any intelligence.

One of the Hall women? So far he had seen only the sorry drudges and the ageing females the Warder had as housekeepers. The Warder's personal woman? He must discover if that man had one. One of the Hold guards' women? F'lar suppressed an intense desire to rise and search.

'You mount a guard?' he asked Fax casually.

'Double at Ruath Hold!' he was told in a tight, hard voice, ground out from somewhere deep in Fax's chest.

'Here?' F'lar all but laughed out loud, gesturing around the sadly appointed chamber.

'Here! Food!' Fax changed the subject with a roar.

Five drudges, two of them women in brown-grey rags such

that F'lar hoped they had had nothing to do with the preparation
of the meal, staggered in under the emplattered herdbeast. No
one with so much as a trace of power would sink to such depths,
unless . . .

The aroma that reached him as the platter was placed on the
serving table distracted him. It reeked of singed bone and charred
meat. The Warder frantically sharpened his tools as if a keen
edge could somehow slice acceptable portions from this unlikely
carcass.

Lady Gemma caught her breath again and F'lar saw her
hands curl tightly around the armrests. He saw the convulsive
movement of her throat as she swallowed. He, too, did not look
forward to this repast.

The drudges reappeared with wooden trays of bread. Burnt
crusts had been scraped and cut, in some places, from the loaves
before serving. As other trays were borne in, F'lar tried to catch
sight of the faces of the servitors. Matted hair obscured the face
of the one who presented a dish of legumes swimming in greasy
liquid. Revolted. F'lor poked through the legumes to find
properly cooked portions to offer Lady Gemma. She waved
them aside, her face ill-concealing her discomfort.

As F'lar was about to turn and serve Lady Tela, he saw Lady
Gemma's hand clutch convulsively at the chair arms. He realized
that she was not merely nauseated by the unappetizing food.
She was seized with labour contractions.

F'lar glanced in Fax's direction. The overlord was scowling
blackly at the attempts of the Warder to find edible portions of
meat to serve.

F'lar touched Lady Gemma's arm with light fingers. She
turned just enough to look at F'lar from the corner of her eye.
She managed a socially-correct half-smile.

'I dare not leave just now, Lord F'lar. He is always dangerous
at Ruatha. And it may only be false pangs.'

F'lar was dubious as he saw another shudder pass through
her frame. The woman would have been a fine weyrwoman, he
thought ruefully, were she but younger.

The Warder, his hands shaking, presented Fax the sliced
meats. There were slivers of overdone flesh and portions of
almost edible meats, but not much of either.

One furious wave of Fax's broad fist and the Warder had the

plate, meats and juice, square in the face. Despite himself, F'lar sighed, for those undoubtedly constituted the only edible portions of the entire beast.

'You call this food? *You call this food?*' Fax bellowed. His voice boomed back from the bare vault of the ceiling, shaking crawlers from their webs as the sound shattered the fragile strands. 'Slop! *Slop!*'

F'lar rapidly brushed crawlers from Lady Gemma who was helpless in the throes of a very strong contraction.

'It's all we had on such short notice,' the Warder squealed, juices streaking down his cheeks. Fax threw the goblet at him and the wine went streaming down the man's chest. The steaming dish of roots followed and the man yelped as the hot liquid splashed over him.

'My lord, my lord, had I but known!'

'Obviously, Ruatha *cannot* support the visit of its Lord. You must renounce it,' F'lar heard himself saying.

His shock at such words issuing from his mouth was as great as that of everyone else in the Hall. Silence fell, broken by the splat of crawlers and the drip of root liquid from the Warder's shoulders to the rushes. The grating of Fax's boot-heel was clearly audible as he swung slowly around to face the bronze rider.

As F'lar conquered his own amazement and rapidly tried to predict what to do next to mend matters, he saw F'nor rise slowly to his feet, hand on dagger hilt.

'I did not hear you correctly?' Fax asked, his face blank of all expression, his eyes snapping.

Unable to comprehend how he could have uttered such an arrant challenge, F'lar managed to assume a languid pose.

'You did mention,' he drawled, 'that if any of your Holds could not support itself and the visit of its rightful overlord, you would renounce it.'

Fax stared back at F'lar, his face a study of swiftly suppressed emotions, the glint of triumph dominant. F'lar, his face stiff with the forced expression of indifference, was casting swiftly about in his mind. In the name of the Egg, had he lost all sense of discretion?

Pretending utter unconcern, he stabbed some vegetables on

to his knife and began to munch on them. As he did so, he noticed F'nor glancing slowly around the Hall, scrutinizing everyone. Abruptly F'lar realized what had happened. Somehow, in making that statement, he, a dragonman, had responded to a covert use of the power. F'lar, the bronze rider, was being put into a position where he would *have* to fight Fax. Why? For what end? To get Fax to renounce the Hold? Incredible! But there could be only one possible reason for such a turn of events. An exultation as sharp as pain swelled within F'lar. It was all he could do to maintain his pose of bored indifference, all he could do to turn his attention to thwarting Fax, should he press for a duel. A duel would serve no purpose. He, F'lar, had no time to waste on it.

A groan escaped Lady Gemma and broke the eye-locked stance of the two antagonists. Irritated, Fax looked down at her, fist clenched and half-raised to strike her for her temerity in interrupting her lord and master. The contraction that contorted the swollen belly was as obvious as the woman's pain. F'lar dared not look towards her but he wondered if she had deliberately groaned aloud to break the tension.

Incredibly, Fax began to laugh. He threw back his head, showing big, stained teeth, and roared.

'Aye, renounce it, in favour of her issue, if it is male . . . and lives!' he crowed, laughing raucously.

'Heard and witnessed!' F'lar snapped, jumping to his feet and pointing to his riders. They were on their feet in the instant. 'Heard and witnessed!' they averred in the traditional manner.

With that movement, everyone began to babble at once in nervous relief. The other women, each reacting in her way to the imminence of birth, called orders to the servants and advice to each other. They converged towards Lady Gemma, hovering undecidedly out of Fax's range, like silly wherries disturbed from their roosts. It was obvious they were torn between their fear of their lord and the desire to reach the labouring woman.

He gathered their intentions as well as their reluctance and, still stridently laughing, knocked back his chair. He stepped over it, strode down to the meatstand and stood hacking off pieces with his knife, stuffing them, juice dripping, into his mouth without ceasing to guffaw.

As F'lar bent towards Lady Gemma to assist her out of her

chair, she grabbed his arm urgently. Their eyes met, hers clouded with pain. She pulled him closer.

'He means to kill you, Bronze Rider. He loves to kill,' she whispered.

'Dragonmen are not easily killed, but I am grateful to you.'

'I do not want you killed,' she said, softly, biting at her lip. 'We have so few bronze riders.'

F'lar stared at her, startled. Did she, Fax's lady, actually believe in the Old Laws?

F'lar beckoned to two of the Warder's men to carry her up into the Hold. He caught Lady Tela by the arm as she fluttered past him.

'What do you need?'

'Oh, oh,' she exclaimed, her face twisted with panic; she was distractedly wringing her hands, 'Water, hot. Clean cloths. And a birthing-woman. Oh, yes, we must have a birthing-woman.'

F'lar looked about for one of the Hold women, his glance sliding over the first disreputable figure who had started to mop up the spilled food. He signalled instead for the Warder and peremptorily ordered him to send for the woman. The Warder kicked at the drudge on the floor.

'You . . . you! Whatever your name is, go get her from the crafthold. You must know who she is.'

The drudge evaded the parting kick the Warder aimed in her direction with a nimbleness at odds with her appearance of extreme age and decrepitude. She scurried across the Hall and out of the kitchen door.

Fax sliced and speared meat, occasionally bursting out with a louder bark of laughter as his inner thoughts amused him. F'lar sauntered down to the carcass and, without waiting for invitation from his host, began to carve neat slices also, beckoning his men over. Fax's soldiers, however, waited until their lord had eaten his fill.

> *Lord of the Hold, your charge is sure*
> *In thick walls, metal doors and no verdure.*

Lessa sped from the Hall to summon the birthing-woman, seething with frustration. So close! So close! How could she come so close and yet fail? Fax should have challenged the dragonman. And the dragonman was strong and young, his face that of a fighter, stern and controlled. He should not have temporized. Was all honour dead in Pern, smothered by green grass?

And why, oh why, had Lady Gemma chosen that precious moment to go into labour? If her groan hadn't distracted Fax, the fight would have begun and not even Fax, for all his vaunted prowess as a vicious fighter, would have prevailed against a dragonman who had her—Lessa's support! The Hold must be secured to its rightful Blood again. Fax must not leave Ruatha alive!

Above her, on the High Tower, the great bronze dragon gave forth a weird croon, his many-faceted eyes sparkling in the gathering darkness.

Unconsciously she silenced him as she would have done the watch-wher. Ah, that watch-wher. He had not come out of his den at her passing. She knew the dragons had been at him. She could hear him gibbering in panic.

The slant of the road towards the crafthold lent impetus to her flying feet and she had to brace herself to a sliding stop at the birthing-woman's stone threshold. She banged on the closed door and heard frightened exclamation within.

'A birth. A birth at the Hold,' Lessa cried.

'A birth?' came the muffled cry and the latches were thrown up on the door. 'At the Hold?'

'Fax's lady and, as you love life, hurry! For if it is male, it will be Ruatha's own lord.'

That ought to fetch her, thought Lessa, and in that instant, the door was flung open by the man of the house. Lessa could see the birthing-woman gathering up her things in haste, piling them into her shawl. Lessa hurried the woman out, up the steep road to the Hold, under the Tower gate, grabbing the woman as she tried to run at the sight of a dragon peering down at her. Lessa drew her into the Court and pushed her, resisting, into the Hall.

The woman clutched at the inner door, baulking at the sight of the gathering there. Lord Fax, his feet up on the trestle table, was paring his fingernails with his knife blade, still chuckling. The dragonmen in their wher-hide tunics, were eating quietly at one table while the soldiers were having their turn at the meat.

The bronze rider noticed their entrance and pointed urgently towards the inner Hold. The birthing-woman seemed frozen to the spot. Lessa tugged futilely at her arm, urging her to cross the Hall. To her surprise, the bronze rider strode to them.

'Go quickly, woman, Lady Gemma is before her time,' he said, frowning with concern, gesturing imperatively towards the Hold entrance. He caught her by the shoulder and led her, all unwilling, Lessa tugging away at her other arm.

When they reached the stairs, he relinquished his grip, nodding to Lessa to escort her the rest of the way. Just as they reached the massive inner door, Lessa noticed how sharply the dragonman was looking at them—at her hand, on the birthing-woman's arm. Warily, she glanced at her hand and saw it, as if it belonged to a stranger: the long fingers, shapely despite dirt and broken nails; her small hand, delicately boned, gracefully placed despite the urgency of the grip. She blurred it and hurried on.

> *Honour those the dragons heed,*
> *In thought and favour, word and deed,*
> *Worlds are lost or worlds are saved*
> *By those dangers dragon-braved.*

> *Dragonman, avoid excess;*
> *Greed will bring the Weyr distress;*
> *To the ancient Laws adhere,*
> *Prospers thus the Dragon-weyr.*

An unintelligible ululation raised the waiting men to their feet, startled from private meditations and the diversion of Bonethrows. Only Fax remained unmoved at the alarm, save that the slight sneer, which had settled on his face hours past, deepened to smug satisfaction.

'Dead-ed-ed,' the tidings reverberated down the rocky corridors of the Hold. The weeping lady seemed to erupt out of the passage from the Inner Hold, flying down the steps to sink into an hysterical heap at Fax's feet. 'She's dead. Lady Gemma is dead. There was too much blood. It was too soon. She was too old to bear more children.'

F'lar couldn't decide whether the woman was apologizing for, or exulting in, the woman's death. She certainly couldn't be criticizing her Lord for placing Lady Gemma in such peril. F'lar, however, was sincerely sorry at Gemma's passing. She had been a brave, fine woman.

And now, what would be Fax's next move? F'lar caught F'nor's identically quizzical glance and shrugged expressively.

'The child lives!' a curiously distorted voice announced, penetrating the rising noise in the Great Hall. The words electrified the atmosphere. Every head slewed round sharply towards the portal to the inner Hold where the drudge, a totally unexpected messenger, stood poised on the top step.

'It is male!' This announcement rang triumphantly in the still Hall.

Fax jerked himself to his feet, kicking aside the woman at his feet, scowling ominously at the drudge. 'What did you say?'

'The child lives. It is male,' the creature repeated, descending the stairs.

Incredulity and rage suffused Fax's face. His body seemed to coil up.

'Ruatha has a new lord!' Staring intently at the overlord, she advanced, her mien purposeful, almost menacing.

The tentative cheers of the Warder's men were drowned by the roaring of the dragons.

Fax erupted into action. He leaped across the intervening space, bellowing. Before Lessa could dodge, his fist crashed down across her face. She fell heavily to the stone floor, where she lay motionless, a bundle of dirty rags.

'Hold, Fax!' F'lar's voice broke the silence as the Lord of the High Reaches flexed his leg to kick her.

Fax whirled, his hand automatically closing on his knife hilt.

'It was heard and witnessed, Fax,' F'lar cautioned him, one hand outstretched in warning, 'by dragonmen. Stand by your sworn and witnessed oath!'

'Witnessed? By dragonmen?' cried Fax with a derisive laugh. 'Dragonwomen, you mean,' he sneered, his eyes blazing with contempt, as he made one sweeping gesture of scorn.

He was momentarily taken aback by the speed with which the bronze rider's knife appeared in his hand.

'Dragonwomen?' F'lar queried, his lips curling back over his teeth, his voice dangerously soft. Glow-light flickered off his circling knife as he advanced on Fax.

'Women! Parasites on Pern. The Weyr power is over. Over!' Fax roared, leaping forward to land in a combat crouch.

The two antagonists were dimly aware of the scurry behind them, of tables pulled roughly aside to give the duelists space. F'lar could spare no glance at the crumpled form of the drudge. Yet he was sure, through and beyond instinct sure, that she was the source of power. He had felt it as she entered the room. The dragon's roaring confirmed it. If that fall had killed her . . . He advanced on Fax, leaping high to avoid the slashing blade as Fax unwound from the crouch with a powerful lunge.

F'lar evaded the attack easily, noticing his opponent's reach, deciding he had a slight advantage there. But not much. Fax had had much more actual hand-to-hand killing experience than had he whose duels had always ended at first blood on the practice floor. F'lar made due note to avoid closing with the burly lord. The man was heavy-chested, dangerous from sheer mass. F'lar must use agility as his weapon, not brute strength.

Fax feinted, testing F'lar for weakness, or indiscretion. The two crouched, facing each other across six feet of space, knife hands weaving, their free hands, spread-fingered, ready to grab.

Again Fax pressed the attack. F'lor allowed him to close, just near enough to dodge away with a back-handed swipe. Fabric ripped under the tip of his knife. He heard Fax snarl. The overlord was faster on his feet than his bulk suggested and F'lar had to dodge a second time, feeling Fax's knife score his wher-hide jerkin.

Grimly the two circled, each looking for an opening in the other's defence. Fax ploughed in, trying to corner the lighter, faster man between raised platform and wall.

F'lar countered, ducking low under Fax's flailing arm, slashing obliquely across Fax's side. The overlord caught at him, yanking savagely, and F'lar was trapped against the other man's side, straining desperately with his left hand to keep the knife arm up. F'lar brought up his knee, and ducked away as Fax gasped and buckled from the pain in his groin, but Fax struck in passing. Sudden fire laced F'lar's left shoulder.

Fax's face was red with anger and he wheezed from pain and shock. But the infuriated lord straightened up and charged.

F'lar was forced to sidestep quickly before Fax could close with him. F'lar put the meat table between them, circling warily, flexing his shoulder to assess the extent of the knife's slash. It was painful, but the arm could be used.

Suddenly Fax scooped up some fatty scraps from the meat tray and hurled them at F'lar. The dragonman ducked and Fax came around the table with a rush. F'lar leaped sideways. Fax's flashing blade came within inches of his abdomen, as his own knife sliced down the outside of Fax's arm. Instantly the two pivoted to face each other again, but Fax's left arm hung limply at his side.

F'lar darted in, pressing his luck as the Lord of the High Reaches staggered. But F'lar misjudged the man's condition and suffered a terrific kick in the side as he tried to dodge under the feinting knife. Doubled with pain, F'lar rolled frantically away from his charging adversary. Fax was lurching forward, trying to fall on him, to pin the lighter dragonman down for a final thrust. Somehow F'lar got to his feet, attempting to straighten to meet Fax's stumbling charge. His very position saved him. Fax over-reached his mark and staggered off balance. F'lar brought his right hand over with as much strength as he could muster and his blade plunged through Fax's unprotected back until he felt the point stick in the chest plate.

The defeated lord fell flat to the flagstones. The force of his descent dislodged the dagger from his chest-bone and an inch of bloody blade re-emerged.

F'lar stared down at the dead man. There was no pleasure in killing, he realized, only relief that he himself was still alive. He wiped his forehead on his sleeve and forced himself erect, his side throbbing with the pain of that last kick and his left shoulder burning. He half-stumbled to the drudge, still sprawled where she had fallen.

He gently turned her over, noting the terrible bruise spreading across her cheek under the dirty skin. He heard F'nor take command of the tumult in the Hall.

The dragonman laid a hand, trembling in spite of an effort to control himself, on the woman's breast to feel for a heartbeat . . . It was there, slow but strong.

A deep sigh escaped him for either blow or fall could have proved fatal. Fatal, perhaps, for Pern as well.

Relief was coloured with disgust. There was no telling under the filth how old this creature might be. He raised her in his arms, her light body no burden even to his battle-weary strength. Knowing F'nor would handle any trouble efficiently, F'lar carried the drudge to his own chamber.

Putting the body on the high bed, he stirred up the fire and added more glows to the bedside bracket. His gorge rose at the thought of touching the filthy mat of hair but none the less and gently, he pushed it back from the face, turning the head this way and that. The features were small, regular. One arm, clear of rags, was reasonably clean above the elbow but marred by bruises and old scars. The skin was firm and unwrinkled. The hands, when he took them in his, were filthy but well-shaped and delicately boned.

F'lar began to smile. Yes, she had blurred that hand so skilfully that he had actually doubted what he had first seen. And yes, beneath grime and grease, she was young. Young enough for the Weyr. And no born drab. There was no taint of common blood here. It was pure, no matter whose the line, and he rather thought she was indeed Ruathan. One who had by some unknown agency escaped the massacre ten Turns ago and bided her time for revenge. Why else force Fax to renounce the Hold?

Delighted and fascinated by this unexpected luck, F'lar reached out to tear the dress from the unconscious body and found himself constrained not to. The girl had roused. Her great, hungry eyes fastened on his, not fearful or expectant; wary.

A subtle change occurred in her face. F'lar watched, his smile deepening, as she shifted her regular features into an illusion of disagreeable ugliness and great age.

'Trying to confuse a dragonman, girl?' he chuckled. He made no further move to touch her but settled against the great carved post of the bed. He crossed his arms sternly on his chest, thought better of it immediately, and eased his sore arm. 'Your name, girl, and rank, too.'

She drew herself upright slowly against the headboard, her features no longer blurred. They faced each other across the high bed.

'Fax?'

'Dead. Your name!'

A look of exulting triumph flooded her face. She slipped from the bed, standing unexpectedly tall. 'Then I reclaim my own. I am of the Ruathan Blood. I claim Ruath,' she announced in a ringing voice.

F'lar stared at her a moment, delighted with her proud bearing. Then he threw back his head and laughed.

'This? This crumbling heap?' He could not help but mock the disparity between her manner and her dress. 'Oh, no. Besides, Lady, we dragonmen heard and witnessed Fax's oath renouncing the Hold in favour of his heir. Shall I challenge the babe, too, for you? And choke him with his swaddling cloths?'

Her eyes flashed, her lips parted in a terrible smile.

'There is no heir. Gemma died, the babe unborn. I lied.'

'Lied?' F'lar demanded, angry.

'Yes,' she taunted him with a toss of her chin. 'I lied. There was no babe born. I merely wanted to be sure you challenged Fax.'

He grabbed her wrist, stung that he had twice fallen to her prodding.

'You provoked a dragonman to fight? To kill? *When he is on Search?*'

'Search? Why should I care about a Search? I've Ruatha as my Hold again. For ten Turns, I have worked and waited, schemed and suffered for that. What could your Search mean to me?'

F'lar wanted to strike that look of haughty contempt from her face. He twisted her arm savagely, bringing her to her feet before he released his grip. She laughed at him, and scuttled to one side. She was on her feet and out of the door before he could give chase.

Swearing to himself, he raced down the rocky corridors, knowing she would have to make for the Hall to get out of the Hold. However, when he reached the Hall, there was no sign of her fleeing figure among those still loitering.

'Has that creature come this way?' he called to F'nor who was, by chance, standing by the door to the Court.

'No. Is she the source of power after all?'

'Yes, she is,' F'lar answered, galled all the more. 'And Ruathan Blood at that!'

'Oh ho! Does she depose the babe, then?' F'nor asked,

gesturing towards the birthing-woman who occupied a seat close to the now blazing hearth.

F'lar paused, about to return to search the Hold's myriad passages. He stared, momentarily confused, at this brown rider. 'Babe? What babe?'

'The male child Lady Gemma bore,' F'nor replied, surprised by F'lar's uncomprehending look.

'It lives?'

'Yes. A strong babe, the woman says, for all that he was premature and taken forcibly from his dead dame's belly.'

F'lar threw back his head with a shout of laughter. For all her scheming, she had been outdone by circumstances.

At that moment, he heard Mnementh roar in unmistakable elation and the curious warble of other dragons.

'Mnementh has caught her,' F'lar cried, grinning with jubilation. He strode down the steps, past the body of the former Lord of the High Reaches and out into the main court.

He saw that the bronze dragon was gone from his Tower perch and called him. An agitation drew his eyes upwards. He saw Mnementh spiralling down into the Court, his front paws clasping something. Mnementh informed F'lar that he had seen her climbing from one of the high windows and had simply plucked her from the ledge, knowing the dragonman sought her. The bronze dragon settled awkwardly on to his hind legs, his wings working to keep him balanced. Carefully he set the girl on her feet and formed a precise cage around her with his huge talons. She stood motionless within that circle, her face towards the wedge-shaped head that swayed above her.

The watch-wher, shrieking terror, anger and hatred, was lunging violently to the end of its chain, trying to come to Lessa's aid. It grabbed at F'lar as he strode to the two.

'You've courage enough, girl,' he admitted, resting one hand casually on Mnementh's upper claw. Mnementh was enormously pleased with himself and swivelled his head down for his eye ridges to be scratched.

'You did not lie, you know,' F'lar said, unable to resist taunting the girl.

Slowly she turned towards him, her face impassive. She was not afraid of dragons, F'lar realized with approval.

'The babe lives. And it is male.'

She could not control her dismay and her shoulders sagged briefly before she pulled herself erect.

'Ruatha is mine,' she insisted in a tense low voice.

'Aye, and it would have been, had you approached me directly when the wing arrived here.'

Her eyes widened. 'What do you mean?'

'A dragonman may champion anyone whose grievance is just. By the time we reached Ruath Hold, I was quite ready to challenge Fax given any reasonable cause, despite the Search.' This was not the whole truth but F'lar must teach this girl the folly of trying to control dragonmen. 'Had you paid any attention to your harper's songs, you'd know your rights. And,' F'lar's voice held a vindictive edge that surprised him, 'Lady Gemma might not now lie dead. She suffered far more at that tyrant's hand than you.'

Something in her manner told him that she regretted Lady Gemma's death, that it had affected her deeply.

'What good is Ruatha to you now?' he demanded, a broad sweep of his arm taking in the ruined courtyard and the Hold, the entire unproductive valley of Ruatha. 'You have indeed accomplished your ends; a profitless conquest and its conqueror's death.' F'lar snorted: 'All seven Holds will revert to their legitimate Blood, and time they did. One Hold, one lord. Of course, you might have to fight others, infected with Fax's greed. Could you hold Ruatha against attack . . . now . . . in her decline?'

'Ruatha is mine!'

'Ruatha?' F'lar's laugh was derisive. 'When you could be Weyrwoman?'

'Weyrwoman?' she breathed, staring at him.

'Yes, little fool. I said I rode in Search . . . it's about time you attended to more than Ruatha. And the object of my Search is . . . you!'

She stared at the finger he pointed at her as if it were dangerous.

'By the First Egg, girl, you've power in you to spare when you can turn a dragonman, all unwitting, to do your bidding. Ah, but never again, for now I am on guard against you.'

Mnementh crooned approvingly, the sound a soft rumble in

his throat. He arched his neck so that one eye was turned directly on the girl, gleaming in the darkness of the court.

F'lar noticed with detached pride that she neither flinched nor blanched at the proximity of an eye greater than her own head.

'He liked to have his eye ridges scratched,' F'lar remarked in a friendly tone, changing tactics.

'I know,' she said softly and reached out a hand to do that service.

'Nemorth's queen,' F'lar continued, 'is close to death. This time we must have a strong Weyrwoman.'

'This time—the Red Star?' the girl gasped, turning frightened eyes to F'lar.

'You understand what it means?'

'There is danger . . .' she began in a bare whisper, glancing apprehensively eastward.

F'lar did not question by what miracle she appreciated the imminence of danger. He had every intention of taking her to the Weyr by sheer force if necessary. But something within him wanted very much for her to accept the challenge voluntarily. A rebellious Weyrwoman would be even more dangerous than a stupid one. This girl had too much power and was too used to guile and strategy. It would be a calamity to antagonize her with injudicious handling.

'There is danger for all Pern. Not just Ruatha,' he said allowing a note of entreaty to creep into his voice. 'And *you* are needed. Not by Ruatha,' a wave of his hand dismissed that consideration as a negligible one compared to the total picture. 'We are doomed without a strong Weyrwoman. Without you.'

'Gemma kept saying *all* the bronze riders were needed,' she murmured in a dazed whisper.

What did she mean by that statement? F'lar frowned. Had she heard a word he had said? He pressed his argument, certain only that he had already struck one responsive chord.

'You've won here. Let the babe,' he saw her startled rejection of that idea and ruthlessly qualified it, '. . . Gemma's babe . . . be reared at Ruatha. You have command of all the Holds as Weyrwoman, not ruined Ruatha alone. You've accomplished Fax's death. Leave off vengeance.'

She stared at F'lar with wonder, absorbing his words.

'I never thought beyond Fax's death,' she admitted slowly. 'I never thought what should happen then.'

Her confusion was almost childlike and struck F'lar forcibly. He had had no time, or desire, to consider her prodigious accomplishment. Now he realized some measure of her indomitable character. She could not have been much over ten Turns of age herself when Fax had murdered her family. Yet somehow, so young, she had set herself a goal and managed to survive both brutality and detection long enough to secure the usurper's death. What a Weyrwoman she would be! In the tradition of those of Ruathan blood. The light of the paler moon made her look young and vulnerable and almost pretty.

'You can be Weyrwoman,' he insisted gently.

'Weyrwoman,' she breathed, incredulous, and gazed round the inner court bathed in soft moonlight. He thought she wavered.

'Or perhaps you enjoy rags?' he said, making his voice harsh, mocking. 'And matted hair, dirty feet and cracked hands? Sleeping in straw, eating rinds? You are young . . . that is, I assume you are young,' and his voice was frankly sceptical. She glared at him, her lips firmly pressed together. 'Is this the be-all and end-all of your ambition? What are you that this little corner of the great world is *all* you want?' He paused and with utter contempt added, 'The blood of Ruatha has thinned, I see. You're afraid!'

'I am Lessa, daughter of the Lord of Ruath,' she countered, stung. She drew herself erect. Her eyes flashed. 'I am afraid of nothing!'

F'lar contented himself with a slight smile.

Mnementh, however, threw up his head, and stretched out his sinuous neck to its whole length. His full-throated peal rang out down the valley. The bronze communicated his awareness to F'lar that Lessa had accepted the challenge. The other dragons answered back, their warbles shriller than Mnementh's bellow. The watch-wher which had cowered at the end of its chain lifted its voice in a thin, unnerving screech until the Hold emptied of its startled occupants.

'F'nor,' the bronze rider called, waving his wingleader to him. 'Leave half the flight to guard the Hold. Some nearby lord might think to emulate Fax's example. Send one rider to the High Reaches with the glad news. You go directly to the Cloth Hall and speak to L'to . . . Lytol.' F'lar grinned. 'I think he would make an exemplary Warder and Lord Surrogate for this Hold in the name of the Weyr and the babe.'

The brown rider's face expressed enthusiasm for his mission as he began to comprehend his leader's intentions. With Fax dead and Ruatha under the protection of dragonmen, particularly that same one who had dispatched Fax, the Hold would have wise management.

'She caused Ruatha's deterioration?' he asked.

'And nearly ours with her machinations,' F'lar replied but having found the admirable object of his Search, he could now be magnanimous. 'Suppress your exultation, brother,' he advised quickly as she took note of F'nor's expression. 'The new queen must also be Impressed.'

'I'll settle arrangements here. Lytol is an excellent choice,' F'nor said.

'Who is this Lytol?' demanded Lessa pointedly. She had twisted the mass of filthy hair from her face. In the moonlight the dirt was less noticeable. F'lar caught F'nor looking at her with an all too easily read expression. He signalled F'nor, with a peremptory gesture, to carry out his orders without delay.

'Lytol is a dragonless man,' F'lar told the girl, 'no friend to Fax. He will ward the Hold well and it will prosper.' He added persuasively with a quelling stare full on her. 'Won't it?'

She regarded him sombrely, without answering, until he chuckled softly at her discomfiture.

'We'll return to the Weyr,' he announced, proffering a hand to guide her to Mnementh's side.

The bronze one had extended his head towards the watch-wher who now lay panting on the ground, its chain limp in the dust.

'Oh,' Lessa sighed, and dropped beside the grotesque beast. It raised its head slowly, lurring piteously.

'Mnementh says it is very old and soon will sleep itself to death.'

Lessa cradled the bestial head in her arms, scratching it behind the ears.

'Come, Lessa of Pern,' F'lar said, impatient to be up and away.

She rose slowly but obediently. 'It saved me. It knew me.'

'It knows it did well,' F'lar assured her, brusquely, wondering at such an uncharacteristic show of sentiment in her.

He took her hand again, to help her to her feet and lead her back to Mnementh. As they turned, he glimpsed the watch-wher, launching itself at a dead run after Lessa. The chain, however, held fast. The beast's neck broke, with a sickeningly audible snap.

Lessa was on her knees in an instant, cradling the repulsive head in her arms.

'Why, you foolish thing, why?' she asked in a stunned whisper as the light in the beast's green-gold eyes dimmed and died out.

Mnementh informed F'lar that the creature had lived this long only to preserve the Ruathan line. At Lessa's imminent departure, it had welcomed death.

A convulsive shudder went through Lessa's slim body. F'lar watched as she undid the heavy buckle that fastened the metal collar about the watch-wher's neck. She threw the tether away with a violent motion. Tenderly she laid the watch-wher on the cobbles. With one last caress to the clipped wings, she rose in a fluid movement and walked resolutely to Mnementh without a single backward glance. She stepped calmly to the dragon's raised leg and seated herself, as F'lar directed, on the great neck.

F'lar glanced around the courtyard at the remainder of his wing which had re-formed there. The Hold folk had retreated back into the safety of the Great Hall. When his wingmen were all astride, he vaulted to Mnementh's neck, behind the girl.

'Hold tightly to my arms,' he ordered her as he took hold of the smallest neck ridge and gave the command to fly.

Her fingers closed spasmodically around his forearm as the great bronze dragon took off, the enormous wings working to achieve height from the vertical take-off. Mnementh preferred to fall into flight from a cliff or tower. Like all dragons, he tended to indolence. F'lar glanced behind him, saw the other dragonmen form the flight line, spread out to cover those still on guard at Ruatha Hold.

When they had reached a sufficient altitude, he told Mnementh
to transfer, going *between* to the Weyr.

Only a gasp indicated the girl's astonishment as they hung
between. Accustomed as he was to the sting of the profound cold,
to the awesome utter lack of light and sound, F'lar still found
the sensations unnerving. Yet the uncommon transfer spanned
no more time than it took to cough thrice.

Mnementh rumbled approval of this candidate's calm reaction
as they flicked out of the eerie *between*.

And then they were above the Weyr, Mnementh setting his
wings to glide in the bright daylight, half a world away from
night-time Ruatha.

As they circled above the great stony trough of the Weyr,
F'lar peered at Lessa's face, pleased with the delight mirrored
there; she showed no trace of fear as they hung a thousand
lengths above the high Benden mountain range. Then, as the
seven dragons roared their incoming cry, an incredulous smile lit
her face.

The other wingmen dropped into a wide spiral, down, down
while Mnementh elected to descend in lazy circles. The dragonmen peeled off smartly and dropped, each to his own tier in
the caves of the Weyr. Mnementh finally completed his leisurely
approach to their quarters, whistling shrilly to himself as he
braked his forward speed with a twist of his wings, dropping
lightly at last to the ledge. He crouched as F'lar swung the girl
to the rough rock, scored from thousands of clawed landings.

'This leads only to our quarters,' he told her as they entered
the corridor, vaulted and wide for the easy passage of great
bronze dragons.

As they reached the huge natural cavern that had been his
since Mnementh achieved maturity, F'lar looked about him
with eyes fresh from his first prolonged absence from the Weyr.
The huge chamber was unquestionably big, certainly larger than
most of the halls he had visited in Fax's procession. Those halls
were intended as gathering places for men, not the habitations
of dragons. But suddenly he saw his own quarters were nearly
as shabby as all Ruatha. Benden was, of a certainty, one of the
oldest dragon-weyrs, as Ruatha was one of the oldest Holds,
but that excused nothing. How many dragons had bedded in

that hollow to make solid rock conform to dragon proportions! How many feet had worn the path past the dragon's weyr into the sleeping chamber, to the bathing room beyond where the natural warm spring provided ever-fresh water! But the wall hangings were faded and unravelling and there were grease stains on lintel and floor that should be sanded away.

He noticed the wary expression on Lessa's face as he paused in the sleeping room.

'I must feed Mnementh immediately. So you may bathe first,' he said, rummaging in a chest and finding clean clothes for her, discards of other previous occupants of his quarters, but far more presentable than her present covering. He carefully laid back in the chest the white wool robe that was traditional Impression garb. She would wear that later. He tossed several garments at her feet and a bag of sweetsand, gesturing to the hanging that obscured the way to the bath.

He left her, then, the clothes in a heap at her feet, for she made no effort to catch anything.

Mnementh informed him that F'nor was feeding Canth and that he, Mnementh, was hungry, too. *She* didn't trust F'lar but she wasn't afraid of himself.

'Why should she be afraid of you?' F'lar asked. 'You're cousin to the watch-wher who was her only friend.'

Mnementh informed F'lar that he, a fully matured bronze dragon, was no relation to any scrawny, crawling, chained, and wing-clipped watch-wher.

F'lar, pleased at having been able to tease the bronze one, chuckled to himself. With great dignity, Mnementh curved down to the feeding ground.

> By the Golden Egg of Faranth
> By the Weyrwoman, wise and true,
> Breed a flight of bronze and brown wings,
> Breed a flight of green and blue.
> Breed riders, strong and daring,
> Dragon-loving, born as hatched,
> Flight of hundreds soaring skyward,
> Man and dragon fully matched.

Lessa waited until the sound of the dragonman's footsteps

proved he had really gone away. She rushed quickly through the big cavern, heard the scrape of claw and the *whoosh* of the mighty wings. She raced down the short passageway, right to the edge of the yawning entrance. There was the bronze dragon circling down to the wider end of the mile-long barren oval that was Benden Weyr. She had heard of the Weyrs, as any Pernese had, but to be in one was quite a different matter.

She peered up, around, down that sheer rock face. There was no way off but by dragon wing. The nearest cave mouths were an unhandy distance above her, to one side, below her on the other. She was neatly secluded here.

Weyrwoman, he had told her. His woman? In his weyr? Was that what he had meant? No, that was not the impression she got from the dragon. It occurred to her, suddenly, that it was odd she had understood the dragon. Were common folk able to? Or was it the dragonman blood in her line? At all events, Mnementh had inferred something greater, some special rank. She remembered vaguely that, when dragonmen went on Search, they looked for certain women. Ah, certain women. She was one, then, of several contenders. Yet the bronze rider had offered her the position as if she and she, alone, qualified. He had his own generous portion of conceit, that one, Lessa decided. Arrogant he was, though not a bully like Fax.

She could see the bronze dragon swoop down to the running herd-beasts, saw the strike, saw the dragon wheel up to settle on a far ledge to feed. Instinctively she drew back from the opening, back into the dark and relative safety of the corridor.

The feeding dragon evoked scores of horrid tales. Tales at which she had scoffed but now . . . Was it true, then, that dragons did eat human flesh? Did . . . Lessa halted that trend of thought. Dragonkind was no less cruel than mankind. The dragon, at least, acted from bestial need rather than bestial greed.

Assured that the dragonman would be occupied a while, she crossed the larger cave into the sleeping room. She scooped up the clothing and the bag of cleansing sand and proceeded to the bathing room.

To be clean! To be completely clean and to be able to stay that way. With distaste, she stripped off the remains of the rags, kicking them to one side. She made a soft mud with the sweet-sand and scrubbed her entire body until she drew blood from various half-healed cuts. Then she jumped into the pool, gasping as the warm water made the sweetsand foam in the lacerations.

It was a ritual cleansing of more than surface soil. The luxury of cleanliness was ecstasy.

Finally satisfied she was as clean as one long soaking could make her, she left the pool, reluctantly. Wringing out her hair she tucked it up on her head as she dried herself. She shook out the clothing and held one garment against her experimentally. The fabric, a soft green, felt smooth under her water-shrunken fingers, although the nap caught on her roughened hands. She pulled it over her head. It was loose but the darker-green over-tunic had a sash which she pulled in tight at the waist. The unusual sensation of softness against her bare skin made her wriggle with voluptuous pleasure. The skirt, no longer a ragged hem of tatters, swirled heavily around her ankles. She smiled. She took up a fresh drying cloth and began to work on her hair.

A muted sound came to her ears and she stopped, hands poised, head bent to one side. Straining, she listened. Yes, there were sounds without. The dragonman and his beasts must have returned. She grimaced to herself with annoyance at this untimely interruption and rubbed harder at her hair. She ran fingers through the half-dry tangles, the motions arrested as she encountered snarls. Vexed, she rummaged on the shelves until she found, as she had hoped to, a coarse-toothed metal comb.

Dry, her hair had a life of its own suddenly, crackling about her hands and clinging to face and comb and dress. It was difficult to get the silky stuff under control. And her hair was longer than she had thought, for clean and unmatted, it fell to her waist—when it did not cling to her hands.

She paused, listening, and heard no sound at all. Apprehensively, she stepped to the curtain and glanced warily into the sleeping room. It was empty. She listened and caught the perceptible thoughts of the sleepy dragon. Well, she would rather meet the man in the presence of a sleepy dragon than in a sleeping room. She started across the floor and, out of the corner of her eye, caught sight of a strange woman as she passed a polished piece of metal hanging on the wall.

Amazed, she stopped short, staring, incredulous, at the face the metal reflected. Only when she put her hands to her prominent cheekbones in a gesture of involuntary surprise and the reflection imitated the gesture, did she realize she looked at herself.

Why, that girl in the reflector was prettier than Lady Tela, than the clothman's daughter! But so thin. Her hands of their own volition dropped to her neck, to the protruding collarbones, to her breasts which did not entirely accord with the gauntness of the rest of her. The dress was too large for her frame, she noted with an unexpected emergence of conceit born in that instant of delighted appraisal. And her hair . . . it stood out around her head like an aureole. It wouldn't lie contained. She smoothed it down with impatient fingers, automatically bringing locks forward to hang around her face. As she irritably pushed them back, dismissing a need for disguise, the hair drifted up again.

A slight sound, the scrape of a boot against stone, caught her back from her bemusement. She waited, momentarily expecting him to appear. She was suddenly timid. With her face bare to the world, her hair behind her ears, her body outlined by a clinging fabric, she was stripped of her accustomed anonymity and was, therefore, in her estimation, vulnerable.

She controlled the desire to run away—the irrational fear. Observing herself in the looking metal, she drew her shoulders back, tilted her head high, chin up; the movement caused her hair to crackle and cling and shift about her head. She was Lessa of Ruatha, of a fine old Blood. She no longer needed artifice to preserve herself; she must stand proudly bare-faced before the world . . . and that dragonman.

Resolutely she crossed the room, pushing aside the hanging on the doorway to the great cavern.

He was there, beside the head of the dragon, scratching its eye ridges, a curiously tender expression on his face. The tableau was at variance with all she had heard of dragonmen.

She had, of course, heard of the strange affinity between rider and dragon but this was the first time she realized that love was part of that bond. Or that this reserved, cold man was capable of such deep emotion.

He turned slowly, as if loath to leave the bronze beast. He caught sight of her and pivoted completely round, his eyes intense as he took note of her altered appearance. With quick, light steps, he closed the distance between them and ushered her back into the sleeping room, one strong hand holding her by the elbow.

'Mnementh has fed lightly and will need quiet to rest,' he said in a low voice. He pulled the heavy hanging into place across the opening.

Then he held her away from him, turning her this way and that, scrutinizing her closely, curious and slightly surprised.

'You wash up . . . pretty, yes, almost pretty,' he said, amused condescension in his voice. She pulled roughly away from him, piqued. His low laugh mocked her. 'After all, how could one guess what was under the grime of . . . ten full Turns?'

At length he said, 'No matter. We must eat and I shall require your services.' At her startled exclamation, he turned, grinning maliciously now as his movement revealed the caked blood on his left sleeve. 'The least you can do is bathe wounds honourably received fighting your battle.'

He pushed aside a portion of the drape that curtained the inner wall. 'Food for two!' he roared down a black gap in the sheer stone.

She heard a subterranean echo far below as his voice resounded down what must be a long shaft.

'Nemorth is nearly rigid,' he was saying as he took supplies from another drape-hidden shelf, 'and the Hatching will soon begin anyhow.'

A coldness settled in Lessa's stomach at the mention of a Hatching. The mildest tales she had heard about that part of dragonlore were chilling, the worst dismayingly macabre. She took the things he handed her numbly.

'What? Frightened?' the dragonman taunted, pausing as he stripped off his torn and bloodied shirt.

With a shake of her head, Lessa turned her attention to the wide-shouldered, well-muscled back he presented her, the paler skin of his body decorated with random bloody streaks. Fresh blood welled from the point of his shoulder for the removal of his shirt had broken the tender scabs.

'I will need water,' she said and saw she had a flat pan among the items he had given her. She went swiftly to the pool for water, wondering how she had come to agree to venture so far from Ruatha. Ruined though it was, it had been hers and was familiar to her from Tower to deep cellar. At the moment the idea had been proposed and insidiously prosecuted by the dragonman, she had felt capable of anything, having achieved, at last, Fax's death. Now, it was all she could do to keep the water from slopping out of the pan that shook unaccountably in her hands.

She forced herself to deal only with the wound. It was a nasty gash, deep where the point had entered and torn downwards in a gradually shallower line. His skin felt smooth under her fingers as she cleansed the wound. In spite of herself, she noticed the masculine odour of him, compounded not unpleasantly of sweat, leather, and an unusual muskiness which must be from close association with dragons.

She stood back when she had finished her ministration. He flexed his arm experimentally in the constricting bandage and the motion set the muscles rippling along side and back.

When he faced her, his eyes were dark and thoughtful.

'Gently done. My thanks.' His smile was ironic.

She backed away as he rose but he only went to the chest to take out a clean, white shirt.

A muted rumble sounded, growing quickly louder.

Dragons roaring? Lessa wondered, trying to conquer the ridiculous fear that rose within her. Had the Hatching started? There was no watch-wher's lair to secrete herself in, here.

As if he understood her confusion, the dragonman laughed good-humouredly and, his eyes on hers, drew aside the wall covering just as some noisy mechanism inside the shaft propelled a tray of food into sight.

Ashamed of her unbased fright and furious that he had witnessed it, Lessa sat rebelliously down on the fur-covered wall seat, heartily wishing him a variety of serious and painful injuries which she could dress with inconsiderate hands. She would not waste future opportunities.

He placed the tray on the low table in front of her, throwing down a heap of furs for his own seat. There was meat, bread, a tempting yellow cheese and even a few pieces of winter fruit. He made no move to eat nor did she, though the thought of a piece of fruit that was ripe, instead of rotten, set her mouth to watering. He glanced up at her, and frowned.

'Even in the Weyr, the lady breaks bread first,' he said, and inclined his head politely to her.

Lessa flushed, unused to any courtesy and certainly unused to being first to eat. She broke off a chunk of bread. It was like nothing she remembered having tasted before. For one thing, it was fresh-baked. The flour had been finely sifted, without trace of sand or hull. She took the slice of cheese he proffered her and it, too, had an uncommonly delicious sharpness. Made bold by this indication of her changed status, Lessa reached for the plumpest piece of fruit.

'Now,' the dragonman began, his hand touching hers to get her attention.

Guiltily she dropped the fruit, thinking she had erred. She stared at him, wondering at her fault. He retrieved the fruit and placed it back in her hand as he continued to speak. Wide-eyed, disarmed, she nibbled, and gave him her full attention.

'Listen to me. You must not show a moment's fear, whatever happens on the Hatching Ground. And you must not let her overeat.' A wry expression crossed his face. 'One of our main functions is to keep a dragon from excessive eating.'

Lessa lost interest in the taste of the fruit. She placed it carefully back in the bowl and tried to sort out not what he had said, but what his tone of voice implied. She looked at the dragonman's face, seeing him as a person, not a symbol, for the first time.

There was a blackness about him that was not malevolent; it was a brooding sort of patience. Heavy black hair, heavy black brows; his eyes, a brown light enough to seem golden, were all too expressive of cynical emotions, or cold hauteur. His lips were thin but well-shaped and in repose almost gentle. Why must he always pull his mouth to one side in disapproval or in one of those sardonic smiles? At this moment, he was completely unaffected.

He meant what he was saying. He did not want her to be afraid. There was no reason for her, Lessa, to fear.

He very much wanted her to succeed. In keeping whom from overeating what? Herd animals? A newly hatched dragon certainly wasn't capable of eating a full beast. That seemed a simple enough task to Lessa. . . . Main function? *Our* main function?

The dragonman was looking at her expectantly.

'Our main function?' she repeated, an unspoken request for more information inherent in her inflection.

'More of that later. First things first,' he said, impatiently waving off other questions.

'But what happens?' she insisted.

'As I was told so I tell you. No more, no less. Remember these two points. No fear, and no overeating.'

'But . . .'

'You, however, need to eat. Here.' He speared a piece of meat on his knife and thrust it at her, frowning until she managed to choke it down. He was about to force more on her but she grabbed up her half-eaten fruit and bit down into the firm sweet sphere instead. She had already eaten more at this one meal than she was accustomed to having all day at the Hold.

'We shall soon eat better at the Weyr,' he remarked, regarding the tray with a jaundiced eye.

Lessa was surprised. This was a feast, in her opinion.

'More than you're used to? Yes, I forgot you left Ruatha with bare bones indeed.'

She stiffened.

'You did well at Ruatha. I mean no criticism,' he added, smiling at her reaction. 'But look at you,' and he gestured at her body, that curious expression crossing his face, half-amused, half-contemplative. 'I should not have guessed you'd clean up pretty,' he remarked. 'Nor with such hair.' This time his expression was frankly admiring.

Involuntarily she put one hand to her head, the hair crackling over her fingers. But what reply she might have made him, indignant as she was, died aborning. An unearthly keening filled the chamber.

The sounds set up a vibration that ran down the bones behind her ear to her spine. She clapped both hands to her ears. The noise rang through her skull despite her defending hands. As abruptly as it started, it ceased.

Before she knew what he was about, the dragonman had grabbed her by the wrist and pulled her over to the chest.

'Take those off,' he ordered, indicating dress and tunic. While she stared at him stupidly, he held up a loose white robe, sleeveless and beltless, a matter of two lengths of fine cloth fastened at shoulder and side seams. 'Take it off, or do I assist you?' he asked, with no patience at all.

The wild sound was repeated and its unnerving tone made her fingers fly faster. She had no sooner loosened the garments she wore, letting them slide to her feet, than he had thrown the other over her head. She managed to get her arms in the proper places before he grabbed her wrist again and was speeding with her out of the room, her hair whipping out behind her, alive with static.

As they reached the outer chamber, the bronze dragon was standing in the centre of the cavern, his head turned to watch the sleeping room door. He seemed impatient to Lessa; his great eyes, which fascinated her so, sparkled iridescently. His manner breathed an inner excitement of great proportions and from his throat a high-pitched croon issued, several octaves below the unnerving cry that had roused them all.

With a yank that rocked her head on her neck, the dragonman pulled her along the passage. The dragon padded beside them at such speed that Lessa fully expected they would all catapult off the ledge. Somehow, at the crucial stride, she was a-perch the bronze neck, the dragonman holding her firmly about the waist. In the same fluid movement, they were gliding across the great bowl of the Weyr to the higher wall opposite. The air was full of wings and dragon tails, rent with a chorus of sounds, echoing and re-echoing across the stony valley.

Mnementh set what Lessa was certain would be a collision course with other dragons, straight for a huge round blackness in the cliff-face, high up. Magically, the beasts filed in, the greater wingspread of Mnementh just clearing the sides of the entrance.

The passageway reverberated with the thunder of wings. The air compressed around her thickly. Then they broke out into a gigantic cavern.

Why, the entire mountain must be hollow, thought Lessa, incredulous. Around the enormous cavern, dragons perched in serried ranks, blues, greens, browns and only two great bronze beasts like Mnementh, on ledges meant to accommodate hundreds. Lessa gripped the bronze neck scales before her, instinctively aware of the imminence of a great event.

Mnementh wheeled downward, disregarding the ledge of the bronze ones. Than all Lessa could see was what lay on the sandy floor of the great cavern; dragon eggs. A clutch of ten monstrous, mottled eggs, their shells moving spasmodically as the fledglings within tapped their way out. To one side, on a raised portion of the floor, was a golden egg, larger by half again the size of the mottled ones. Just beyond the golden egg lay the motionless ochre hulk of the old queen.

Just as she realized Mnementh was hovering over the floor in the vicinity of that egg. Lessa felt the dragonman's hands on her, lifting her from Mnementh's neck.

Apprehensively, she grabbed at him. His hands tightened and inexorably swung her down. His eyes, fierce and amber, locked with hers.

'Remember, Lessa!'

Mnementh added an encouragement, one great compound eye turned on her. Then he rose from the floor. Lessa half-raised one hand in entreaty, bereft of all support, even that of the sure inner compulsion which had sustained her in her struggle for revenge on Fax. She saw the bronze dragon settle on the first ledge, at some distance from the other two bronze beasts. The dragonman dismounted and Mnementh curved his sinuous neck until his head was beside his rider. The man reached up absently, it seemed to Lessa, and caressed his mount.

Loud screams and wailings diverted Lessa and she saw more dragons descend to hover just above the cavern floor, each rider depositing a young woman until there were twelve girls, including Lessa. She remained a little apart from them as they clung to each other. She regarded them curiously. The girls were not injured in any way she could see, so why such weeping? She took a deep breath against the coldness within her. Let *them* be afraid. She was Lessa of Ruatha and did not need to be afraid.

Just then, the golden egg moved convulsively. Gasping as one, the girls edged away from it, back against the rocky wall. One, a lovely blonde, her heavy plait of golden hair swinging just above the ground, started to step off the raised floor and stopped, shrieking, backing fearfully towards the scant comfort of her peers.

Lessa wheeled to see what cause there might be for the look of horror on the girl's face. She stepped back involuntarily herself.

In the main section of the sandy arena, several of the handful of eggs had already cracked wide open. The fledglings, crowing weakly, were moving towards . . . and Lessa gulped . . . the young boys standing stolidly in a semi-circle. Some of them were no older than she had been when Fax's army had swooped down on Ruath Hold.

The shrieking of the women subsided to muffled gasps. A fledgling reached out with claw and beak to grab a boy.

Lessa forced herself to watch as the young dragon mauled the youth, throwing him roughly aside as if unsatisfied in some way. The boy did not move and Lessa could see blood seeping on to the sand from dragon-inflicted wounds.

A second fledgling lurched against another boy and halted, flapping its damp wings impotently, raising its scrawny neck and croaking a parody of the encouraging croon Mnementh often gave. The boy uncertainly lifted a hand and began to scratch the eye ridge. Incredulous, Lessa watched as the fledgling, its crooning increasingly more mellow, ducked its head, pushing at the boy. The child's face broke into an unbelieving smile of elation.

Tearing her eyes from this astounding sight, Lessa saw that another fledgling was beginning the same performance with another boy. Two more dragons had emerged in the interim. One had knocked a boy down and was walking over him, oblivious to the fact that its claws were raking great gashes. The fledgling who followed its hatch-mate stopped by the wounded child, ducking its head to the boy's face, crooning anxiously. As Lessa watched, the boy managed to struggle to his feet, tears of pain streaming down his cheeks. She could hear him pleading with the dragon not to worry, that he was only scratched a little.

It was over very soon. The young dragons paired off with boys. Green riders dropped down to carry off the unacceptable. Blue riders settled to the floor with their beasts and led the couples out of the cavern, the young dragons squealing, crooning, flapping wet wings as they staggered off, encouraged by their newly acquired weyrmates.

Lessa turned resolutely back to the rocking golden egg, knowing what to expect and trying to divine what the successful boys had, or had not done, that caused the baby dragons to single them out.

A crack appeared in the golden shell and was greeted by the terrified screams of the girls. Some had fallen into little heaps of white fabric, others embraced tightly in their mutual fear. The crack widened and the wedge head broke through, followed quickly by the neck, gleaming gold. Lessa wondered with unexpected detachment how long it would take the beast to mature, considering its by no means small size at birth. For the head was larger than that of the male dragons and they had been large enough to overwhelm sturdy boys of ten full Turns.

Lessa was aware of a loud hum within the Hall. Glancing up at the audience, she realized it emanated from the watching bronze dragons, for this was the birth of their mate, their queen. The hum increased in volume as the shell shattered into fragments and the golden, glistening body of the new female emerged. It staggered out, dipping its sharp beak into the soft sand, momentarily trapped. Flapping its wet wings, it righted itself, ludicrous in its weak awkwardness. With sudden and unexpected swiftness, it dashed towards the terror-stricken girls.

Before Lessa could blink, it shook the first girl with such violence, her head snapped audibly and she fell limply to the sand. Disregarding her, the dragon leaped towards the second girl but misjudged the distance and fell, grabbing out with one claw for support and raking the girl's body from shoulder to thigh. The screaming of the mortally injured girl distracted the dragon and released the others from their horrified trance. They scattered in panicky confusion, racing, running, tripping, stumbling, falling across the sand towards the exit the boys had used.

As the golden beast, crying piteously, lurched down from the raised arena towards the scattered women, Lessa moved. Why hadn't that silly clunk-headed girl stepped aside, Lessa thought, grabbing for the wedge-head, at birth not much larger than her own torso. The dragon's so clumsy and weak she's her own worst enemy.

Lessa swung the head round so that the many-faceted eyes were forced to look at her . . . and found herself lost in that rainbow regard.

A feeling of joy suffused Lessa, a feeling of warmth, tenderness, unalloyed affection and instant respect and admiration flooded mind and heart and soul. Never again would Lessa lack an advocate, a defender, an intimate, aware instantly of the temper of her mind and heart, of her desires. How wonderful was Lessa, the thought intruded into Lessa's reflections, how pretty, how kind, how thoughtful, how brave and clever!

Mechanically, Lessa reached out to scratch the exact spot on the soft eye ridge.

The dragon blinked at her wistfully, extremely sad that she had distressed Lessa. Lessa reassuringly patted the slightly damp, soft neck that curved trustingly towards her. The dragon reeled to one side and one wing fouled on the hind claw. It hurt. Carefully, Lessa lifted the erring foot, freed the wing, folding it back across the dorsal ridge with a pat.

The dragon began to croon in her throat, her eyes following Lessa's every move. She nudged at Lessa and Lessa obediently attended the other eye ridge.

The dragon let it be known she was hungry.

'We'll get you something to eat directly,' Lessa assured her briskly and blinked back at the dragon in amazement. How could she be so callous? It was a fact that this little menace had just now seriously injured, if not killed, two women.

She wouldn't have believed her sympathies could swing so alarmingly towards the beast. Yet it was the most natural thing in the world for her to wish to protect this fledgling.

The dragon arched her neck to look Lessa squarely in the eyes. Ramoth repeated wistfully how exceedingly hungry she was, confined so long in that shell without nourishment.

Lessa wondered how she knew the golden dragon's name and Ramoth replied: Why shouldn't she know her own name since it was hers and no one else's? And then Lessa was lost again in the wonder of those expressive eyes.

Oblivious to the descending bronze dragons, uncaring of the presence of their riders, Lessa stood caressing the head of the most wonderful creature on all Pern, fully prescient of troubles and glories, but most immediately aware that Lessa of Pern was Weyrwoman to Ramoth the Golden, for now and for ever.

AFTERWORD

Unlike many aficionados, I do not ready every science fiction story published. Ergo, I've probably missed some good things, as well as some real dogs. Because of this, I'm in no position to comment on the year 1967 in science fiction, as I do not know everything that happened in it. Therefore, let me talk of other matters.

It is a Good Thing, as I see it, that Chip Delany has—within the past two years—received the Papal blessing. He deserves recognition, and now he's got plenty of it.

Good Thing No. 2: I am pleased to have the opportunity to publish here something of Gary Wright's. He is a newcomer who I think will do many a goodly thing as time wears on. I eagerly await his first novel. I tip my hat to him on the eve of what I think will be a grand career.

Last year, the editors of *Nebula 2* spoke of the problems that were or were not getting into science fiction. Viet Nam seems to be ever with us. And all the big problems of all the big cities. And progressive bureaucratization, computerization of life as we know it. And the outflow of gold. Race relations. I could use a full page just listing them. They are still with us and we don't have any handy answers. We can only guess at possible outcomes.

Science fiction, as I see it, though, isn't here to provide handy answers. We may comment upon or extrapolate a particular thing, but it doesn't provide a solution, it simply points a finger. This is what I believe Theodore Sturgeon meant when he referred to a class of stories as being of the 'If this goes on . . .' type.

So maybe it's a Good Thing that most people do not pay much attention to their *ad hoc* future planning committee. We are not that much different from the medicine men predicting fire, famine, plague and war. They're always safe bets.

As for the year in science fiction, God knows, there's more of it with us as a result thereof. Some of it is good and some isn't. That which is good shall prevail.

So what am I to say, here and now? I am going to tell you that our special form of literature is an invitation, an indication, a pastime. Sometimes we push the right buttons and sometimes we don't. You're looking at literature, not social commentary. If some of the latter gets mixed in—well, good. It was probably not intentional, though. Some future historian will chuckle at all our mistakes. Like the man who crashes the party, we just want to be on the scene.

So here are our words, impure and unsimple. We enjoyed putting them together in the order in which they exist. Should they give you pleasure, emotional or intellectual, that's all we can really ask. Thanks for coming along for the ride.

This year, as I see it, was a good one. There were more of us around.

Roger Zelazny

NEBULA AWARDS 1967

Best Novel: 'Einstein Intersection' by Samuel R. Delany.

Best Novella: 'Behold the Man' by Michael Moorcock.

Best Novelette: 'Gonna Roll the Bones' by Fritz Leiber.

Best Short Story: 'Aye, and Gomorrah' by Samuel R. Delany.

ROLL OF HONOUR

'Chthon' by Piers Anthony.

'Thorns' by Robert Silverberg.

'Hawksbill Station' by Robert Silverberg.

'Weyr Search' by Anne McCaffrey.

'If All Men Were Brothers, Would You Let One Marry Your Sister?' by Theodore Sturgeon.

'Flatlander' by Larry Niven.

'Pretty Maggie Moneyeyes' by Harlan Ellison.

'Baby, You Were Great' by Kate Wilhelm.

1966 NEBULA AWARDS

Best Novel: (tie) 'Flowers for Algernon' by Daniel Keyes and 'Babel-17' by Samuel R. Delany.

Best Novella: 'The Last Castle' by Jack Vance.

Best Novelette: 'Call Him Lord' by Gordon R. Dickson.

Best Short Story: 'The Secret Place' by Richard McKenna.

1965 NEBULA AWARDS

Best Novel: 'Dune' by Frank Herbert.

Best Novella: (tie) 'The Saliva Tree' by Brian Aldiss and 'He Who Shapes' by Roger Zelazny.

Best Novelette: 'The Doors of His Face, the Lamps of His Mouth' by Roger Zelazny.

Best Short Story: ' "Repent, Harlequin!" Said the Ticktockman' by Harlan Ellison.

Famous SF Names in Panther Books

Brian W. Aldiss

Poul Anderson

Issac Asimov

J. G. Ballard

John Bowen

John Brunner

Algis Budrys

William R. Burkett

William Burroughs

John W. Campbell (editor)

Avram Davidson (editor)

Philip K. Dick

Thomas M. Disch

I. O. Evans (editor)

Philip José Farmer

Rex Gordon

Robert Heinlein

Zenna Henderson

Damon Knight (editor)

Charles Eric Maine

Walter M. Miller

Robert P. Mills (editor)

Michael Moorcock (editor)

Rick Raphael

Eric Frank Russell

Arthur Sellings

Clifford Simak

Theodore Sturgeon

William F. Temple

William Tenn

Jack Vance

A. E. van Vogt

Jules Verne

Henry Ward

Robert F. Young

Roger Zelazny